Author's Note

This is a work of fiction, set in the United States of America, in the early 1900s. However, many of the incidents did happen. All characters in the novel are fictitious. Any name of or resemblance to a person or event is coincidental.

Shaft Number Four

The faint glow from oil lanterns hanging outside the opening to the mine entrance illuminated it and the rough muddy road that ran downhill to Shanty Town. A whistle blew at precisely six-thirty a.m., shattering the cold, damp, foggy morning as a reminder that a tired, weary, and hungry coal-mining crew would soon emerge from four mine shafts. However, another crew would enter the mine immediately after the night shift had exited and would perform the same type of grueling work for ten hours.

The majority of the miners who lived in Shanty Town, as well as the miners working above ground level, heard the whistle. The miners donned their work coats and caps and kissed their wives before picking up their lunch pails and walking to the mine. As they passed the clapboard shanties, others going to the mine joined the line. To no one in particular, George Gibson complained, "Another day of sweating beneath the bowels of the earth to earn a living."

Bill Dykes said to his family, "It's time to go to work." He was twenty-six years old with Indian piercing eyes that he had inherited from his father. He stood six feet, two inches tall, was handsome and muscular, with wavy black hair, and was dedicated to his family and job. He left his wife, Betty, his son, Clyde, age ten, and his daughter, Mona, age eight, to join the line of miners. Bill was classified as a skilled worker and held the titles as a dynamiter and metalworker. Bill's father, Homer Dykes, had worked in the mine since its inception, but he had died of the dreaded black lung disease. When Bill was not drilling holes in the walls of a mine shaft and skillfully placing dynamite, he was working at repairing coal carts, pumps, electrical wiring, elevators, and railway tracks that traversed the floors of each mine shaft in order to bring the small loaded carts of coal to the mine entrance.

The relief men on the day shift waited beside the cave entrance and watched the night crew exit the mine. The tired workers' clothes, faces, hands, and necks were covered with coal dust, with only their eyeballs displaying a color of white. The moment the last of the night shift emerged from the mine, fifteen fresh men stepped onto the elevator and descended to the fourth mine shaft. Quickly the process was repeated until the forty-seven workers were several hundred feet below ground, mining coal in four different mine shafts.

Bill, using a chisel and hammer in the number four shaft, was cutting a narrow hole to place a dynamite charge inside it when the foreman, Mort Sermons, approached him. Mort, called Iron Gut by the miners, was known for two things—drinking large quantities of beer and assuring the coal-mine owners that his shift of men would meet their quota of coal each day.

Mort said, "Bill, someone cut an electrical wire in the number three shaft and most of their lights are out. Go above and repair it before you set off these charges of dynamite."

Bill put his tools in a canvas bag and caught the elevator going up to the number three mine shaft.

It was dark when Bill exited the elevator, so he switched on his headband light. He could not see any lights burning farther down the shaft but a voice said, "Come down here, Bill. This is where the break in the wire is. Somehow the wire got pushed onto the railway tracks, and a coal cart ran over it and cut it in half."

Bill made his way to an electrical control panel and closed the main switch, extinguishing all electrical power within that tunnel. Cautiously he stepped over and around workers and chunks of coal before returning to the broken wire. Quickly he spliced the wire, wrapped it with tape, and moved the wire to the edge of the wall before returning to the breaker box and throwing the switch. Immediately after the lights came on, the miners began working, some shoveling coal into carts, some used sledgehammers to pound huge chunks of coal into smaller pieces, while others pushed loaded carts of coal to the elevator.

Bill returned to the number four mine shaft and finished cutting the last of three small holes in the wall before pushing a stick of dynamite into each one. Mort Sermons yelled, "Fire in the hole. Take cover for a dynamite blast." He looked at his pocket watch and waited one minute before striking a match and lighting the fuses protruding from the dynamite. He quickly took cover beside Bill, who had already retreated about thirty yards from where the explosion would take place. When the explosion went off, workers in tunnels above and below heard it.

The miners waited a few minutes for some of the coal dust to settle and then began working. The procedure never changed, break up huge chunks of coal, load coal into carts, extend narrow tracks in order to keep the coal carts close by, roll three loaded carts onto the bed of the elevator, and then blow another hole beneath the mountain in order to extract the coal.

"Mort," Bill said, "there is a huge crack in the ceiling caused by the explosion. Don't you think we should install some braces and shore up this shaft to protect the miners?"

Before answering, Mort shined his headlight across the crack and finally said, "No. The crack is wide but it is not very deep. Let's keep a sharp eye on it, but to maintain our quota, we have to keep the loaded carts of coal going to the surface. Bill, they need you in the number one shaft to prepare for another blast."

Bill knew better than to argue with a foreman if he wanted to keep his job. He grabbed his canvas tool bag and walked away, thinking about Cliff Goodbread, who was fired two weeks ago for disagreeing with a foreman. The year was 1928 and jobs were hard to find in Coldsburg, Virginia.

Today was Friday, so when the whistle blew at the end of the ten-hour shift, the miners left the mine and lined up outside the payroll window. The night shift who was relieving them had already picked up their wages. The line moved slowly as each man was identified before the paymaster handed him a small envelope which contained his pay in cash. The paymaster reminded each employee that the ten dollars for renting a shanty house for the past month and the money for anything he or his wife had charged at the general store had been deducted from his wages.

After conversing with the paymaster, the man in front of Bill said, "Ten dollars rent for that shack is ludicrous, and three dollars and eighty cents for a pair of high-top shoes is ridiculous."

The paymaster said, "You forgot to gripe about the four dollars and twenty cents I deducted for groceries and the two dollars you charged for a pair of coveralls. William, you need to learn that this coal mine is not a charity organization. Your gross pay was forty dollars for last week. You owed our company twenty dollars, which has been deducted from your pay. After the deductions, your envelope contains twenty dollars, the correct amount. Move on so I can pay the other men."

William walked away, tearing the two-by-three-inch manila

envelope and counting his twenty dollars as he mumbled to himself.

Later in the day a foreman knocked on William's door and said, "William, your services are no longer needed at the mine. You have two days to vacate this house and move on. You know what happens to you and your family if you refuse to move?"

William hung his head as he said, "Yes. I'm aware of what the company thugs do to anyone who crosses the company. We'll be gone tomorrow."

The following day William and his family walked away from Shanty Town with their belongings in six sacks dangling from their hands.

The owners of the coal mine had it shut down at six-thirty a.m. each Sunday in order to give the employees a day of rest. Betty Dykes was adamant about her family spending a half hour in front of a silver cross for a family devotion. She always insisted that her husband read scripture from the Bible and lead the family in a discussion about the Holy words. When the devotion ended on this day, Betty said, "Bill, it's a beautiful day. I've already told the children you and I are planning to go into Coldsburg to shop for groceries and do some window shopping. Do you mind if the children come with us?"

Bill nodded indicating the affirmative.

Shortly the Dykes family was walking the bumpy two-mile road to Coldsburg. They had walked a distance when Clyde read aloud a sign in front of a farmhouse. "Smith's Hog Farm. Hogs and pigs for sale, inquire at front door. Dad, does the general store at the mine buy hogs from Mr. Smith?"

"Yes, son, they buy hogs, chickens, and eggs. But the general store in Coldsburg sells their products cheaper than the store at the mine. Years ago, Mr. Gibson, who owns the general store in Coldsburg, delivered food and supplies to Shanty Town until the owners of the mine put a stop to it. His cheaper goods were cutting into the mine owners' profits."

They walked another mile in silence, and just outside of Coldsburg, Clyde helped Mona to read the signs at a gasoline station.

Their first stop was the general store where a cold drink box was located outside. Bill opened and handed a bottle of orange soda to each member of his family. As they entered the store, Mr. Gibson said, "The Dykes family, good morning."

"Good morning to you, Mr. Gibson," Betty said. While Bill looked at knives, guns, tools, and hardware, Betty took a wheelbarrow from beside the front door and began loading it with various foods. While shopping, she gazed at women's clothes, shoes, and hats. Mona and Clyde were interested in toys and board games. Before leaving the store, Bill paid Mr. Gibson five dollars and ninety cents for a Barlow pocketknife, a checkerboard set, four bottles of pop, and four large sacks of groceries.

Bill waited outside and talked with miners about the unsafe conditions within the mine while his family looked around in several stores. Their last stop was the bookstore where Betty purchased two math books for her children. There was no school in the area, so Betty taught them arithmetic, reading, spelling, and geography three hours each day for five days a week. She did this because she didn't want her children to be illiterate.

After saying farewells, the family departed for Shanty Town. Each was carrying a bag of groceries as they walked toward their shack. The family had traveled about two blocks when Luke Spears stopped his flatbed truck beside them. "Get in," Luke said, "I'll save you a walk."

Betty stepped into the cab beside Luke, and her family took seats on the rear of the truck. She said, "Thanks, Mr. Spears. Every time we make this walk, Bill reminds us that a good stretch is good for anyone."

Luke laughed.

Minutes later Bill's family exited the truck and Betty said, "Thanks again, Luke," as she watched him drive to his shanty. While Betty put her groceries on shelves, Bill sharpened his new knife.

Clyde went to the porch stoop and put the checkerboard on top of an empty wooden cable spool, and Mona pulled two benches up to it. Clyde asked, "Dad, will you teach us how to play checkers?"

Bill wiped the blades of his new knife and pocketed it. For several minutes he demonstrated to his children how to set up a checkerboard, how to move the pieces, and when it was mandatory to move or jump the opponent's checkers. "Okay, kids," Bill said, "I want the two of you to set up the board and play a game."

Quickly Mona put her red pieces on the correct squares while Clyde assembled the black checkers. Bill took a seat on the steps, packed his pipe, lit it, and watched his children play a game. He was amazed at the concentration they displayed before moving a checker. Clyde barely won the contest, but Mona was anxious for another game.

Bill went behind the house to check on their winter garden

where Betty had different types of vegetables growing. She had cut two cabbages and was busy pulling carrots from the ground. At two o'clock, she had a meal on the table. Later in the day the children at Shanty Town gathered in a nearby field for a game of touch football while the adults stood on the sidelines and watched.

The hour was past noon the following day when Iron Gut lit the three dynamite fuses that Bill had placed inside a wall in the fourth mine shaft. After the explosion and the dust had settled, Bill said, "Mort, I hear an eerie noise above us. I believe we need to stop mining and erect some bracing to prevent a cave in."

"Quiet everyone," Iron Gut yelled. Intently he listened until the creaking noises stopped before saying, "Bill, you suggested the same thing the other day, but the answer is still no. The creaking sounds have subsided, so let's go to work. Everything is safe."

The miners went to work, and Bill began checking and renewing turnbuckles that enabled the elevator to be raised and lowered at proper levels. The day shift ended without incident, and the last chore Bill performed was to check the oil level on the three motors that powered water pumps to transfer water from shaft number four to a holding pond on the surface behind the mine office.

At precisely four a.m., Caleb Hicks, a foreman on the night shift working in the number four shaft, yelled, "Fire in the hole. Clear out for a dynamite charge."

Caleb let one minute pass before he lit the fuses to the five sticks of dynamite and darted for cover. After the explosion and the coal dust began to settle, the sixteen miners, believing everything was normal, started back to work. Suddenly an eerie stressful noise caused them to focus their attention on the ceiling above them.

A shattering noise that sounded exactly like lightning bolts echoed within the shaft as twelve huge cracks skyrocketed across the ceiling. Six of the miners bolted toward the elevator, but they were not quick enough. The first section of the ceiling collapsed, burying them under several tons of coal. For a few seconds, groaning, screaming, and cries for help could be heard. Quickly the remaining ten uninjured miners, knowing that the chance of finding anyone alive was slim, began rolling and shoveling chunks of coal from the heap.

The men worked rapidly, hoping to find their friends alive. At the same time, they tried to imagine what had happened to cause the ceiling of the number four shaft to collapse. As the shaft gradually began filling with water, the men realized that the three water lines running up to the surface pond behind the mine office had been severed.

When the cave-in happened, the ten shacks located near the cave entrance slipped off their foundations. The emergency whistle outside the mine office was blasting ten times a minute. Everyone at Shanty Town had been awakened when the catastrophe took place.

The worst of all fears for any coal miner had happened, and everyone at Shanty Town, except the small children, had experienced this before. The entire day shift crew arrived at the mine entrance. The access to the number three elevator was clear on the surface, but number one, two, and four had been partially filled with coal.

Iron Gut said, "Bill, go below with fourteen men and see if you can reach the trapped miners."

Fifteen miners rode the elevator over four hundred feet downward before stopping at the fourth shaft. Coal from the dynamite blast had caused a large part of the floor of the number three shaft to collapse. Bill had no way of knowing if the entire shaft was plugged, or if there were surviving miners on the other side of the coal in the number four shaft, trying to dig their way out.

While Bill's crew loaded carts of coal, they found the severed water hoses. As soon as three carts were loaded, Bill said, "I'll take these carts to the surface and get a few pieces of water hose and more men. Continue breaking the large chunks until I get back."

When Bill reached the entrance to the mine and stepped from the elevator, a crowd of people with faces of anticipation were assembled, waiting and hoping for good news, but it was obvious that a silent deadly pandemonium gripped them. Questions from different men, women, and children echoed from the crowd, "Did you find my daddy? How far down is the cave-in? Have you found any of the trapped miners? How long will it take before you rescue the miners?"

Quickly a few men rolled the three loaded carts of coal off the elevator and replaced them with three empty ones. Bill noticed miners removing coal from the other elevator shafts, but he knew it would take at least two weeks before they had them cleared.

Bill yelled, "Hold the elevator for me until I get some supplies. Sam, get me three sections of water hose and eight clamps from the storage shed."

Bill went to the supervisor of the mine who was standing next to Mort and said, "Mr. Coleman, we took the elevator down to the exit of the fourth shaft, but the tunnel is blocked with coal. There is no way for anyone to know exactly how many tons of coal has to be moved in order to get to the trapped miners. But, if we work around the clock and extract coal from one end of the shaft and if there are surviving miners digging from the other side, we should be able to clear the coal out of the way in three to four days, providing we don't have another cave-in.

"We found the water discharge lines from the number four shaft cut in half. By now the number four shaft is starting to fill with water, so I will repair the water line promptly. If there are any survivors down below, they know to disconnect the water line at twelve noon tomorrow, so we will be able use the same hose to pump oxygen into the shaft. Before noon tomorrow, I will need several full oxygen tanks. My opinion is we should stop work on the other two elevator shafts and concentrate our efforts at digging out the number four shaft. Do either of you have any suggestions or comments?"

Mr. Coleman said, "No, Bill, I don't. You seem to be doing everything that can be done for those men. Mort, do you have anything to add?"

Mort shook his head.

The moment Bill and several other miners were on the elevator and out of sight, Mort said, "Mr. Coleman, at the moment, we have too much help. I'm going to send half of these men home and have them report tonight to relieve the ones I'll keep here for the day shift."

Mr. Coleman nodded his approval.

Within the next few minutes, Mort assigned thirty-nine men to continue working a twelve-hour day shift. He also gave orders for thirty-nine miners to report to the mine at six-thirty p.m. to relieve the day shift.

While relatives and curiosity seekers waited near the mine entrance, a four-door Ford sedan parked beside the mine office, and three men from the Bureau of Mines exited the car and went into the office. Minutes later another car arrived, and two newsmen stepped out.

Behind closed doors, Mr. Coleman vaguely answered questions for the three bureau men about guidelines for the mining industry, but the bureau representatives pressed him for detailed answers.

Before leaving, Carson Hitchwell, the top agent for the

Bureau of Mines in Virginia, said, "Mr. Coleman, in a few minutes four of my employees will arrive here to interview everyone who comes out of that mine. We expect your complete cooperation on this case. Our men will remain here until everyone is out of the mine."

Mr. Hitchwell handed Mr. Coleman a document and then said, "When the last miner or corpse is removed from the mine, this business is closed until the State Mining Commission gives its approval for you to continue mining coal and doing business in this state."

"But …" Mr. Coleman started to say.

"There are no buts, alibis, or excuses," Mr. Hitchwell interrupted. "When the entrance to the mine is closed, anyone who enters without permission from the bureau will be jailed. If you have any questions, just read the document I just handed you."

When the state inspectors exited the office, they spoke with four other bureau men before driving away. Two of them erected a tent for their living quarters, while the other two photographed the entrance to the mine.

Shortly the elevator came to the surface and Bill pushed a cart of coal onto an unloading track while two other men followed with the other carts. As the miners pushed three empty carts onto the elevator, Herman Sanks, a bureau man, asked, "Are you Bill Dykes?"

"Yes, I am," Bill said. "Sam, bring me a keg of drinking water. Sir, I suspect that you are either a newsman or a bureau man. But we have a life-or-death situation down below. I don't want to be rude, but I have to go. Six of you miners who are assigned to the day shift come with me."

As Bill and the other miners stepped onto the elevator, Sanks asked, "Mr. Dykes, have you rescued any of the trapped miners?"

"No, sir, so far we haven't found anyone." Moments later the elevator was out of sight.

The hour was past four p.m. when the surviving miners uncovered three bodies. With extreme caution they moved them to a clearing in the shaft, washed their faces for recognition, and covered their heads and faces with their handkerchiefs. A deeper state of depression fell over the miners as they returned to their tasks and worked with an intense ferociousness without the utterance of a word.

At the mine entrance, the shift change was completed before seven p.m. The older half-worn-out miners remained on the surface to make sure the coal carts were empty and nothing would slow down the operation. Bill was with the last crew who exited the elevator. Herman Sanks approached him and said, "Mr. Dykes, my superiors asked me to interview you as soon as possible. Will you answer some questions for me?"

"Yes, sir, I will try," Bill said. "However, I will not speculate or offer opinions on any of my statements until after we rescue my fellow employees and I have a look at the number four mine shaft."

"Very well," Sanks said. "For the time being, I will ask you pertinent questions about the situation at hand." He looked at Bill intently and asked, "Where is the cave-in within this mine?"

"It occurred on the ceiling of shaft number four which was the floor for shaft number three," Bill answered.

"Did the walls of the shaft cave-in?" Sanks asked.

"Sir, my crew has cleared out approximately eighty feet inside the number four shaft," Bill said. "The walls are intact, but most of the ceiling for the number four shaft has collapsed."

"Mr. Dykes, have you seen or heard from anyone who was working in the number three or four shafts?" Mr. Sanks asked.

"Sir," Bill answered, "according to the foreman, only two men were in the number three shaft. So far we have not found them." Unknown to Bill the two men survived by standing on a ledge when the floor collapsed. After the cave-in, they climbed down and joined the trapped miners.

"Bill, are you going to use timbers and brace up the eighty feet you have cleared inside the shaft before you move any more coal out of the mine?" Sanks asked.

"No, sir, I'm not planning to," Bill answered. "But, if I'm ordered to brace up the shaft, I will do so. Mr. Sanks, if there are any survivors in that shaft, time is of the essence, and we must continue to dig coal, not perform carpentry work, unless it is absolutely necessary at this time."

"Bill, tomorrow when you pump oxygen to the number four shaft, will any of the miners who are alive hear your voice? And do you have any prearranged signals so the trapped miners can communicate with you?"

"Yes, we have a few signals, and if I contact someone down there who is alive and able to communicate with me, I should be able to tell you something about any surviving miner's plight," Bill said.

"Thanks, Bill, I appreciate your forthright answers. When the bureau is given the results of this investigation, several of them will want to question the miners. At noon tomorrow, I'll be with you, hoping for a safe report about the trapped miners. Good day," Mr. Sanks said.

While walking to his shanty, at the end of his shift, Bill was stopped and questioned by family groups, including the wives and children of the trapped miners. To each group he said, "At noon tomorrow, we will attempt to communicate with the trapped miners. We will not be able to hear their voices, but by using clanging noises, we will know if they are alive and waiting to be rescued." Bill left each group by giving them a feeling of hope that their husbands and fathers would exit the mine alive.

Bill went to his back stoop and closed the canvas curtain around a half-filled wooden drum of water. He shed his black clothes, eased into the cold water, submerged himself, and lathered his body with a bar of lye soap. Shortly he dried himself, put on clean clothes, and joined his family at the kitchen table.

"Before we eat," Betty said, "let's each say a silent prayer for the trapped miners and their families."

Moments later Betty said, "Amen."

As the family ate in silence, Bill could feel the tension and the anticipation on his family's faces as they waited to hear some good news about the trapped miners. He knew that anything he said would probably be repeated to his neighbors by his children, so he would have to carefully choose his words.

At the conclusion of the meal, Bill said, "The cave-in is the worst one I have ever seen. The number one and two elevator shafts are half plugged with coal but the miners who were in those shafts escaped through a small tunnel in the coal. The number three elevator shaft is partially open. The number four tunnel is filled with coal, which was caused by the ceiling of the number four shaft collapsing. But men are working around the clock moving the coal to the surface. All we can do is hope and pray we find the trapped men alive."

"Dad," Clyde asked, "would support timbers have prevented the cave-in at the number four shaft?"

Bill didn't answer the question, but said, "At noon tomorrow, I will try to communicate with the trapped miners. We are hoping and praying to get each of them out of the shaft alive. If we don't have another cave-in, or if nothing happens that we don't anticipate, we should have the miners out within two more days. Now, you children help your mother with the dishes." He went to the front stoop, took a seat, packed his pipe, and lit it. He mumbled, "This is no way to make a living, and this is a horrible place to raise a family."

At precisely twelve o'clock the following day Bill disconnected the water line and attached the hose to an oxygen tank that ran down to the number four shaft. He gradually opened a valve releasing the oxygen from a tank that had one hundred twenty pounds of pressure on it.

The trapped miners had already removed the hose from the water and tied the end of the water hose to a railway track. They stood against the walls of the shaft and watched the water spew from the hose, adding to the amount they were standing in. Instantly the oxygen made a whistling sound within the shaft and created dust when the fresh air burst around the miners. The men breathed deeply, appreciating the fresh air because they had been laboring on the thin air for the past several hours.

When the oxygen tank was empty, Bill quickly closed a valve and connected another one to the hose. While the second tank of air was flowing into the number four shaft, the trapped men's hope of being rescued was restored. Holt Mosby said, "Thank God, someone above is using his head and trying to save us." The twelve men smiled for the first time since the cave-in.

After Bill had pumped four tanks of oxygen into the shaft, he disconnected the hose. When a minute passed, he pulled a whistle from his pocket, held the loose end of the hose up to his mouth, and blew the whistle three times into the open end of the hose. The trapped miners were squatting, holding their end of the hose out of the water, enabling them to hear the whistle. "That has got to be Bill Dykes," Holt said. "Dick, when I say 'now,' hit your two spud wrenches together twelve times."

Bill heard the metallic noise come through the hose, but he was hoping to hear eighteen sounds. He gave another long blow on the whistle, which meant, "Repeat your message." Again, twelve metallic sounds came from the trapped miners at the end of the hose. Bill gave five short blasts on the whistle, and the trapped miners knew that he was connecting the hose to continue pumping water from the shaft.

Shortly Bill stepped from the pump and women, children, newsmen, and mining officials were in the road, anxiously awaiting the news he had received from the trapped miners. Bill motioned for Mr. Hitchwell, Mr. Coleman, and Iron Gut to come to him. He said, "The trapped miners have enough oxygen for two days. Unless I misinterpreted their signals, twelve of the men are alive, which means six are seriously injured or dead. At the rate we're removing coal from the number four shaft, we should have them out tomorrow."

"That is terrible news, but it could have been worse," Mr. Coleman said. "Bill, how many feet do you estimate our men have dug into the number four shaft?"

"Mr. Coleman," Bill said, "from the mouth of the elevator to the pile of coal, we have cleared at least three hundred feet. And, with twelve miners digging from the other side, we should reach them sometime in the morning."

While Mr. Coleman stepped up on the office porch to address the miners' families, onlookers, and newsmen, Bill went to a table laden with bologna sandwiches and hot coffee with Mr. Hitchwell following him. He asked, "Bill, are you sure about only twelve miners surviving the cave-in?"

"Yes, sir, unless I've forgotten how to count to twelve, I'm positive," Bill answered.

They both drank coffee, as they listened to Mr. Coleman stating the news he had about the miners below. When Coleman was asked about all the miners being alive, he answered, "At this time we cannot be certain about the condition of all the men. By this time tomorrow we will have the answers all of us are waiting for."

At eleven o'clock the following morning, Bill's crew of men could hear the trapped miners digging on the opposite side of the pile of coal. Shortly, a huge chunk of coal rolled away from the relief miners toward the rear of the mine shaft, and Holt Mosby stood facing them. With tears in his eyes he said, "Bill, your ugly face is a welcome sight. In fact, all of you look good to me." Bill's crew filed through the opening, greeting their friends and asking them questions about the cave-in.

Bill said, "Holt, you and your crew get on the elevator with the three carts of coal and we will load the six corpses. There are quite a few people up top waiting for all of you. When the elevator returns, we'll join you." Within a few minutes the bodies of six miners were lying on top of the coal in the carts and moving toward the entrance to the mine.

While the relief crew waited for the elevator, Bill used his headlight to study the result of the last dynamite blast and the cave-in. He recalled showing Iron Gut the huge crack in the ceiling which supported and was the floor in the number three shaft. And now the ceiling for the number four shaft was on the floor of the wrong mine shaft. He was thinking, "It is a miracle that any of the miners survived."

When the elevator returned, Bill and his crew went to the surface. Mining families were being restrained while the six corpses were being loaded into three pickup trucks. The relatives of the dead miners were assembled into small groups with their friends. Some were weeping, some wailing, and some cursing the mine. Other groups clung to each other, thankful to be alive. Bill and his crew went to the families of the deceased miners and tried to console them. Quickly the bodies of the dead miners were taken to the mine clinic where a nurse and her assistant stripped, washed, dressed, and placed the corpses in wooden caskets.

Decomposition of the six corpses was apparent, and Mr. Coleman had already been given permission by the relatives of the deceased to bury them at five o'clock in the miners' cemetery.

Heart of Decisions

At five o'clock, miners, relatives of miners, mine and state officials, people from Coldsburg, and a Methodist preacher, Lance Green, stood facing the six pine boxes that sat on top of sawhorses located at the head of the six graves that had been dug earlier.

Lance stepped to the top of a clump of freshly dug dirt and said, "Let us pray. Lord, today we commit to you the souls of Hank Sterns, Cliff Goodbread, Jason Smart, Carlile Smith, Johnny Sims, and Seth Yomans. Lord, these six men were taken from us while they were in their prime of life and working hard to support their families. We don't pretend to know why these men were taken, but your will be done. Lord, as these men join you, help us to support and comfort their loved ones. Amen."

Lance noticed tears on adults' faces, children crying, miners flexing their hands, and mining officials and bureau men standing like statues. After reading a Psalm from the Bible, he said, "As great as this loss is, we can comfort ourselves in knowing that all of these men were professing Christians. Yes, I had the privilege of speaking with each one at least twice at church services within the past six months. Their souls now reside in Heaven, but their loss is ours. As the Psalmist said, 'Work hard, do your Master's bidding, love and care for your family, and above all, love and live according to God's plan.'" Indicating the caskets, Lance continued, "These six departed souls loved the Lord and tried to live by his instructions."

Lance stepped from the mound of dirt and said, "Let us pray. Lord, we have had the privilege of living with and knowing the deceased that you entrusted to us. And now we ask your guidance in sustaining us to continue to keep and live by your ordinances. Amen."

Lance went to the families of the deceased and spoke with each group before they went to their shacks. Minutes later the caskets were lowered into the ground, covered with dirt, and a cross bearing the deceased name was erected at the head of his grave.

Bill and his children were walking toward their shack when Herman Sanks spoke to them. He said, "Bill, members of the state mining board want to interview you in the mining office at ten o'clock in the morning, providing that time suits you."

"Herman, I'll be there. Will the bosses of the mine be present?"

"Yes, Bill, they will. However, you can speak to the bureau personnel without any mine executives or foreman being present if you wish," Herman said.

"No, sir," Bill said adamantly, "years ago my father tried to tell the bureau men about mine safety and was chastised for his efforts and was passed over for a promotion. As you know, the three bureau men I'm referring to were taking bribes from mine officials. Later the three were discharged but that did not prevent several miners from being killed. Sanks, whether or not anyone wants to hear it if I speak at that meeting the truth will be heard. I'll see you at ten in the morning." It was obvious Bill was disgusted with mine owners and bias state officials.

As Bill passed the shacks of each miner who had just been buried, he softly called their names. The last name he whispered was that of the man who lived beside him, Jason Smart.

As Bill was about to enter his own shanty, Betty came to the stoop of a neighbor's porch and called out, "Bill, Laurabeth is about to give birth. We need you in here."

Bill rushed into the shanty, and Betty led him into a bedroom that was enclosed with blankets. "Bill, her water has already broken," Betty said.

Ruby, Laurabeth's fifteen-year-old daughter, was frightened as she sat next to her mother, holding her right hand.

Bill timed Laurabeth's breathing and said, "Ruby, your mother will be fine. Would you and Betty bring me some towels, two basins of hot water, and two pieces of string?"

When they returned to the bedroom, Bill was wiping sweat from Laurabeth's face and head. He had already propped her knees up and had checked the position of the unborn child, whose head was trying to make an entrance into the world.

"Laurabeth," Bill said, "take deep breaths and push downward as hard as you can. The pain will be over shortly."

Moments later Bill grasped the head of the baby and pulled the male child from his mother's womb. He tied off the umbilical cord in two places, cut the cord twice, and tapped the child on the rump in order to force him to take deep breaths. Then he and Betty cleaned the infant before laying him on a towel.

"Ruby," Bill announced, "you have a new brother and he has all of the right parts. While Betty cleans your mother, let's go to the kitchen and get a cup of coffee."

After washing their hands, Bill sat with Ruby on the front stoop. "Mr. Dykes," Ruby said, "thanks for helping my mother. But I worry about what will become of us. With Papa gone, I don't know how we will survive. Did the pastor mentioned Papa's name at the funeral?"

Ruby had tears in her eyes, so Bill put his arm around her and answered, "Yes, he not only mentioned his name, but he also spoke of Jason's being a Christian, loving and supporting his family, and never shirking his duties. Ruby, your father loved his family. Your father and mother have given you a beautiful brother. What is your mother going to name him?"

"We discussed several names but with the loss of Papa, I think we should name him Jason. Mr. Dykes, I don't want my brother to be a miner. Our family has lost both of our grandfathers and now Papa to the mines."

Betty came to the door and said, "Ruby, you and Bill can come in now."

As they entered the bedroom, Laurabeth had the sleeping infant cradled in her arms. She smiled and said, "Thanks, Bill, and if Jason were here, he would also thank you."

Ruby asked, "Mama, what are you going to name my brother?"

"Ruby, I think we should name him either Bill or Jason. Do you have a name in mind?"

"Yes, Mother, I do. Let's name him Jason Bill Smart."

"Ruby, that is a splendid idea," Laurabeth said. "Betty, move your chair closer to the bed and help me make some plans."

Bill knew the women wanted to talk so he eased out the door. Betty remained with the Smart family for two nights, teaching Ruby how to prepare milk bottles, change diapers, and bathe little Jason Bill, among other things.

Bill entered the mining office just before ten o'clock the following morning. He spoke to three other miners who were also waiting to give statements to the mining commission. He couldn't help but notice the pot of hot coffee and donuts on a tray. He had observed this goodwill gesture before, and each time a cave-in had occurred at the mine. After pouring a cup of coffee, he took a seat.

Shortly, Herman Sanks poked his head out from a private office and said, "Come in, Bill."

Seated at a long rectangle table were John Coleman, Mort Sermons, and Cason Hicks, all mining bosses. They sat facing Carson Hitchwell, Herman Sanks, and a man Bill didn't know. Bill took a seat at the end of the table, facing a young lady with a friendly looking demeanor.

"Mr. Dykes," Carson said, "you know everyone here except Jack Cook, a federal government representative, and our recording secretary, Miss Grace Simpson."

Jack and Grace nodded.

"Grace will not intervene in any of our conversations, but she will record every word spoken at this meeting.

"Mr. Dykes," Carson continued, "you were asked to attend this meeting because the bureau mining officials for the state of Virginia and the federal government want to know why we are having so many catastrophes in coal mines. Mr. Sanks told us you offered to answer any questions we have about the cave-in."

Bill nodded.

"We realize the only way to stop accidents is to interview miners and learn from their experience as to what takes place in coal mines before we issue mandates to make mines safer," Carson continued. "When the cave-in occurred, we know you did everything you could to rescue the trapped men. When you testify, no one will interrupt you, but after you give your testimony, everyone except Grace will be permitted to question you. Are you prepared to do this?"

Bill nodded again.

Carson pointed at Herman Sanks and said, "Herman, since you have already been interviewing various miners involved in the cave-in, you can ask the first questions."

Herman said, "Bill, what is your title and how many years have you been working at this mine?"

"I've been working here for eight years," Bill said. "Four years ago I was given the title as a dynamiter and metalworker."

"Bill, just exactly what encompasses the work of a dynamiter and metalworker?" Carson Hitchwell asked.

"Sir, while working inside the mine, I drill holes, set dynamite charges, install new electrical lines, repair old wiring, repair coal carts, maintain the elevators, install water lines, grease bearings and wheels on different pieces of equipment, maintain pumps, and supervise the installation of new tracks for the carts to traverse. On the surface of the mine, I maintain the water pumps and submit a material list once a month for items needed to keep the machinery operating."

"Mr. Dykes," Jack Cook said, "from what I've heard about you, I believe you are an unusually skilled worker. I know you were not in the mine when the cave-in occurred, but do you have a theory as to why the number four ceiling caved in and took the lives of those six men?"

"No, sir, I don't have a theory," Bill answered. "I know exactly what caused the cave-in."

The group at the table sat erect and stared at Bill.

John Coleman shouted as he stood up. "There's no way you can positively know this."

"Sit down, Mr. Coleman," John Cook said calmly. "You have a right to question Mr. Dykes, not shout at anyone in this room. One more outburst and you will be removed from this meeting. Mr. Dykes, would you continue with your theory."

"Gentlemen," Bill said, "I worked the day shift on Friday before the cave-in. After blasting a hole in the wall in order to extend the mine shaft in number four tunnel, at least a three-inch crack was visible on the ceiling above the mine shaft." Pointing, Bill continued, "I asked our foreman, Mort Sermons, if he didn't think we should install braces and shore up the ceiling to protect the crews in number three and four shafts. Mort shined his head light on the crack and answered, 'No. The crack is wide, but it is not very deep. Let's keep an eye on it, but to maintain our quota we have to keep the loaded carts of coal going to the surface.'"

Bill paused to take a swallow of coffee and Carson Hitchwell asked, "Mr. Dykes, when Mr. Sermons denied your request, did any of the other miners hear the two of you speak?"

"Yes, sir," Bill said. "The entire crew in that shaft heard us, including the three men waiting outside. And, just after the dynamite explosion, eerie creaking noises could be heard by everyone in the mine shaft."

"When Mr. Sermons refused your request, why didn't you insist on bracing up the mine shaft?" Mr. Cook asked.

"Sir," Bill answered, "every time a miner insists or is adamant about installing posts and beams to keep the mine shafts safe, that employee is discharged within a few hours. The employee records will substantiate my statements. I am well aware that the performing of carpentry work in a mine shaft costs the mine owners a few tons of coal, but a few tons of coal is not worth men's lives. That was the eighteenth request I have had refused for wanting to brace up different mine shafts."

"Mr. Sermons," Jack Cook asked, "do you disagree with Mr. Dykes's statements?"

Staring at the table Mort answered, "No, sir, I don't. He spoke the truth, but you need to know that we foremen are under pressure to extract so many tons of coal from the coal mine each shift."

"Mr. Dykes," Jack continued, "as you know, we have statements from the twelve surviving miners. These reports substantiate what you said about the crack in the ceiling in the number four shaft being the first indication that a cave-in was imminent unless some bracing was installed. When the cave-in happened, you didn't wait for orders or instructions from mining officials or anyone—you went to work giving orders and trying to save the trapped men. The bureau and the government executives want to know if there are any prior written or verbal orders to follow in a disastrous situation like the one that has just happened."

"No, Mr. Cook," Bill answered, "we don't have any orders or statements. However, any miner who gets trapped in a mine knows that everyone on the surface will do everything possible to get him out alive. Miners work on the theory and hope that someday the state and federal government will impose the adequate safety regulations for coal, iron ore, copper, tin, silver, gold, or anything else that comes from beneath the earth. But, until the law mandates some rigid requirements for mine owners, this will not come to pass."

"Mr. Dykes, I don't agree with the part of your statement about the law being idle," Mr. Hitchwell said.

"Of course, you don't," Bill answered. "However, just to dig out the loose coal in order to inspect this mine will take several weeks. Then a bureau inspector who will risk his life will go below and come out with a report stating exactly how much bracing and shoring up needs to be done before the mine can continue to operate. For your records, I will tell you this. Inside each mine shaft you will find areas of at least one hundred yards where there are no posts or beams supporting the floors above. The mining commission should mandate that support structures be erected in mine shafts no more than a few yards apart. "

"Mr. Dykes, are you sure about your statements?" Herman Sanks asked.

"Herman, I've been working in these mine shafts for eight years. Many times while walking, I count my steps. Inside the number four shaft, there is one area that extends for one hundred twenty-four yards without a post or a beam for support. Yes, I'm positive."

The men stared at Bill as if they were in a trance.

"Are there any other questions for Mr. Dykes?" Mr. Hitchwell asked.

Each man shook his head as if to say "No."

"Gentlemen," Bill said, "before I leave, there is one other thing I would like to say." Mr. Hitchwell nodded in the affirmative so Bill continued. "When the cost is calculated for shutting down this business, digging out the mine, installing the proper bracing in each mine shaft, obtaining the state permits to continue mining, paying insurance payments for the deceased miners, and adding up the lost time for this accident, it is a huge sum to pay because a few post and beams could have prevented all of it. We've just buried six good men and we can't bring them back. If this is going to be prevented in the future, mandates from the government and the bureau must establish guidelines for mining. Good day, gentlemen."

Sanks followed Bill out as he was leaving and said, "Bill, I want to thank you for being forthright."

Bill shook Sanks's hand and left the office as another miner went into the meeting.

The miners worked four weeks, days and nights, removing loose coal caused by the cave-in. Then the state bureau inspectors went into the mine and wrote their report on safety violations—there were eighty-nine. Miners went to work moving timbers into the mine and erecting framing to support the mine shafts. As a result, several thousand tons of coal were piled beside freight cars, waiting to be loaded and shipped to customers.

When John Coleman asked permission to load the coal and ship it to customers, Jack Cook said, "No. This business will stay shutdown until the bureau men give their approval for the mine to operate."

Coleman was livid.

For two more weeks under the bureau men's direction, the miners performed carpentry work and installed posts and beams in the mine shafts. The mining commission gave Mr. Coleman permission to resume business six weeks after the accident. However, Mr. Coleman was aware that his mine would be scrutinized constantly for safety violations.

Bill Dykes entered his shanty on this Friday evening with an expression of forlorn hope. Betty knew something was on his mind, but she didn't ask him. When the family finished eating supper, he said, "After we clear the table, I have news for all of you." Bill hardly ever lectured or made speeches, so the family quickly cleared the table and took their seats.

Bill said, "Next week, the mine will start operating again. I will return to work, but the company might discharge me for the statements I made to the mining commission about the unsafe conditions within the mine. I've decided that regardless of what happens, I'm going to stop worrying about a bad situation. If I should lose my job, we will have to leave Shanty Town, but there are other jobs and looking at other towns might be good for all of us."

One month later, the news of Black Friday, a gloomy Monday, and the stock market crash in 1929, starting the Great Depression did not reach the residents of Shanty Town until the following day when Luke Spears came from Coldsburg with a newspaper. With the passing of each day, the miners read the dreadful news about unemployment on a massive scale everywhere across the United States. Small and large corporations were shutting down, sending the unemployment rate to record numbers. Businesses were closing, the stock market was going broke, people were losing their life savings, banks were closing, and the citizens of the United States were trying to prepare themselves for the gigantic struggle it would take to survive.

Four weeks later the company notified the miners that the coal mine was shutting down due to the cancellation for coal orders. At the end of the week, the miners drew their last pay and were told to vacate Shanty Town within ten days. However, four miners were retained by the coal company to work as security guards.

The few miners who had a savings account in the bank went to withdraw their money. A sign inside the glass window of the bank read, "Gone out of Business." The miners were furious when they went home with empty pockets.

For two days, Bill Dykes and Betty discussed what they could do to support themselves and their children in a depression. They outlined a plan of action which encompassed a life of traveling while searching for jobs. The family had a savings of two thousand two hundred sixteen dollars buried in a tin container—their wisdom of not completely trusting banks or the US federal government proved to be right.

When Luke Spears posted his flatbed truck for sale, Bill purchased it for two hundred dollars. Bill, Clyde, and Mona went to the lumberyard and bought enough material to build living quarters on the fourteen-foot bed of the truck.

Bill and his family worked six days building a room that contained four bunk beds and a multitude of shelves with slats to keep things from falling to the floor while traveling. Bill used screws to secure every piece of wood on the project, including the shelves. While building the room, Bill marked the timbers, and Betty and Clyde did the cutting using a crosscut saw.

They installed a cast-iron stove with a flat top for heating and cooking and vented it through the floor. A new fifty-five-gallon water drum was bracketed next to the door at the rear end of the truck. The small bathroom contained a lavatory and a commode, and was enclosed with a piece of canvas. When the job was finished, Bill said, "Let's dust, sweep, clean the two windows, and get our home ready before we load our contents in the morning."

As the family stepped down from the room on the truck, Bill folded the steps to the rear bumper and tied them securely. At the same time, Mike Waters, his wife, and three children were leaving Shanty Town. They stopped to look at the new room on the truck. Mike exclaimed, "Bill, it appears that you are one man who has a plan! Where are you and your family headed?"

Bill smiled and said, "Far enough south where there aren't any coal mines or snow. If I can't find a job, my family will try to find work picking peaches or cotton in Georgia and citrus fruit in Florida. Mike, where are you going?"

Mike said, "My brother, Oliver, has a ninety-acre farm eleven miles down the road. We're going to move into a section of his barn until I can find work. Betty, take care of this family, and I hope to see all of you again in better times."

Bill's family watched their friends with their children leading goats, trudging down the road with their few possessions in their hands. Since the closing of the mine people leaving Shanty Town was a familiar sight each day. Betty stood watching that family and thought about the few meager possessions they had to show for Mike's twelve years of turmoil. She turned and sadly said, "While the rest of you pack our belongings, I've got to build a fire and cook supper in the truck."

"I'll help you," Mona said. Mona and Clyde could hardly wait to leave Shanty Town and see the sights of the world.

At daylight the following morning, Bill and Betty were in the cemetery, weeding and rearranging the stones around their family members' graves. When the weeding was finished, Betty put wildflowers on each one. They took each other's hand and said a silent prayer. Still hand in hand, the two went home to wake their children. After breakfast, slowly but methodically, the family put their belongings in the truck and stored them where each knew exactly where his or her items were. Bill unloaded his shotgun and stored it and the shells over the rear door of the truck.

Bill said, "Family, tonight we will sleep in the truck to familiarize ourselves with the compact quarters. Clyde, be sure the water drum and wood box are filled before dark. Mona, it is your job to set the table and help your mother with the dishes."

Just before the family went to bed, Bill shut off one oil lantern, but he cut the wick down on another one to reflect a light glow. He didn't want anyone tripping in the dark.

At daybreak the following morning, Bill went through the house to be sure they didn't leave anything of value behind. The only thing he found was a hatchet on the ground beside a log in the backyard. He heard Mona yell, "Breakfast, Papa."

An hour later, the family was leaving Shanty Town. As the truck rolled through Coldsburg, Clyde counted six shops and the one bank that had gone out of business. Just outside of Coldsburg, the family noticed that a warehouse where different grains were bought and packaged was closed.

When Bill entered a good highway, he kept the International truck under forty-five miles per hour. Before nightfall, he stopped at a service station and Clyde jumped from the truck. He pulled and pushed a long metal handle which forced gasoline into a glass cylinder located on top of the gas pump. When the cylinder contained five gallons, he put the gas nozzle in the mouth of the truck tank and squeezed the trigger.

The gasoline was feeding into the truck tank by gravity, and it drained slowly. "Dad, is five gallons all you want?" Clyde asked.

"No, son, put another five gallons in the tank."

Bill turned and a station attendant behind him smiled and

said, "Hello. Do you need my help?"

"Thank you, but no, sir. This truck is our first vehicle, and pumping the gas is a first for my boy," Bill answered.

The station worker checked the oil and water levels in the engine and then cleaned the windshield. When Clyde finished, Bill paid the attendant one dollar eighty cents for the gas and twenty cents for four bottles of pop. Before dark, Bill left the main highway and parked about six blocks away in a stand of pine trees. After checking the area for snakes and other varmints, Clyde chopped wood and filled the wood box, while Betty and Mona cooked a meal.

Before sunset, Bill returned with three rabbits and one fox squirrel. After supper, he cleaned the game and put it into a small wooden refrigerator and noticed the block of ice had melted considerably. He sat down with his back to a pine tree and listened to the peaceful sounds of the night as a cool breeze vibrated through the pine needles above him creating a sound like no other from any musical instrument.

Shortly Betty took a seat beside him and said, "Well, are you having second thoughts about all of us going south?"

He burst with laughter and said, "Oh, no. While I was driving today, I cherished every word and motion the children said and made as they kept pointing and commenting about things they had never seen before. Betty, we have God, each other, our vehicle, and some money hid under the floorboards of the truck, and the way prices are dropping, if I didn't earn a dime, we could eat for the next six years. We are a very fortunate family." Bill put his arm around Betty and kissed her passionately.

The following morning, Bill observed his children performing the chores that needed to be done. They were in a hurry to get rolling and see the sights along the highway. On the outskirts of Richmond, Bill reduced the speed to watch a man posting a sign in front of a lumberyard. After tacking the notice to a bulletin board, the man nodded to the family and returned to the mill.

Clyde read the sign aloud. "Wanted, one first class electrician to install electrical wiring, wire electrical motors, and install chain drives for conveyor belts. Apply at mill office. Dad, this may be a job for you!"

Bill parked the truck between a Packard and a Hudson automobile and went to the front door of the office. He knocked and a voice behind the door called out, "Come in."

A massive built man with hanging jowls asked, "How may

I help you?"

"Sir, my name is Bill Dykes and I'm inquiring about the opening for the electrical job posted on the bulletin board."

"Mister Dykes, I'm William Carney, the owner of this lumberyard. Several weeks ago we installed new transfer motors and cutting tables to expand our production. But none of the new equipment has the wiring installed and we didn't know a depression was coming. My additions are complete except for the wiring and the installation of the motors and belts. The lumberyard is shutdown, but I've decided to finish my additions so if and when the economy improves, this mill will be ready to supply lumber to our customers. Young man, tell me about your qualifications for this job."

"Mister Carney, for the past eight years I've worked at electrical wiring, elevator work, maintaining electrical motors and pumps and, of course, dynamite blasting. I was employed at a coal mine in Coldsburg, but the mine shut down."

"The Coldsburg mine," Mr. Carney said. "Is that the mine where the cave-in occurred and killed six men?"

"Yes, sir, I was in charge of rescuing the twelve miners who made it out alive," Bill said.

"All right, Bill. You have the job, providing you can perform the work. The pay is one dollar per hour and your working hours are fifty hours per week, Monday through Friday. I can see through the window that you and your family are traveling in some type of rolling home. In these uncertain times, that is very smart. Bill, where do you plan to park your truck?"

"Sir, I was going to ask you where I could find a suitable place where we could rent a spot and be out of the way."

"Bill, continue up the dirt road for about six city blocks and you will come to four small houses on your right. Park your truck right there on any suitable place you want to. We maintain those dwellings for four security guards who work here. There is a clear freshwater river east of the houses and the woods are full of small game. You may use a shotgun for hunting, but no rifles. I will look for you Monday morning."

"Thank you. I will be here Monday morning."

Bill was elated as he left the office and got into his truck. Within three hours, he had parked his truck west of the houses, used a swing blade to cut the underbrush away from the truck, tied a rope up for a clothesline, and dug a latrine. Betty was using hot water and a scrub board for washing and rinsing dirty clothes while Mona hung them up to dry. Clyde had filled the water drum and was busy chopping wood. This was the weekend, so the family dug a few worms and went fishing. While Betty and Mona carried the fish to the truck, Bill and Clyde went into the woods and killed two rabbits and four squirrels.

On Monday morning, Bill reported for work and was surprised when William Carney worked beside him. Later in the day, William said, "Bill, you don't seem to miss a stroke or make mistakes. A few of the electricians we have used in the past seem to work on a trial-and-error basis."

"William, when an electrician makes mistakes in a coal mine, it can cost lives. If anyone is unsure about installations in that place, he had better stop and think about the job. With the number of new motors you are planning to operate, the breaker panel you have is too small."

"You're right," William said. "Some of the breakers in the one we've been using trips out from time to time. When we finish these installations, I will have you tie in a larger panel with more breakers."

Wild Bill Harrigan

Bill worked for Mr. Carney for three and a half weeks—enjoying the work on top of the earth, rather than beneath it. When the job was complete, William paid him and said, "Bill, if you and your family come north again, stop by and see me. At the moment, the economy is growing weaker, but who knows, the situation may get better quicker than we think."

The two shook hands and Bill said, "I want to thank you for everything: the work, allowing us to live on your property, and the fishing and hunting here. My family looks upon this sawmill property as a vacation spot. Good luck with your business."

Shortly, Bill and his family were cruising toward North Carolina. Late the following evening, they stopped to read a sign posted at a tobacco farm north of Raleigh. After reading it Bill applied for the job. A farmer, Mr. Simmons, hired him to repair two farm tractors and do some welding on four farm implements. The job lasted two days and the Dykes family took to the road again.

With the passing of each day, the Dykes family passed dozens of homeless people walking on the shoulder of the highway, carrying their few possessions. Small children who had been abandoned by their relatives were walking in both directions. South of Columbia, South Carolina, Betty was looking in her side-view mirror and said, "Bill, for me to sit here watching those barefooted children step into those sandspurs on the side of the road in order to let us pass is a pitiful sight. They are sitting in the road crying as they pull the thorns out of their feet."

"Betty," Bill said, "we have discussed this before. I truly wish we could stop and help everyone in transient. But, if we stop every time we see someone in need, I won't be able to make a living and support this family. I promise you that if and when I secure a steady job for a few days, we will do what we can to help the children."

Betty smiled.

At that very moment, Colonel Lawrence Bentley Harrigan, a veteran of World War 1, strode from his mansion and took a backseat in an immaculate Packard automobile. Simple Sipes, an eighty-five-year-old field hand, closed the door and took a seat behind the steering wheel. "Colonel, where do I drive you?" Simple asked.

"Drive to that blasted water dam my son is having built," the colonel bellowed. "My grandfather, father, and I operated this plantation for almost two hundred years without disturbing the fish and wildlife, and now my son thinks he has a right to alter the rivers and the land. If I find anything wrong at that dam, I will see that it comes down."

Simple shook his head.

Simple was driving twenty miles per hour on the clay road between the fields of corn, cotton, tobacco, and Bermuda grass where livestock was grazing. As he turned onto the highway, the colonel ordered, "Speed up, I want to get there before the sun sets!" Simple increased his speed to forty miles per hour, but the colonel shouted, "Drive faster!"

The Packard was moving at sixty miles per hour when the right front tire blew out. Simple was a large man yet it was all he could do to hold the steering wheel in check as the car went into a ditch beside the road. The car came to a stop without either man being injured, but the right front rim hit a small boulder, bending it badly. The front tires were resting in a mud-bog and buried in two feet of water. Simple tried to back the car up a small embankment, but the heavy automobile would not budge.

"Simple," the colonel ordered as he packed his pipe, "you go to the mansion and return with my son's Rolls Royce, and tell Claven to send someone here to tow this car. I'll wait for you."

Simple was about to walk away when Bill Dykes drove up and parked his truck on the shoulder of the road. As he stepped from the cab Bill asked, "Is anyone hurt?"

"No, sir," Simple replied. "But we have a flat tire and a bent rim."

Bill said, "I have a rope in my truck. I'll pull you onto the road and then we can change the rim and tire."

"Wait just a minute, youngster," the colonel yelled as he stepped from the car. "Are you a Hun?"

Bill was taken aback as he gazed at the old gentleman

who was dressed as if he were a judge headed for court. He was wearing an expensive brown suit, a vest, a gleaming white shirt, shiny brown shoes, and a yellow bow tie with brown dots. He had a gray handlebar mustache and his silver gray hair showed under a cream-colored hat with a dark brown band.

Bill said, “No, sir, I’m not a German. Two of my older cousins fought the dreaded Hun at Verdun in World War One, but both of them were killed in battle.”

“What were your cousins’ names and rank?” the colonel asked.

“Sir,” Bill answered, “one was named Captain Joe Prigle and his brother, a lieutenant, was named Ben.”

“Yes, I fought with your cousins,” the colonel boomed, smiling. “In fact, Joe and I planned two missions together before executing our plan. You and the rest of this country should be very proud of them. Why didn’t you fight the scoundrels?”

“Sir, at the time I was an adolescent, and the military authorities would not accept me.” The colonel was still gazing at Bill, sizing him up.

“Sir, I’m Bill Dykes and this is my wife, Betty, my daughter, Mona, and my son, Clyde.”

Bill extended his hand and the colonel shook it before saying, “I’m Colonel Bill Harrigan and this darkie is Simple Sipes. You can pull my car on the road and help change the tire, but I will pay you for the trouble.”

Bill started to protest about the pay but somehow knew it would be a waste of time. He looked at Clyde and said, “Son, get the rope out of the truck.”

Shortly the Packard was on the shoulder of the road and Bill and Simple were mounting the spare whitewall tire. While working, Bill answered the colonel’s questions about his life and work. They had just finished changing the tire when the colonel’s son, Claven Harrigan, parked a Rolls Royce behind them. As he exited the car he asked, “Has anyone been hurt?”

“No one’s hurt,” the colonel answered, “but another sorry tire blew out and sent us into the ditch. Claven, this is Mr. Dykes and his family. Bill is an out-of-work coal miner.”

Claven nodded, acknowledging the family.

“He pulled my car from the ditch and helped Simple change the tire. Simple and I are going to check on your dam, and I will talk with you about the project later. Take this dollar, Mr. Dykes, along with my thanks. Good day.”

As the Packard pulled away, Claven asked, “Mr. Dykes,

what is your destination?"

"Mr. Harrigan, I'm looking for a job. Since leaving the coal mine, I have had several small jobs but nothing of any consequence."

"Since you are not obligated to anyone at the moment," Claven said, "if you are knowledgeable in carpentry, electrical, plumbing, and pump work, I can offer you a few weeks of work. Since this depression moved into this country like a tornado, top wages are one dollar per hour."

"Mr. Harrigan, no man should brag, but I'm proficient in all those skills."

"When will you be able to begin working?" Claven asked.

"Sir, I can start tomorrow morning providing I can find a place to park my truck which serves as our home."

"Bill," Claven said, "follow me and I'll show you a high dry spot under some oak trees beside the river. There are five tenant houses behind the mansion where my other workers live, and all of them are excellent people. You may as well live next to your neighbors, and your children can socialize with theirs."

Bill followed the Rolls Royce. They passed a two-story southern mansion with five brick chimneys with a manicured lawn and beautiful flowers. "Betty," Bill said, "I looked at the design of the mansion and the outbuildings. They were all built before or during the Civil War. If the Yankees had seen them, they would have been burned."

"Perhaps the northern troops bypassed this area and didn't see the mansion," Betty remarked. "We're not farmers but anyone can see the crops are gorgeous and everything seems to be well planned. The livestock is fat from feeding on the different grains they are grazing on. Did you notice the field to the left side of the mansion with all the trees? I saw pecan, pear, persimmon trees, and a huge grape arbor."

"No, I didn't," Bill said, "but one thing is for sure, if the Harrigan family owns all this, they must be rich." The tenant houses were behind a rolling knoll, out of sight of the mansion. Bill stopped his truck when Claven parked in front of a house.

Claven walked over to Bill's truck and said, "Mr. Dykes, I don't have an empty tenant house, but you said the structure on the truck is your home. You can park it under the oak trees. There is a well for water in front of the houses. You may use the river behind you for fishing or swimming. My employees are allowed to hunt on my land, but they can't use rifles—I don't want rifle slugs in my livestock."

Claven paused to light a cigar and Bill asked, "Where or to whom do I report for work in the morning?"

"Speed Searcy lives in the house next door. Speed is the only employee I have who is capable of helping a top-notch technician like you. I will notify him that you will meet him on his front stoop at seven o'clock. Speed will work with you on a daily basis. He knows the jobs I want done and the order in which they are to be completed. Don't concern yourself about tools; we have plenty of them. Bill, do you have any more questions?"

"No, sir," Bill replied. "I think you have covered everything and thanks for the job."

"Bill, there is one thing I need to mention because you will hear it from others on the farm or when you go into our nearby settlement. My father, who many refer to as Wild Bill Harrigan, has a reputation as being a good man, but, at times, he is very unpredictable. Two weeks before the Great War ended in 1918, he was blinded by chlorine gas when a bomb exploded near him. I was told that although he was blind, he exited his foxhole swinging a bayonet in the direction of the enemy. Another bomb exploded, killing nine of his companions and severely wounding my father in the head."

Claven paused to pull on his cigar and continued, "Bill, when my father came home from a military hospital, he had regained his sight, but he had four body wounds from shrapnel and a six-inch metal plate in his head. I love my father, and until the war came along, he was a very productive man. Most of the time, the colonel is civil and responsive to people—with the first exception being the German race. However, several times he has gone on a tangent and created havoc. Last year when the local citizens refused his request to hold a celebration on the date the Great War ended, he had Simple drive him to town. He was so angry he shot out a few storefront windows and the only streetlight in the settlement of Gloomburg.

"Most of the time, Simple has kept my father in check, and so far, he has not harmed anyone," Claven continued. "I do not wish to put him in an institution and restrict his freedom, but I can't let him harm innocent people. Bill, you aren't aware of it, but my father hardly ever talks with a stranger. I was surprised to see him talking with you, much less accepting your help. He is a stubborn and proud man, but he seems to like you and your family."

"Claven, I appreciate men like your father, and if there is anything I can do to help him just ask. I will be waiting for Speed in the morning."

Claven went next door and told Speed's wife that Bill would be looking for him the following morning.

Bill backed his truck under the oaks and his family went to work establishing another homesite. Before dark, the five families adjoining the Dykes walked over and introduced themselves. Bill and Betty answered the tenant farmers' questions about the coal mine shutting down and what little they knew about the state of the economy. All of their news was bad.

Bill was surprised the following morning when he walked over to Speed's stoop to find two saddled horses waiting for them. Speed was sitting on the steps, drinking coffee, his feet resting on top of two canvas bags filled with tools. "I can see you are ready for work," Speed remarked. "Bill, attach one of those bags of tools to the saddle horn of the spotted horse while I take care of the other one. Claven wants us to go to the barn and repair the tractors and farm implements first."

They mounted and rode between the fields where men, women, and teenagers were hoeing weeds out of the corn. Upon reaching the barn, they carried the tool bags inside and then unsaddled the horses and put them into stalls. "Bill," Speed said, "Claven wants us to tune up these two tractors and then weld some cracks on the harrow frames before we install the new discs. I'll get the grinder, welding rods, and face shields while you uncoil the hoses."

Bill said, "If you agree, we will tune up one of the tractors first and that will enable us to raise the harrow framework for welding."

Before eleven o'clock that morning, both tractors were running smoothly. "Speed," Bill said, "get in the tractor and raise the harrows framework until I signal you to stop." Moments later the harrows were raised so the men could perform their welding without squatting or bending over.

While Speed watched, Bill used a grinder to remove the paint, rust, and slag away from the supports on the harrows. When he put on a face shield and started to perform his first weld, Speed put one on and said, "If you don't mind, I want to see how this is done. I want to learn how to weld."

"Speed, it is easy to learn, providing you pay close attention to the crack and the tip of the rod. Move directly in front of me and you will have a better view of the job." Before noon Bill had made one weld on a muffler bracket and nineteen on the farm implements. He found Speed to be a congenial man to work with who was anxious to learn other trades.

Bill was about to start another weld when Speed said, "Let's eat lunch, it's past noon."

As the men picked up their lunch bags, Claven entered the barn, nodded, and took a seat on one of the tractors. He cranked the machine and let the engine warm up. After he looked at the gauges on the instrument panel, he shut the engine off. He repeated his inspection of the other tractor and then looked at the welds Bill had finished.

"Those welds look good," Claven said. "A professional welder is hard to find in these parts. Bill, did you find anything else wrong with the tractors?"

"Well, yes, sir," Bill said. "The fan belts need to be replaced on both of them. Within a year, both tractors will need new mufflers."

Claven pulled a note pad from his jacket pocket and made notes.

"The machines cranked easily and seem to run well," Claven said. "Exactly what did you do to them?"

Speed said, "We changed oil, oil filters, air filters, antifreeze, and replaced spark plugs, rotary, distributor caps, sparkplug wires, points, and Bill reset the timing on both engines."

"That's good work," Claven said. "Speed, tomorrow when you finish repairing these two machines, you and Bill drive them to the fifty-acre field we're clearing, and leave them with that crew of men. Then drive the two tractors they are using back to the barn and repair them."

From a distance, the sounds of three explosions captivated the attention of everyone on the farm. "Bill," Claven said, "those explosions are coming from a field I'm having cleared. Usually they explode one dynamite charge at a time to remove stumps from the ground, but my father is intrigued by explosives. Wild Bill is with that crew today. He has taken charge of the dynamiting, and is probably demonstrating how he did things in the Great War. I'm on my way to the dam and will pick him up so I can keep him out of trouble. I'll see you tomorrow."

At quitting time, Speed and Bill saddled their horses and rode home. After removing the saddles, they put the animals in a shed behind Speed's house and fed them. Speed said, "I can see my boy Steve and your son Clyde cleaning fish."

"That is a welcome sight," Bill replied. "Our wives and other children are coming down the road carrying baskets of vegetables. Speed, where did they buy them?"

"No one on this farm has to buy vegetables or fruit," Speed said. "The Harrigan family maintains a fifteen-acre garden a short distance down that road. Anyone working here is welcome to it as long as he does his share of the work, planting and maintaining the garden, and picking fruit from the orchard."

Two hours later, Speed's and Bill's families were sitting on a picnic bench in Speed's backyard enjoying fried fish, grits, corn on the cob, sliced tomatoes, hushpuppies, and lemonade. While eating, the families watched Simple stop the Packard beside the river a short distance away and Wild Bill stepped out. He quickly assembled two fishing rods and handed Simple one. After baiting their hooks with worms, they cast their lines into the river, took a seat under an oak tree, and lit their pipes.

"Daddy," Mona asked, "why does Mr. Harrigan wear a jacket and bow tie to go fishing?"

"Mona, I suppose Mr. Harrigan is a rich man and he can wear anything he wants to. Before you were born, Mr. Harrigan was severely injured in a world war. However, he seems to be a fine old gentleman who lives by his own code of ethics."

The families continued eating, while the two fishermen pulled bream and catfish from the river. When the meal was over, Bill noticed that Clyde and the other boys had disappeared.

The families were talking when Wild Bill told Simple to put their fish in the trunk of the car. The boys reappeared, with each one holding a four-foot stick. Wild Bill approached the families and greeted each one by name and then said, "Boys, unless you have chores to perform, it is time to drill. Simple, hurry up and get over here."

The boys lined up quickly in a straight line and Wild Bill said, "Stand at attention." Fourteen boys stood erect with their sticks resting on the ground on their right side. "Left face," Wild Bill ordered. "Right shoulder arms. Forward, march, and move to the cadence. By the numbers and rhythm, count to yourself, one, two, three, four. To the rear, march, and sharply turn one hundred eighty degrees." For several minutes Wild Bill issued commands and the boys tried to execute precision movements. Clyde was among the boys, and it was obvious he was having trouble turning on the exact foot to the commands being issued by Wild Bill.

"Bill," Betty said, "I didn't know our son had fashioned a make-believe weapon and was training to be a soldier, did you?"

"No, I didn't either," Bill answered. "But, as you constantly say, boys are hard to keep up with."

"Squad halt," Wild Bill ordered. "Occupy your foxholes and prepare for the enemy." The boys ran to seven foxholes which they had dug earlier, with two of them occupying one hole. "Ammo bearers supply our troops." Betty was startled when Mona and the other girls ran to the foxholes and handed each boy several rocks which had been painted blue. "Ammo bearers retreat."

"Fire at will," Wild Bill shouted.

The boys pretended their wooden sticks were rifles as they pointed their weapons and shouted, "Bam, boom, bam, bam," aiming across the river at a fictitious enemy who was shooting at them. Downstream, Simple had forded the river and crept up to the area directly across from where the boys were pretending to shoot. When he pulled a rope taut through a pulley, seven large white targets which had been made from plywood rose to a vertical position. Each target had a sketch of a German soldier painted on it. Simple lit three firecrackers and threw them in the vicinity of the targets to give the boys the impression the soldiers were firing at them.

Wild Bill yelled, "Throw your grenades at the Huns." The boys hurled the blue rocks, which represented hand grenades, at the white boards. Some of the rocks fell into the river but a few scored direct hits. Shortly a whistle blast filled the area and Wild Bill ordered, "Cease fire and assemble here." Immediately the boys stood at attention facing the river. "Parade rest," he shouted at them. "Simple, give us a count of the hand grenade hits on the Huns."

From across the river, Simple shouted, "Colonel, we have three direct hits and eleven hand grenades within four feet of the targets."

"Soldiers, this has been one of our better drills," Wild Bill said. "Come to attention. You are dismissed until next week." Each boy went home to put his weapon away before returning to the group.

"Speed," Bill asked, "how long has this military training been taking place?"

"Bill, to my knowledge, about three years. But Wild Bill hardly ever executes his mock battles when adults are around. I have given my sons strict orders to drop out of the group if Wild Bill supplies them with dynamite or live weapons."

At twilight the families returned home with a few of the adults concerned about their children and military training.

Mona and Clyde went inside and bathed before going to bed, but Betty remained outside with her disgruntled husband. She said, "Bill, I know that you are as upset as I am about our children learning about war. But, they are easily influenced because they respect adults. How do you plan to handle this problem?"

"Betty, for the time being, let's don't say or do anything. You told me that Speed's wife, Clair, works in the mansion three days each week. You also said the Harrigans have a small library and they will lend books to any of their workers. Ask Clair if you can borrow any books they have about the Great War."

"What makes you think the Harrigan family would have such books in their possession?" Betty quickly asked.

"Because Wild Bill sees himself as a student of war and a commander who believes another conflict is imminent, so he tries to keep himself and anyone he can influence prepared for battle," Bill said. "Betty, with your help, I plan to let our children learn and see for themselves how senseless and wasteful war really is."

"Bill, you are right. When our children read about the nations that joined together and defeated the Germans, they might think that war is anything but glamorous and then they will cease to have anything to do with anyone who advocates death and destruction. In the beginning of this dilemma Mona and Clyde could be misled, but when they answer your questions, hopefully the lessons they learn will be engraved on their brains. Although they are young and learning to glorify destruction, it is up to us to teach them about war, cannibalism, and mass destruction."

The Dykes family embraced the hard work on the farm while enjoying the privileges the Harrigan family granted. Two weeks had passed since Wild Bill and the children had given their demonstration on a war game. Bill and Speed returned home from work late one evening because they had stopped at the mansion to tune up the Packard. When Bill entered the room, Mona was putting supper on the table and Clyde was reading a history book about the Great War.

At the conclusion of the meal, Bill said, "Clyde, you and Mona take a seat. The history books you are reading were borrowed at my request. Your mother and I were shocked when we saw you take part in a make-believe war game because neither of us knew that you were taking part in tactical training. How long have you been training in Wild Bill's military maneuvers?"

"Papa, we've been members of the squad since the second day we got here," Mona said. "We drill three times each week."

"Have both of you been reading these books?" Bill asked. The children nodded in the affirmative. "You are reading about the bloodiest and costliest conflict in the history of mankind. I want you to write down the answers to these questions for me no later than next week." Quickly the children retrieved pencils and paper from a drawer.

"My first question is, how long did the Great War last?" Bill paused after each question in order for his children to have time to write. "How many states or nations participated in the Great War?" Betty refilled Bill's coffee cup and he continued. "How many soldiers died in the Great War? How many soldiers were presumed dead? How many soldiers were wounded? How many civilians were killed in the war? How many soldiers were taken prisoner during the war? As a result of the war, how many orphans, widows, and refugees were in Europe? How many buildings were destroyed?"

"Papa, please slow down," Mona said.

Bill took a drink of coffee, paused, and continued. "How many men were mobilized to go to war in the deadly struggle? What was the cost of the Great War? What nation suffered the worst as a result of the Great War? As a result of the Great War, what happened to Germany's homes, factories, and lands? What was the name of the treaty imposed on Germany when the war ended? Clyde, Mona, do you have any questions?"

"Yes, I do," Clyde said. "How many days do we have before we must give you the answers to these questions?"

"Ten," Bill answered. "In the days ahead, obey your mother and do your chores. But until you answer my questions, I want both of you to read these history books and learn about war, the outcome of senseless struggles, and the pain, suffering, disease, waste, hatred, destruction, and above all, the total cost of human lives and economic wealth that goes down a sewer pipe. Now you may go back to your reading."

Betty stepped into the yard with Bill and said, "I realize you didn't enjoy that talk with the children, but it was necessary. No one should believe that war is glamorous and children should not be trained to commit havoc. Bill, are you going to permit them to continue participating in the war games?"

"Yes, Betty, I am. Once our children learn what war does to human beings and their countries, I sincerely hope they will forsake the evil phenomenon on their own accord. I could easily forbid them from taking part in the mock battles and tell them why. But, if they study and learn for themselves, I believe the true facts will remain with them. To my knowledge, they have never been exposed to people like Wild Bill or his beliefs and I sincerely hope this will be a lesson Mona and Clyde will not forget."

"When will your work here be finished?" Betty asked.

"Betty, two days ago, Claven told Speed and me to report to the dam on Monday morning. We have about thirty metal beams to cut and weld flanges on one end which will be used for pilings to support the dam. I haven't been to the dam yet, but according to Speed, my first job will be to make repairs on a Bucyrus dragline which is not running. Then Speed and I will take a multitude of measurements and return to the barn and continue fabricating metal braces and beams. Speed told me, 'When the dam is finished, Claven will have a walkway built across the top of it.' I assume we will be here at least another month."

"Darling, in the morning the children and I are going to the Harrigan's garden with the other families to pick vegetables," Betty said. "But, I will require Mona and Clyde to study the history books for at least two hours per day."

"That sounds like a good plan. But don't let them forget that I am expecting them to answer my questions."

On Monday morning, Speed and Bill loaded thirty-two metal beams on two trailers. "Bill, let's go to the dam," Speed said. They pulled the trailers with tractors, so Speed drove one and Bill the other. They drove across the plantation between cultivated crops with Bill anxious to see the dam. Finally Speed drove up a steep hill and down the other side and was momentarily out of Bill's sight. Bill stopped on top of the hill because Speed had stopped waiting for him.

Below them, on the edge of the narrow river, were boxes of hardware, wooden piling, metal beams, a storage shed, rolls of cable, stacks of lumber, and fourteen men. Sandbags were piled on one side of the dam, stopping the flow of the water. Claven said, "Speed, park the tractors near the river and these men will unload the trailers while you and Bill work on the dragline."

After parking the tractors, Speed and Bill went to the dragline with Claven. "Mr. Harrigan, do you have an operations manual for this dragline?" Bill asked.

"Speed, the manual and spare parts for the machine are in the storage shed," Claven said.

Bill and Speed went to work on the machine. Before two o'clock, they had adjusted the values on the diesel engine, reset the timing, replaced two gaskets, replaced two gauges, changed oil and filters, and removed one link from the chain to the power takeoff. Next they applied lubricant to the turntable and greased each bearing on the machine.

Claven approached and said, "Speed, we will need to use

the dragline tomorrow, providing I can find someone to operate the machine. Will it be ready for service?"

"Yes, sir," Bill said. "The dragline will be ready tomorrow but for the moment, several strands of cable are broken on the drag cables and two cable clamps need to be replaced. No one working under the boom will be safe until those cables are renewed."

"I don't want anyone getting hurt," Claven responded, "so renew the cables." It was six o'clock when the last cable clamp was tightened on a cable that finished the job. To the surprise of everyone on the job, Bill stepped up into the cab of the dragline, cranked the engine, raised and lowered the boom, checked the gauges on the instrument panel, moved the machine forward and backward in order to check the tracks, and swung the machine three hundred sixty degrees to check the turntable.

When Bill shut the machine off and stepped to the ground, Claven asked, "Bill, when did you learn to operate a dragline?"

"While working at the coal mine, I loaded coal into freight cars for thirteen months with a machine exactly like this Bucyrus."

"Good," Claven said, "when you and Speed finish with the metal beams, both of you will be a welcome asset on this project if my dragline operator fails to come to work. I'll see you tomorrow."

The Theory

Unseen by the men leaving the dam, Wild Bill and Simple stood beneath an oak tree overlooking the dam. To Simple, Wild Bill said, "I don't care for that project because it isn't necessary. Wait for me at the car." He went to the jobsite and looked everything over, while kicking several of the boxes containing supplies. He remembered ordering his troops during the Great War to blow up two dams which had forced the Huns to either retreat or advance into a murderous machine-gun fire. He looked at the body of water, searching for ducks that had once lived in and around the river. There were none. As Simple drove home, he knew by the look on Wild Bill's face that he was disgusted.

On the way home, Bill Dykes asked, "Speed, how much land does Claven own on the other side of the river?"

"I've heard approximately seventy-eight hundred acres more or less. His survey line extends the entire length of his property, which is twenty-two thousand acres. Bill, when the dam is completed, Claven intends to clear the land across the river and plant crops. That floodgate located in the center of the dam will allow water to flow constantly to the swamps downstream."

"How many farms are downriver from Claven's property?" Bill asked.

"There are four, but all of their farms have large lowland swamps bordering the river. Claven's dam will not harm any of their land. In fact, should they need more water during a dry spell, he will open the floodgate. Claven's dam project is an extensive plan that encompasses irrigating all of his crops. According to Claven, farming techniques will drastically change in the near future with improved machinery and fertilizers."

"Speed, exactly where does the water that feeds the river come from?"

"Bill, there are two hills on the southeastern edge of Claven's property. The river, which can't be seen from the dam, runs between them. Rainwater, four small creeks, and nine ditches from Gloomburg maintain the amount of water flowing into the river. We know of three artesian wells on Claven's land running into the river but he plans to cap the wells and stop wasting that water."

Claven and his workers met Speed and Bill in the barn the following morning. Claven said, "Speed, we're going to load the welding equipment and all of these metal beams and move them to the dam. You and Bill can continue the fabricating work at the job site. If we should have another breakdown with machinery, I need both of you there."

Two hours later, everyone was working at the dam.

That same morning, Clara, Claven's wife, met the ladies and children at the garden. She said in her soft pleasant voice, "Good morning, everyone. Since the summer is about gone, you may pick anything and everything you want from this field. If you want to preserve the vegetables, do so. Shortly I will have a house servant bring a tractor and two trailers here so you can carry your vegetables to your homes. Within three days, we will pick any remaining vegetables and send them to a church to be distributed to the needy in Gloomburg. Then this field will be fertilized, plowed under, and a winter garden planted. If there are no questions, I will return in a few hours." There were no questions so the ladies and their children went to work picking vegetables.

At the end of the day, the crew at the dam had started home when a biplane, flying just above the river, gained altitude and flew above the dam, clearing it by no more than twenty feet. "Oh, no," Claven said, "it's One Arm Charlie. I don't need him on the premises to incite my father."

From the edge of the river, the men watched the biplane gain altitude, bank, descend, and drop behind a cultivated field.

"Speed, where did the airplane land?" Bill asked.

"One Arm Charlie always lands on the clay road in front of the mansion," Speed answered. "Charlie, Wild Bill's younger brother, lost his left arm in an air battle over France during the Great War. While Charlie is visiting, these next few days won't be boring because he and Wild Bill will celebrate and relive the battles of their past. Charlie owns a farm on the Georgia–South Carolina state line. I've been told it is larger than this one."

One Arm Charlie taxied the biplane onto the lawn of the

mansion and cut the engine. He stepped down from the front cockpit, wearing a leather flying hood with goggles, an exclusive leather jacket, a shiny black cross-button shirt topped with a long white scarf, dark gray English-style riding pants, brown high-top leather boots, and a wide belt with two holsters holding forty-five-caliber pistols. As Charlie removed his hood, Wild Bill said, "Brother, it's time you paid us a visit. We have some work for your aircraft."

Before Charlie could respond, Clara and her children and grandchildren embraced the old flyer. While walking to the house, One Arm said, "Steve, you, William, and Herman get the three boxes of gifts out of the second cockpit." On each visit, Charlie always brought candy and perfume for the females and knives and fishing gear for the males. The brothers took a sip from the flask Charlie pulled from his coat before joining the family in the parlor.

"Charlie," Clara said, "tell us how your wife and family are doing. Do you have any more grandchildren? Did you bring pictures of them with you?" Charlie pulled a large packet of papers and photos from his pocket.

When Bill got home, he noticed several hampers of vegetables as he approached his truck. Mona, Clyde, and Betty were shelling peas and butterbeans. Bill remarked, "That is enough food to feed this family for months. What is going on?"

"Papa," Mona said, "Mr. Harrigan's wife gave the workers permission to pick all the vegetables from the garden. All the families on this plantation are going to preserve vegetables. Except for the string beans, next week the summer garden will be plowed under and made ready for winter crops. Any excess vegetables that the workers don't want will be given to the needy."

Bill looked at four bushels of vegetables beside the truck and six more in the shade of a big tree. He said, "My family has a lot of work to complete in the next few days. Betty, do you have everything you need to preserve all of this food?"

"No, I do not," Betty replied. "Speed's wife and I are going into Gloomburg the first thing in the morning to pick up some supplies and ice. Bill, the children won't have time to study their history books for the next few days because they will be helping with our vegetables."

"We will make an exception for now," Bill said. "But the

questions about war must be answered." Bill worked with the family until dark. Then he bathed, ate supper, turned out one oil lantern, and went to bed. However, his family continued working for another three hours.

The following morning, except for the Harrigan family and babies, everyone on the plantation had breakfast before daylight and went to work. Later, the massive table inside the mansion was filled with food as the entire family took their seats, expecting Wild Bill to be dressed in his flying attire. Before a servant could pour coffee for the adults, One Arm picked up a decanter of brandy and half-filled his and Wild Bill's cups. Breakfast was jovial as One Arm teased Claven's grandchildren about going up with him in his flying machine. When the meal was finished, Claven asked, "Father, what will you two be doing today?"

"My brother wants to fly over a few of our bordering counties and see what has changed," Will Bill answered. "I'm going with him to point out a few objects such as the two new water towers and we're also going to take care of a job for you. We will see you shortly."

Claven headed for the dam, very concerned about what job the old brothers would take care of.

The remaining Harrigan family went outside to watch the biplane take off. They observed Wild Bill as he put a bag in the second cockpit. Simple was waiting beside the biplane with four containers of gasoline.

"Brother," One Arm said, "have Simple fill the gas tank while I check the engine, struts, cables, and flaps." One Arm opened a small door on each side of the engine and checked it first. The last items he checked were the flaps. "Are we ready to take off?" One Arm asked.

"The gas tank is full and the cap is on," Wild Bill answered. The brothers put on their parachutes, climbed into the cockpits, pulled their goggles over their eyes, and buckled themselves in.

"Simple, give the propeller a spin," One Arm ordered. Simple gave the propeller a strong pull and quickly stepped back as the engine cranked and the wooden prop began spinning. One Arm increased the throttle as he observed the oil pressure gauge and checked the controls. As he slowly taxied to the clay road, the family huddled together and shielded their eyes because the wind from the prop would blow grass and particles of dirt flying through the air. Moments later, the biplane raced down the road and was airborne.

One Arm climbed to an altitude of four hundred feet before

he banked the aircraft, dived to eighty feet, and buzzed just over the heads of the family. Horses ran around the corral and whined, chickens crowed, ducks quacked, and the hogs in the parlor honked. The grandchildren cheered the heroics at the display of danger from the daredevils in the aircraft.

One Arm gained altitude and banked the biplane again in order to make another pass over the family. He inverted the aircraft, hoping the family could see inside the cockpit as he flew over them. One of Will Bill's boots rested on the bundle of dynamite in order to keep it from falling from the biplane. At ninety miles per hour, seventy feet above the road, Wild Bill dropped several bags of soft candy near the children as the aircraft flew over. The sky was a clear blue and the family watched the aircraft until it was just a speck up toward the stratosphere.

Minutes later One Arm turned his head toward his brother and nodded up and down. Wild Bill knew he was about to dive and fly under the supports of Turners Bridge, which looked like an outhouse from the sky. The fishermen below had seen those antics before, and they knew to get out of the way. While the biplane dived, gaining speed, four fishermen in two small boats paddled furiously in order to make room for the aircraft to pass beneath the bridge. Six men, who had been fishing from the top of the bridge, ran for the bank.

The aircraft was level just above the water and passed under the bridge as Wild Bill waved at the fishermen. Immediately the biplane gained altitude and One Arm executed an outside loop. He leveled off above the river before making another pass under the bridge and then flew out of sight of the fishermen.

Wild Bill pointed and yelled the name of the first obstacle he wanted to fly between. "Fly between the water towers." As the plane went between them, a flock of pigeons flew away. "Buzz the school yard." When the aircraft passed the flagpole, the wind from the propeller caused the flag to fly horizontal momentarily. "Make a pass over the train." The airmen could see the faces of passengers looking through the windows when they flew over it for the second time. "Circle the cotton factory." After buzzing the main street of Gloomburg and startling its citizens, One Arm flew over three other small settlements. Hours later he landed the plane on the only major highway just past a gas station outside of Gloomburg.

Two young boys, each carrying two cans of gasoline, approached the plane and One Arm said, "Fill her up, and when you finish, treat yourselves to a bottle of pop." The boys had performed this chore many times and they welcomed the radical brothers who always amused them.

The flyers went into a diner adjoining the station and ordered beans, watermelon juice, and barbecue. They poured brandy into their juice and while they ate, several of Gloomburg's citizens walked around the biplane, discussing the capabilities of the contraption. A ninety-eight-year-old man said, "One thing is certain, things around here won't be boring while that aircraft is in the sky with those old veterans."

Shortly the brothers paid the waitress and the station attendant and gave each one a gratuity. Approaching the aircraft, One Arm said, "Brother, check the gas tank and cap while I look at the flaps." As soon as the old brothers strapped themselves into the cockpits, One Arm said to a station attendant, "Give her a spin and move out of the way."

The engine roared, but there was a gradual curve in the road so One Arm taxied a short distance and stopped on the shoulder of the road to let a truck pass. However, the truck went a short distance and turned around. By that time, One Arm had already eased the biplane onto the road and increased the RPM on the engine. The bystanders stood in awe as the biplane raced down the road toward the oncoming truck. Both truck doors flew open and the two occupants dived onto the road, holding their hands over their heads.

One Arm was laughing as he pulled the stick back and flew over the truck, clearing it by ten feet. The group around the station was cheering, but the occupants of the truck were shaking their fists and cursing. One Arm flew past the dam, dropped to fifty feet above the river, and decreased the speed of the aircraft in order to get a good look at the massive construction site.

"I can see the first beaver dam," One Arm yelled. "I will pass it on the left side." As the aircraft approached the pile of limbs, logs, and other debris, the brothers were amazed as to how such a small group of animals could build such a large structure. The beaver dam was protruding about thirty feet out into the river. One Arm held his course, pretending he was making a bomb run over German troops.

Wild Bill had already tied four sticks of dynamite together with a short fuse, hoping to destroy the dam and he had seven more bundles in a bag at his feet. Just before the aircraft reached the dam, he used his cigar and lit the fuse. "Hold her steady," Wild Bill yelled. He threw the bundle of dynamite and it landed at the edge of the beaver dam and wedged between several small logs. A horrific explosion erupted, sending chunks of wood and limbs into the river and onto the bank. The concussion from the explosion shook the tail-end of the aircraft.

"Make a low pass over the river," Wild Bill yelled. "We may need to drop another charge on the dam." The plane passed over the river at seventy miles per hour and the only thing left from the beaver dam was floating logs, smoke, and a few flames on the shoreline. One Arm gunned the engine, heading downriver, looking for the next beaver dam.

At Claven's dam project, Bill asked, "Speed, what are the brothers blowing up?"

"I think they are destroying beaver dams," Speed said. "There are four of them in the river, no, I should say there are only three. Shortly there won't be any obstructions in this river."

Claven shook his head and added, "Destroying the beaver dams is all right, but when One Arm goes home, I usually pay a fine for his and my father's antics and the many things they buzzed in and around this community."

When Claven walked away, Bill asked, "Speed, what were the other antics Claven was referring to?"

Another explosion occurred, sending noises over the farmland and surrounding areas. "Bill," Speed answered, "every time One Arm comes for a visit, he and his brother take off and buzz everything in this area, including the citizens of Gloomburg. After One Arm leaves, the county sheriff visits us and Claven has to pay a fine for the daredevils' exploits. On one occasion there was a school parade on the main street downtown and the brothers buzzed them."

Bill shook his head in disbelief.

The aircraft was flying up the middle of the river and Wild Bill yelled, "Slow down, this is a huge beaver dam." When One Arm saw the dam, he banked the plane and turned around to make a bombing run. Wild Bill lit the fuses to two bundles of dynamite. As the aircraft approached the animal's fortification, he dropped both charges and they landed dead center of the dam. Simultaneously, the charges erupted and the noise could be heard for miles around, but the beaver dam ceased to exist. As the smoke cleared, One Arm circled the area and saw piles of debris floating down river.

"One more to go," Wild Bill yelled, "and then it will be toddy time."

As the aircraft flew around a bend in the river, One Arm saw the fourth dam and yelled, "There are three children fishing near the dam. We can't drop the charges of dynamite here, so let's go home."

"Did you see that herd of wild hogs grazing behind the dam?" Wild Bill yelled.

One Arm turned his head, nodded in the affirmative, and yelled, "We will come back in the morning and try to kill a few."

Minutes later the biplane landed, and One Arm taxied to the front lawn and cut the engine. Most of the family greeted them, including four teenage boys. Wild Bill said to the boys, "We could not blow up the last dam because of three children fishing near it. But we did see a herd of wild hogs feeding on acorns under oak trees on this side of the river. Herman, tomorrow is Saturday. Would you, Frank, Seth, and George like to go hunting with me and my brother?"

"Yes, sir," the boys answered in unison. They were excited about the hunt, because Claven rarely trusted them with firearms.

"Simple," Wild Bill continued, "at six o'clock in the morning, meet us at the barn with a tractor and trailer gassed up and ready to go. While we are in the woods hunting, clean two worktables, heat two 55-gallon drums of water and two cast-iron pots of water, and be sure to sharpen our knives and saws."

Supper at the mansion was jovial, with the old veterans answering questions about their exploits during the day. However, neither of them mentioned buzzing the school, the Gloomburg citizens, or frightening the occupants of a truck and a train. Finally, Claven's granddaughter, Mary, asked, "Granddaddy Bill, when will you blow up the last beaver dam?"

One Arm said, "Mary, if no one is near the dam, we will destroy it the day after tomorrow. When that chore is complete, I have to go home."

Just before seven the following morning, Wild Bill parked the tractor, and One Arm, along with four boys, stepped off the trailer near the riverbank. Wild Bill cautioned the boys about being careful with the single-shot twenty-two rifles they were carrying. Then he said, "Boys, if or when a group of hogs comes from the palmetto bushes, shoot the lead hog first. When their leader is disabled, the other hogs will remain with him for a short time. That's when you can easily get several more shots."

Shortly all six hunters were sitting in or around different oak trees looking for hogs. Their wait was short. Several hogs came from the brush and started feeding below Herman, while several more appeared before One Arm. "I'll nail the lead hog," Herman said to himself. He shot and killed a large sow, then quietly and quickly he reloaded and dropped two more.

One Arm was equipped with a repeating twenty-two rifle, which was lying across an oak limb, and he easily ended the life of four hogs. Within the next hour, the hunters killed five more of the wild beasts.

Wild Bill climbed down from a tree and yelled, "Okay, boys. We have a total of eleven hogs. Let's unload our weapons and drag these hogs to the trailer." While the boys moved the animals, Wild Bill and One Arm castrated a wild boar and then gutted the hogs and put the intestines in sacks. After slitting the underbellies of the other hogs and removing their entrails, the boys put their intestines in a burlap bag. They loaded the hogs on the trailer and Wild Bill drove toward the mansion.

When Wild Bill stopped the trailer behind the mansion, Simple and the younger boys had two huge cast-iron pots with boiling water and two 55-gallon drums of hot water. Two worktables had been washed and the buckets, knives, saws, and straight razors had been sharpened.

"Look at all those hogs!" Mary said. "That was a good hunt."

Without being told, Herman and Seth cautiously submerged a hog in the cast-iron kettle and held the animal steady while Frank and George scrubbed it with brushes. Next, the four of them shaved the hair from the hog, rinsed the animal again, and placed it on a clean table where Simple and Wild Bill began butchering the animal. The cleaning and butchering process continued, while two hound dogs grabbed the scraps on the ground and buried them behind the barn.

When ten hogs were cut into hams, shoulders, sides, bacon slabs, brisket, and other parts, Wild Bill said, "Let's hang the boar to a limb and skin him. His hide is tough, and his shoulders are covered with shingles. Herman, you and George get the sausage grinder and grind up the tubs of small pork parts while Seth and Frank clean the intestines so we can pack them with the sausage meat. Brother, would you season the meat as they grind it?"

When the last hog was butchered, Simple had a huge fire going under the kettle, cooking out hog fat, which would be used for lard. Before noon, the process was finished, and the pork and sausage had been treated with a brine solution and were hanging from hooks in the smokehouse. After the cans had been filled with lard, Wild Bill said, "Let's clean up and eat."

Quickly the cutting tools, tables, and tubs were cleaned and put away, finishing the hog-butchering process. The children had been arguing among themselves about the species of the wild hogs. George said, "No. Four of the hogs had the markings and color of the three pigs that escaped from the pen two years ago, which makes part of their bloodline domesticated stock. The large boar with the big tusks was the only thou-bred wild hog we killed."

Most of the Harrigan family was eating breakfast the following morning when they heard the biplane take off. "Today will be the last of the beaver dams," Herman said. "Dad, when is One Arm going home?"

"Tomorrow morning, providing the weather is clear and your uncles can't find anything else to blow up, kill, or buzz," Claven said.

One Arm flew at a very high altitude over the construction dam looking for ducks before descending for a closer look. No ducks were in sight. Minutes later he circled the beaver dam to be sure no one was around it. He then signaled to his brother to drop the dynamite on the next pass. Wild Bill dropped one bundle of dynamite on the dam and destroyed it.

After One Arm landed at the mansion, Wild Bill said, "Brother, after we get a cup of coffee, I'll get Simple to drive us to the construction site."

An hour later, the brothers were walking around the edge of the huge body of water, backed up and held in place by Claven's dam. "I don't see one duck or any other wildlife," Wild Bill said. "I've been thinking about blowing that dam into little bitty pieces and sending it downriver. We could easily do it with your biplane, or I could dynamite it myself."

"We could do that," One Arm said. "But if we did, Claven would have my license taken away and I could never fly again. He would put you in an old folks' home where you would spend the balance of your life being told what to do by guards or mean nurses. Instead of having brandy with coffee, sorghum, pork chops, biscuits, and fried foods for breakfast, nursing homes would serve you oatmeal or some other mush to eat."

"Brother, I wouldn't stay in a place like you just described!" Wild Bill retorted. "If I were put in an institution, I would burn it down. When three or four of them burned to the ground, no one would tolerate me. What are you laughing at?"

One Arm lit his pipe and said, "The old folks' homes are accustomed to handling what they call unruly patients. The first thing they do is prescribe some very strong medications for any newcomer."

"If I were forced into an institution, I wouldn't take their medications or orders," Wild Bill said.

One Arm was still laughing as he said, "Yes, you would be forced to take their pills and shots. The old folks' homes have goons to hold their patients' arms, legs, and heads very still. While the goons hold a patient, a nurse clamps his nose shut. When he opens his mouth to breathe, the nurse drops the pills in his mouth and then rubs his throat in order to make him swallow the medicine. They have pills to keep anyone lifeless or drowsy, take away his sex drive, curb his appetite, reduce his thinking ability, and partially keep him in a catatonic or zombie state. Anytime a patient is in an old folks' home for three months, he or she will be weaving baskets or trying to draw pictures of bears or horses for the rest of his life."

"Where did you get that stupid information?" Wild Bill asked.

"Remember Johnny Sizemore, who was shot down and wounded in the Great War?"

Wild Bill nodded.

"I ran into Johnny's two daughters shortly after he came home from Europe. They told me that when he came home, he was unruly and uncontrollable. A lawyer helped those two vipers put Johnny into a nursing home where he will be for the balance of his life. His daughters now have control of his businesses and all of his property. I drove to Claxton to visit with him and I carried him a box of cigars and a gallon of corn liquor.

"In the reception room at the nursing home," One Arm continued, "they searched my bag and refused to let me give Johnny his gifts. I was mad and thought about pulling my revolver from my shoulder holster and cleaning house, but something held me in check. Finally I was taken to Johnny's room and, except for his face, I wouldn't have known him. His once bushy black hair was steel gray, he had lost at least fifty pounds, and it took him five minutes to recognize me. Johnny just sat there, his face drawn with pit marks and his eyes glazed over staring at the walls. Brother, don't do anything to give your family an excuse to put you in an old folks' home."

After lunch, One Arm carried several members of the family for a ride in the biplane. To everyone's surprise, Clara said, "I'm going up, but don't do any loops."

This would be her first and last flight. After the plane landed, she stepped down and said, "Never again will I leave the ground."

Early the next morning, One Arm said his farewells to the

family and took off. When he was high above the mansion, he performed two crazy eights for the children before flying out of sight.

Claven returned from the dam site the following evening to find Sheriff Coleman waiting for him. Claven said, "Sheriff, come into the parlor and I will write you a check."

"Claven, I'm sorry to keep coming here and collecting fines," the sheriff said, "but this time we've had seven complaints. I'm also against One Arm flying too close to schools, bridges, trucks, trains, water towers, and the pedestrians in Gloomburg."

"Sheriff, part of the blame falls on me for permitting my father and his brother to fly around and scare the wits out of people," Claven responded. "When One Arm visits us again, I will have a talk with him and my father about their circus maneuvers in the biplane. However, if they won't listen to reason, with your help, we can have them grounded."

Claven poured two glasses of brandy and handed the sheriff one along with a check for fifty dollars. Sheriff Coleman noticed the sincere look on his face as he said, "Claven, I would truly hate to be a party to stopping those two old war veterans from enjoying their twilight years on this earth. But, I wouldn't want to see anyone get hurt." He paused and then said, "When you have the time, I would like to see the dam you are building."

"Sheriff, I came home to get a drawing my crew needs. If you have the time, you can follow me to the job site."

Shortly they exited their cars and Claven gave the drawing to a foreman. He said, "Sheriff, this body of water you see is the one I plan to pump water from to irrigate my crops when we have a drought."

"This is a project to be proud of," the sheriff said. "I saw the new man who is operating the dragline and his family in Gloomburg. Who is he?"

"That's Bill Dykes. He's was an out-of-work coal miner I hired to do electrical, carpentry, and maintenance work on my machinery. William Sizemore, my dragline operator, had to have an appendix operation, so Bill replaced him. Bill is an excellent worker and has a wonderful family. I was planning to install a paved walkway across the top of the dam but Bill convinced me to put twenty-four steel beams on each side of the dam in order to support a roadbed to drive trucks and tractors across it. It will be much easier to cultivate the land on the other side of the river and grow crops with heavy equipment over there."

"Claven, when this dam is completed, will you keep Bill on

your payroll?" the sheriff asked.

"Sheriff, as you know, I have six full-time tenant families living here and I employ the head of each family. Not one of them has the skills Bill has to offer. But with this depression and farm products almost impossible to sell, reluctantly I will have to let him go."

"Claven, I've heard about the rolling home Bill built for his family. For a man who has to job hop and has to carry his family with him, that was some good planning. Thanks for the tour and being so considerate." The sheriff drove away.

The following day was Sunday and Bill had planned to test his children about the Great War. After breakfast, Bible study, and a family devotion, he said, "Clyde, Mona, after dinner, I expect you to give me the answers I requested about the Great War."

The children were apprehensive, and Mona said, "Papa, we are ready."

"All right, we will see what the two of you have learned. Get your study material and take a seat." Moments later Bill continued. "Mona, refer to the first few questions I gave you and answer them for us."

Mona opened her notebook and read, "The Great War lasted for four years and three months. The great powers of the world plus thirty sovereign states participated in the war. Ten million soldiers were killed in the fighting. Three million were presumed to be dead because they were missing in action and never found. As a result of the war, there were thirteen million dead civilians. There were twenty million soldiers wounded in the war and three million prisoners were captured. At the end of the conflict, there were nine million orphans, five million war widows, and ten million refugees."

"Mona," Bill asked, "as a result of what you have learned about the so-called Great War, what is your opinion about the conflict?"

"Papa, war is a devastating sin that neither rewards nor benefits anyone. When I think about all the people killed and the families without a father or mother I realize what a terrible waste war really is. I truly hope that the leaders of every nation will learn to settle their differences at a peace table. When I think of the wounded, dead, widows, orphans, prisoners, and refugees, I'm at a loss as to what will become of those people, because they need help."

"Clyde," Bill said, "give me the answers to the other questions that I assigned."

"Father, there were sixty-five million men mobilized for the Great War. Forty percent of them became casualties. The estimated cost of the war was three hundred thirty-one billion, six hundred million dollars. But, the numerical term does not include billions of dollars in interest payments on loans, pensions, veterans care, and economic rebuilding. After the war, the countryside of France was devastated and received the most destruction. The country of Germany received very little destruction. The Versailles Treaty was imposed on Germany when the war ended."

"Now, what becomes of the wealth that is invested in any war?" Bill asked.

Mona and Clyde huddled together a few seconds and then Mona said, "Papa, the resources invested in any war is a total waste because mankind profits nothing from discord, lies, propaganda, butchery, disease, carnage, property damage, and barbarism."

"Very good," Bill said. "When your mother and I saw you taking part in a war game a few weeks ago, we were shocked. We will tolerate your taking part in Wild Bill's war games until we leave here. But never forget, there is nothing good that comes from war. No war is glamorous, so keep that thought out of your heads. As you know, we will be leaving here in about two weeks. The Harrigan family has been very nice to all of us, and I appreciate it. And don't forget to pray for Wild Bill and One Arm. Last but not least, what is the Versailles Treaty?"

Clyde answered. "The treaty of Versailles is the demands, regulations, penalties, alliances, and restrictions imposed on Germany by the free nations at the end of the World War."

"One other item," Bill asked. "Do either of you plan to enhance or support a war unless it is thrust upon this nation?"

In unison Clyde and Mona said, "No, sir."

Salty Shores

On Saturday morning, three weeks later, Bill drew his last pay from Claven, and he and his family began getting ready to continue their southward journey. At noon the following day, the Harrigan family, along with Bill's neighbors, came to his truck to say farewell and wish the Dykes family a safe and successful journey.

Claven said, "Bill, I have a relative in Brunswick, Georgia, who operates a seafood business. He has about two months of work for a man with your qualifications. If you are interested, you should look him up." After giving Bill the name and address of his cousin, he added, "Again, I appreciate the work you have accomplished here, and if you come this way again, please stop by and chat with us."

As the Dykes family drove away, Bill noticed the forlorn look on his children's faces. A half hour later he turned the truck onto highway 17 and Mona read a sign, "Savannah, Georgia." Then she remarked, "Papa, there seems to be more people walking on the shoulders of the road carrying bundles than before. I wish we could give them a ride."

"Mona," Betty explained, "the economic situation over the country is getting worse. Not everyone is as fortunate as we are. Your father has promised me that we will help as many of the unfortunate children as we can when it is possible."

Just past five o'clock, Bill stopped at a gas station and said, "Clyde, fill up the tank and I'll get us a bottle of pop. While we stretch our legs, I will ask the manager of the station if he knows of a place where we can park our truck in this area."

Betty and Mona walked a few paces to where a roadside vendor was selling vegetables and fruit. Mona read a sign written on a piece of cardboard, "Corn, cucumbers, tomatoes, okra, peaches, peas, butterbeans, peanuts, all ten cents per bushel." Although Betty had an abundance of food in the truck, she purchased three bushels of peaches from the vendor and a gallon of milk from the store. The vendor's son helped Mona carry the fruit to the truck.

Bill bought a block of ice and put it and the milk in the icebox and the peaches on the floor. He then said, "Betty, the station owner told me that a tropical disturbance is predicted to hit this area early in the morning. He gave me permission to park our truck on that piece of open ground several yards up the road away from the trees. I offered to pay for the use of the land, but he refused. I heard part of a radio broadcast and the announcer said, 'Everyone should stay off the highway for at least two days, because the winds will be in excess of eighty miles per hour.' According to the station attendant, the highway will be impassable after the storm passes."

Shortly, Bill had the truck parked on a knoll facing downhill toward the highway. He helped Clyde gather and cut enough firewood for four days and then filled the wood box. Before nightfall, the wind increased and a steady rain began to fall.

After supper Betty said, "Clyde, you and Mona help me peel these peaches. This will be a good time to preserve them since we have to sit here and wait for this storm to pass."

Bill opened the rear door to the truck, latched the screen, and watched the rain as it blew past and hit the ground and gushed toward the road. The wind increased following flashes of lightning, and a violent crash echoed from the wooded area. "Two trees just hit the ground, along with several limbs," Bill said. "We made the right choice by parking the truck away from the trees." The air was cool and it was past eleven o'clock before the family went to bed.

The next morning the family was busy cooking peaches so Bill put on his rain gear and went to the station. As he entered, he noticed that oil lanterns and candles were being used to light the room. During the storm a tree had destroyed the rear wall, knocking out the electrical panel. Several people were gathered around an old man, listening to his comments. "Highway 17 is closed due to pine trees blocking the road, and all electrical power is out in this area. The bridge between here and Midway has been temporarily closed. The newscaster has warned everyone to stay where he is until the storm passes and the roads are safe. At the moment, the eye of the storm is giving us a lull in the wind, but it will become stronger later in the day."

Bill returned to his trailer and gave his family the old man's weather report. He and Clyde then carried the garbage and the human waste from his tank into the woods and buried it. When they returned to the trailer, Clyde said, "Look, Dad, there's a puppy under the truck. He's a Boston bulldog. Can I bring him inside?"

Reluctantly Bill said, "Yes, but we will try to find his owner. Clyde, look and see if there is a name on his collar."

Clyde read, "Snuffy, owner, Shane Wiggins. Dad, can I carry Snuffy inside?"

"Yes, and give him a bath before you feed him. I'll put on my rain gear and check with the owner of the station and try to find the family to whom Snuffy belongs."

Bill entered the station and asked, "Does anyone know Shane Wiggins? We found his dog named Snuffy under our trailer."

The owner said, "By the way, my name is George Green."

Bill extended his hand and said, "I'm Bill Dykes."

"Two days ago," George continued, "a man drove away and left a puppy here. That makes four dogs that have been left here this past month. If you want the dog, keep him. Bill, as you can see, a tree fell on the back wall and destroyed the electrical panel. When the storm is over, I have a lot of work to do."

"Sir," Bill said, "I can't go anywhere until the highway is cleared. If you will accept my help, I can be of service to you with the carpentry work and the wiring."

"Are you an electrician?" George asked anxiously.

"Yes. I did electrical work in a coal mine for many years."

"Wonderful," George said. "When the weather clears, I can certainly use you to repair this damage."

When Bill returned to the trailer, Mona was on the floor with Snuffy, watching him devour his food. "The wind and rain are increasing," Bill announced. "At the moment, I'm feeling better about constructing this room with bolts and screws." However, the trailer shook, plates rattled, a wooden box blew across the ground behind the trailer, and Snuffy barked. For the next several hours, the Dykes family read, played checkers, and kept looking through the screen door at the havoc being wrought by the storm. The howling wind and the sounds caused by Mother Nature kept the family tense.

The following morning, the family had an early breakfast and Clyde said, "The sun is coming up; it's going to be a beautiful day." Snuffy ran to the screen door and started barking. "I'm going to take Snuffy outside."

"You had better wait a minute," Bill said. "Clyde, fasten the rope to Snuffy's collar and keep him inside." He looked through the door and then grabbed his shotgun and a handful of shells before going to the yard. Bill watched a rattlesnake coil up as he cautiously approached. He took a careful aim and fired the weapon, killing the reptile. "Clyde, let's look under and around the trailer for other snakes. This storm has caused the reptiles to move to higher ground." After a thorough search, they found nothing, so Bill hung the snake on a limb behind the trailer.

"Is it safe to come outside?" Betty asked.

"Yes, it's safe for now," Bill said. "But each time any of you come out, look where you are walking. With this storm passing, snakes will be crawling." The family watched Snuffy sniff the spot where the snake had coiled up. "Betty, I'm going to help the owner of the station repair a wall. You know where I am if you need me, and all of you stay alert for snakes."

When Bill entered the station, George asked, "What did you shoot?"

"A four-foot diamond-back rattlesnake," Bill answered.

Two huge young men heard the conversation and one of them asked, "Can we have the reptile?"

"Sure," Bill said, pointing. "He's hanging on that oak limb to the left of my trailer." As the two men went toward the tree, Bill asked, "George, do they collect snake hides?"

George grinned and said, "No, they eat them. In fact, they eat gator tail and just about anything that lives in the swamps."

Three days later, the carpentry work and the wiring at the station was finished. George said, "Bill, since this project is finished and the highway has been cleared, I suppose you and your family will be going. What do I owe you for helping me?"

Bill answered, "The same thing I paid you for using your land, nothing. I was glad to help. Since the highway is passable, we will be leaving at daylight." Farewells were said and Bill left the station.

The following morning, the Dykes family left. They had just passed Midway, Georgia, when a flatbed vehicle with a canvas covering the bed of the truck passed them, racing down the highway. Moments later a state patrol car, with the siren screaming, passed Bill in pursuit of the speeding truck. Bill slowed down and moved his vehicle over to the side of the road. He and his family watched as the speeding truck attempted to pass a produce truck. Suddenly the speeding truck turned sharply in order to get back into the right lane because a car was in the left lane heading straight toward him.

"My heavens," Betty said. "The speeding truck has hit the front end of the produce truck, scattering hampers of vegetables over the highway! Oh my! It is turning over! Bill, look at all those large glass jugs hitting the ground! Some kind of liquid is spilling everywhere!" The produce truck had run into a ditch and stalled.

Bill drove closer to the wreck and parked on the shoulder of the road and said, "Betty, the driver of the produce truck is standing outside his vehicle. You and the children get the medical box and see if he needs medical attention. I'm going to help the police officer get the driver out of the other truck." Bill and the deputy could not open the bent door on the vehicle, so they dragged the driver through the broken windshield. Moments later the driver stood up and was coherent, but he had several cuts on his face and arms.

When Betty finished bandaging the produce driver's right arm, she said, "Mona, you and Clyde pick up these vegetables and help this man load them in his truck. I'm going to attend to the other driver."

With the deputy's help, Betty disinfected the speeding driver's cuts and bandaged them. "Okay, Lawrence," the deputy said, "put your arms behind your back. I'm going to handcuff you and put you on the ground before I clear the highway." The highway was impassable, and five other vehicles had stopped. The occupants of the cars helped Bill and the deputy clean the debris, jugs, and the last of the produce off the road.

When the job was finished and the cars drove away, the deputy said, "I'm Seth Thomas, a deputy out of Savannah. Who might you be?"

"Sir, I'm Bill Dykes and this is my wife, Betty, and my children, Mona and Clyde. I'm on my way to Brunswick to inquire about a job."

"Mr. Dykes, let's go to my car where you and your wife can write out an affidavit for the county as to what you saw happen here. With my testimony in court and your affidavits, Lawrence Harrison, the driver of this truck, is going to prison for several violations of the law including transporting moonshine."

"Deputy Thomas," Betty said, "don't you need my husband and his truck to pull the produce vehicle onto the highway?"

"Mrs. Dykes, you and your family have been very helpful, but that won't be necessary. I asked the driver of one of those vehicles that just left to call for a tow truck and a clean-up crew.

They will be here in a few minutes." After giving the deputy their affidavits, Bill and his family drove away.

An hour later, Bill drove past a naval stores plant and shortly turned into the city of Brunswick, Georgia. After asking directions, he parked the truck in front of a seafood building on the edge of Brunswick River. Mona read the sign in front of the building, "Smith's Crab and Shrimp House. Papa, this is the business you are looking for." As the Dykes family exited the truck, they saw shrimp houses, boats, two slips to pull vessels from the water, men sitting on the dock sewing nets, a boat easing under the unloading chute at Smith's dock, and three other seafood houses.

"Betty," Bill said, "you and the kids wait here. I'm going inside to inquire about the job Claven told me about."

Shortly, Bill returned, and Betty asked, "Well, did you get the job, or do we keep driving south?"

"Yes, I go to work Monday morning, but salaries are dropping. I will be paid seventy-five cents per hour for building tables to be used for shucking crabs and heading shrimp. Then I will install some wiring, do some welding, and perform carpentry work on several of the boats. After Mr. Clark hired me, he said I could rent a lot from his wife to park our truck." Pointing Bill continued, "They own those houses and vacant lots about four blocks over there, and each site has running water and an outhouse."

Bill quickly found Mrs. Clark and rented a lot. The cost was two dollars per month. A few hours later he had established a homesite and looked forward to going to work two days later.

Betty said, "Bill, the downtown area of Brunswick is just a few blocks from here. We've been cooped up for several days, so let's clean up and go look the town over." Shortly they walked toward brick buildings and turned onto Gloucester Street and then turned left on Newcastle Street.

"Look, Dad," Clyde said, "several stores have gone out of business. A café, grocery store, and a bank are closed. Dad, this is the largest town we have stopped in. Hey, I see a movie house."

The family walked by several shops and stopped on the corner, observing a magnificent hotel with a railway station behind it. Clyde read aloud, "Oglethorpe Hotel."

At that moment, a train pulled into the station, and shortly, patrons began exiting the Pullman cars. After their luggage was secure, many of the passengers got into taxis. The Dykes family watched several cabs go from the rear to the front of the hotel and stop. Young men who had been waiting on the porch quickly went to the cabs to handle the luggage while the patrons paid the drivers. Bill laughed as he said, "Betty, had the customers who just exited the train and got into those taxis known that the train had stopped at the rear door of the hotel, they could have saved themselves a taxi fare."

"I've never witnessed anything like this," Betty said. "The design of that hotel is gorgeous, with amazing brickwork, flower gardens, walkways, and large porches with ceiling fans. Those waiters seem to be standing by for the commands from the patrons."

As the family walked in front of the hotel, Mona read a framed sign. "Sunday special, beef or turkey, mashed potatoes or dressing with gravy, corn, string beans, squash, carrots, cucumbers, salad, ice tea or coffee, and an assortment of pie or cake for dessert. Price sixty-five cents."

After a period of silence, Betty said, "Bill, we seldom treat ourselves to a luxury or waste anything. Could we afford to eat in this luxury hotel before we leave Brunswick?"

"Betty, you are right," Bill responded. "We are poor and sixty-five cents per meal is about an hour's work for me. But the Lord has blessed us on this journey. If the weather is clear on Sunday, we will try to eat here." The family crossed the street, looked at the Ford Motor Company, and then moved on. Citizens on the street either spoke or nodded to the Dykes family as they passed. At the east end of Newcastle Street, the family walked through a park containing statues, flower gardens, brick walkways, and bleachers beside a large platform with a roof.

Betty read the sign in front of the platform, "'Concert each Sunday at four o'clock.' Darling, since you won't be working Sunday, could we attend the concert?"

Bill nodded his approval, but kept walking toward home.

Betty continued. "You have a job to keep you busy, but the three of us have very little to do except to maintain our small home. While you inquired about a job, I noticed signs in front of those seafood houses advertising for shrimp headers and crab shuckers. Those are piecemeal jobs the children and I could perform. I realize the pay would be trivial, but every penny would help."

Bill frowned and said, "Yes, Betty, they have jobs for shucking crabs and heading shrimp, but all of you would have to learn to perform the job with speed in order to make it worthwhile. However, if the three of you can get a spot at the heading tables, you will receive two cents for each bucket of shrimp you head. Mr. Clark told me that the shrimp boats start unloading their seafood about three o'clock each day. If you and the children want to try your skills, good luck."

"Yes, we will. The work will be good for us," Betty added quickly. "I think the children should learn and remember what it takes to survive in hard times." After the family returned home, Bill tied a rope between two trees for a clothesline while Clyde and Snuffy searched for wood. Later in the evening, the family watched the fishing boat's masts as they docked at different seafood houses.

"Bill," Betty said, "it has just dawned on me that you will get home each day before the children and I do. With the boats docking late, we will be off in the early part of the day, but we will be working late in the evening. I will leave your supper on top of the stove each day."

On Monday morning, Mr. Clark was waiting for Bill in the shucking room. "Bill, here is a drawing for a shucking table. We will need six of them. This is Gicho Smith. He will work with you as your helper. You will find tools in the storeroom and the hardware and lumber is stacked just outside the folding doors. If you should have any questions or need anything, I'll be in the office."

Bill and Gicho went to work sawing, drilling holes, and bolting the timbers together. The table was huge and sturdy because it had to support in excess of two thousand pounds of seafood at different times. The hour was past three when they started covering the tabletop and edges with sheet metal. Shortly, the sound from a diesel engine echoed through the seafood house as a shrimp boat tied up at the unloading chute to unload its catch.

Bill and Gicho were using braces and bits when they saw Mona wave. Bill acknowledged his daughter with a nod as he watched his family head shrimp and putt them into a bucket. At quitting time, he went home and let Snuffy out for a short walk. After bathing and eating, he sat down with a newspaper and scanned it, but thoroughly read each article about the state of the economy. The only good news in it was the funny page. He and Snuffy were sitting on the back steps when his family arrived later in the evening.

Betty and the children quickly washed, ate, and dressed for bed. "Tell me," Bill said, "has this been a profitable day for the three of you?"

Mona responded, "Yes, we headed ten buckets of shrimp

and made twenty cents. As soon as we gain some speed, we will do better. I watched a black lady who would grab a shrimp in each hand and pinch their heads off with her thumbs. She headed twenty-one buckets. We have also learned many things about the seafood business."

"Mona, what have you learned?" Bill asked.

"Shrimp fishermen leave the dock between three-thirty and four o'clock each morning and work long hours. Each boat has a limit imposed on it. Each boat is allowed to catch and sell one hundred bushels of shrimp each week and shrimp fishermen get one dollar per bushel for their shrimp. The fishermen try to catch their limit in three to four days in order to save on fuel and ice. Clyde and I have decided that all shrimp fishermen are getting rich."

"I'm proud of all of you," Bill said. "But, each night I expect to hear about an increase in the amount of shrimp that you head. By the way, why do you think shrimp fishermen are getting rich?"

"Papa," Mona answered, "when the captain of a shrimp boat sells one hundred bushels of shrimp, he receives one hundred dollars. That is a lot of money for one week's work. Some days the boat crews sell their fish for one and a half cents per pound and their crabs for two cents, which adds more money to the shrimp sale."

"Mona," Bill said, "that is a lot of money, but you need to think about the expenses each boat incurs in order to fish on the high seas. Each boat captain has to buy diesel fuel, ice, twine, nets, rope, groceries, various types of expensive hardware, fishing license, and the deckhand has to be paid. If the boat crew is fishing another owner's boat, they receive half of the proceeds from seafood sales after they pay for fuel, groceries, and ice. Periodically, each boat has to go to a railway for corking, bottom repairs, zinc plates, painting, replacing rudders and propellers. These maintenance costs fall to the boat owner."

Mona and Clyde were shaking their heads as they went to bed in deep thought.

Bill rose late Sunday morning to find every household chore completed. He asked, "Betty, why are our children so energetic and thoughtful this morning?"

"Perhaps you have forgotten, but they are looking forward to dining in the Oglethorpe Hotel. Today will be a new experience for them. And, we have made enough money to pay for our own meals. What time do you think we should dine?"

Bill grinned; he had forgotten his obligation.

Betty continued, "Twelve-thirty will be fine, don't you think? It's time for our family devotional so finish your breakfast."

At noon, Bill and Clyde dressed in bow ties and dark suits while Mona and Betty wore print dresses for the occasion. As the family walked toward the main streets of Brunswick, they noticed that the town looked deserted, except for all the cars parked in front of the hotel. They entered the hotel and passed through a set of double doors, a huge foyer, a gift shop, and down a hallway toward a sign pointing to the dining room.

As they entered the dining room, the maitre d' said, "Good day, sir. I see this is a party of four. Please, follow me." After the Dykes family was seated, a young black man appeared and the maitre d' said, "This is Homer. He will be your waiter."

As Homer poured ice water into glasses, the family read the elegant menu. "Bill," Betty said, "the children and I have decided we will have turtle soup, the green salad, roast beef, mashed potatoes with gravy, string beans, squash, cucumbers, corn bread, blueberry pie with ice cream, and ice tea."

Bill said, "Homer, I will have the same thing except for the ice tea. I will have coffee instead."

Homer retrieved a small silver pitcher of coffee from a sideboard and filled Bill's cup before putting the coffee canister, cream pitcher, and sugar bowl on the table. He then removed the other three coffee cups and saucers from the table.

As Mona and Clyde looked at the arrangement of the silverware on the table, they remembered the table manners their mother had taught them. The silverware was set with the precise instrument from right to left to be used in the order the food would be served. As Homer pushed a cart to the table and placed a bowl of soup in front of the diners, the family laid napkins across their legs. Betty nodded her approval when the children selected the soup spoon, which was on the outside of the arrangement. As Homer put hot rolls and butter on the table, a young lady took a seat at a huge piano and began playing soft soothing music from a Mozart collection which engulfed the dining room.

The dining room service was superb, the food scrumptious, the music fulfilling, the ambience perfect, and Betty was pleased that her children had selected the right spoons, salad fork, and other instruments for dining.

"Mama," Mona said, "this dining room is filled, but no one talks above a whisper. When you taught Clyde and me how to use good manners in public, you never said other people were so courteous."

"Mona," Betty said, "I said most people are thoughtful of others, most of the time. I'm guessing, but the visitors to this city are probably educated and well mannered. The local patrons dining here have probably just attended church and are on their best behavior."

Bill said, "Homer, would you bring our check please?"

Bill paid the check, which amounted to two dollars and sixty cents. He left Homer a twenty-five-cent gratuity. As the family quietly left the dining room, Bill shook hands with the maitre d' and said, "Thanks for the service and a wonderful meal." When the maitre d' released Bill's hand, he had received a tip. "Young man, is it permitted for visitors to browse through this hotel?"

"Yes, sir," the maitre d' replied. "When you are ready to go upstairs, there is an elevator at the end of the lobby."

The family meandered around, soaking up the luxury. They stopped and observed a sitting room with elaborate furniture, books, a large fireplace, brass lamps, and three beautiful chandeliers. Patrons were reclining, reading either a book or a newspaper. Each room on the first floor was massive with exceptionally large windows, drapes, oak walls, ceiling fans, and the unique trim used for crown mold, chair rails, and baseboards was massive.

"Let's go upstairs," Mona urged.

When the family entered the elevator, a bellboy asked, "Sir, which floor?"

"The top floor, please," Bill said.

As the family roamed through the halls, Betty said, "I didn't expect to see anything except closed bedroom doors up here, but there are sitting rooms, restrooms, and flowers everywhere. Let's go to the rear balcony." The family stepped to the covered balcony and stood behind an iron enclosure looking down at a train pulling into the railway station.

"Papa," Mona said, "with a train station in the backyard this hotel is in the right spot. This place will soon have a few more customers."

On their way home, Betty remarked, "After we rest and read the paper, it will be time to go to the concert in the park. A man at the heading tables told me that a twelve-piece band will be playing today. He said the band takes requests and they play folk, jazz, classical, country, and ballads for entertainment."

When the Dykes family arrived at the park, the bleachers were filled and a large group of people were either standing or sitting on the grass, listening to the band play a waltz written by an Austrian composer. Mona and Clyde were enthralled by the music, so they joined the children who were perched at the edge of the band platform. The band played continuously for over an hour before a man circulated among the crowd, holding a straw hat upside down taking contributions. Bill noticed that most of the men put a few cents into the hat. An hour later, the concert was over and the musicians received a tremendous applause before everyone departed.

When the Dykes arrived home, Clyde said, "Dad, when I read a newspaper or listen to adults talk about the state of the country, everything I hear or read is bad. Since we left the coal mine, the signs indicate that many businesses have shut down, but almost everyone I've met seems to have a job, and their families are doing fine. Mona and I don't understand why the people we see in transit don't go to a state that is prosperous."

"Son," Bill answered, "you and Mona take a seat and I will try to explain the situation to the two of you. This depression is not only in this country but also in many countries overseas. The reason for this is that the demand for products for the world trade market is not available, and this has caused a tremendous loss of jobs within the United States, as well as many foreign countries. We are a mobile family and since we left the coal mine, I have been very lucky and fortunate. You have seen people beside the highway who are probably hungry, children and animals who have been abandoned, farmers selling their goods for ten cents per bushel, many businesses are at a standstill, and large corporations going out of business, which ends jobs.

"The depression has just begun, and the worst is yet to come," Bill continued. "That's because the leaders of this country do not have the answers as to how to fix our economy. Clyde, no state within this country is prosperous at this time. Most of the jobs I have had since leaving the coal mine has in some way been associated with the production of food or industry. Everyone you have been in contact with has had plenty to eat.

"But the majority of the people in this country do not work at growing, catching, or processing food. In the days to come, we will see many towns where there are no jobs to be found," Bill continued. "Our family is not tied to any one state or city and we have the ability to keep moving and looking for work. Your mother and I don't like living like vagabonds and not sinking roots in one place, but at the present time, we are doing what we think is best for this family. Now, fill the wood box and get ready for bed."

Two months and two weeks later, Bill finished his work at Smith's Crab and Fish House. However, he found work at two other shrimp processors and the jobs lasted for two more months. On a Sunday evening in early fall, Bill's family attended a baseball game and watched the Brunswick team play a nearby settlement called Arco. There was no charge for admission, but during the seventh inning, a hat was passed among the spectators for contributions. The organized ball game was a first for the Dykes children and they thoroughly enjoyed it.

When the family returned home, Mona asked, "Papa, was the ball game what you refer to as organized baseball?"

"Yes, Mona, it is. The Brunswick team is sponsored by several stores, and the Arco team has a pulp mill to support it."

"Papa, if the players have a sponsor, why do they pass the hat for contributions?" Mona asked.

"Mona, the sponsor pays for their uniforms, bats, and balls. The players have to purchase their own gloves, shoes, and transportation."

"Dad," Clyde said, "Mom told us that tomorrow morning we will leave Brunswick, and you will look for work in the small town of Fernandina, Florida. Do you have another job waiting for you?"

"Son, I hope so," Bill said. "Mr. Clark said that he recommended me to a friend who is in charge of a fertilizer plant. The factory uses a fish called pogeys and a few other items to produce fertilizers for the world market."

"What are pogeys?" Mona asked.

"Pogeys are a fish that are caught by large trawlers in the ocean. The fish makes some of the best fertilizer in the world, but it is very expensive. It's time for the two of you to help your mother pack up and store everything on shelves before we start rolling."

The children went inside to help their mother, so Bill lifted the hood on the truck and checked the water, oil, and battery levels.

When Bill finished, he bowed his head and thanked the Lord for blessing him in finding work and keeping his family healthy. He knew that he had been extremely lucky since leaving the coal mine, and he hoped the politicians would soon turn the economy around. However, for the moment the job market was bleak, and every prediction from the so-called experts was that the worst was yet to come.

Good Times in Florida

As they drove away from Brunswick the following day, Bill again noticed the forlorn looks on his children's faces—the look that said, "Will we never stay in one place long enough to make friends again?" As they passed people walking beside the highway, no one spoke. Bill thought about Mona and Clyde at the Oglethorpe Hotel, the concerts, ball games, riding on a shrimp boat, playing in the park, browsing through shops, working at the heading tables, saving their pennies, and attending the First Baptist church where they willingly gave some of their pennies to the Lord.

An hour later, Betty demanded, "Bill, stop the truck!"

Bill quickly pulled to the side of the road and asked, "Betty, what's wrong?"

"That lady we just passed is sitting on her suitcase beside the road. She looks pregnant and she has two children with her. We can't pass them without offering our help."

Bill slowly backed the truck up until he reached the lady. Betty stepped out and said, "Could we offer you and your children a ride?"

"Yes, but we don't want to be a burden to anyone. We're going to my father's home at Fernandina Beach. If you could give us a ride to the turn-off at Yulee, it would be a big help. By the way, I'm Gloria Sikes and these are my children, Sam and Cynthia."

"I'm Betty Dykes. My family and I are going to Fernandina Beach, looking for work. Let's load your luggage and I will ride in the body of the truck with you, Mona, and Cynthia. Sam can ride in the cab with my husband and show him where your father lives." After introducing the family and explaining their situation to Bill, Betty mounted the steps and helped Gloria into the trailer.

After getting her settled on a bunk, they were on their way again.

At Yulee, Florida, Sam said, "Mr. Dykes, turn left off highway 17 because that road goes to Fernandina Beach." After they passed over two wooden bridges, Sam said, "Turn right on this tram road. This is where my grandfather Winston Johannsen lives."

Bill parked in front of a small rundown slab house with about ten acres of cultivated ground around it and a saltwater creek on the back side of the property. He helped Gloria to the ground, and said, "Clyde, help Sam put the luggage on the porch."

An old man dressed in overalls approached and said, "Gloria, you finally made it! I was getting worried!"

"Yes, we did," Gloria said, "thanks to the Dykes family." Gloria introduced her father, Winston Johannsen, to the Dykes family and then said to Bill and Betty, "I want to thank you for being so considerate."

Bill asked, "Gloria, how do I get to the fertilizer factory?"

"Mr. Dykes, go back to the main road and turn right. Take another right on the first road you come to. Approximately one mile down the road, you will see the factory, river, and several boats tied to the dock behind it." She laughed before saying, "You will also smell it."

"Gloria," Bill said, "before we leave, I need to ask Winston a question. Assuming that I get a job today, I will need to rent a spot to park my truck. Would you consider renting me a place to park and live for a short time?"

"Yes, sir, I surely will," Winston replied. "I don't have an income, and every little bit helps."

"Thanks," Bill answered. "If I find a job we will be back shortly."

In less than thirty minutes, the Dykes family returned, and Winston rented Bill a parking place for two dollars per month. After parking the truck, Bill said, "Clyde, as soon as we get everything set up and some wood cut, we will go fishing."

The weather was cold, but shortly the Dykes family was sitting beside the creek bank, using artificial bait trying to catch fish. Winston approached and asked, "Bill, what days are you off from the factory?"

"Winston, I will be off every Saturday and Sunday, unless they change my schedule. What do you have in mind?"

"This coming Saturday, the tide will be high at eight-fifteen a.m.," Winston said. "If you and your family will help Sam, Cynthia, and me, I will show you how to catch a lot of big fish.

However, let me warn you, when the fishing trip is over, your work will have just begun."

Bill went to work at the fertilizer factory installing metal brackets, conveyor belts, electrical motors, chain drives, and rubber belts. The shop manager, Dole Billings, assigned a man named Smiggins to assist Bill. Smiggins was a strong young man with a good demeanor, a great disposition, and an eagerness to learn. The fourth day on the job, Smiggins said, "Bill, I don't know if Dole mentioned it to you, but we're also going to run new wiring and install a large panel box. After that we are going to erect a new loading dock, construct an office and two storage rooms, and pour a concrete driveway behind the warehouse."

"Smiggins, good news is always welcome when it sounds like job security for a few weeks. Thanks for letting me know. Let's pull these four belts taut and clamp them before we staple the ends together." The day being Friday, Bill drew his pay and left the job, looking forward to the fishing trip Winston had promised.

Later, after supper, Bill remarked, "Betty, you haven't said a word about Gloria Sikes's situation. Where is her husband?"

"Darling, I check on Gloria each morning and evening. She told me that her husband, Jack, left home four weeks ago, pretending to look for work and she has not seen him since. She said that he is a womanizer, gambler, drunk, thief, and a con artist. She checked their money box after he left and could only assume that the twenty-eight dollars they had saved went with him. Gloria said that Jack may be gone for two weeks or three months, but he always returns with wonderful stories about how different men stole from him. Bill, Gloria warned me about our being cautious when Jack returns. According to her, Jack will steal anything."

"Betty, these economic times cause enough trouble for people, and I for one will not tolerate a troublemaker. In the morning when you go to Gloria's house, I'm going to take Clyde and Mona with me on a fishing expedition. Winston said for us to meet him, Cynthia, and Sam in the yard at seven o'clock and to bring our rubber boots."

The following morning, the sky was clear. It was the first week of fall and the air was crisp, with a northwest wind blowing in excess of twenty knots. Winston came into Bill's yard, pushing a homemade wheelbarrow that contained a net. Sam and Cynthia were behind their grandfather, pulling a wagon loaded with eight bushel baskets, six small planks, two shovels, and two hoes. "I see you're ready," Winston said. "Follow us and we will try our luck."

Bill poured the remainder of his coffee on the ground and picked up his thermos bottle and boots before saying, "Yes, sir, the children and I have been looking forward to this trip. Clyde, you push Winston's wheelbarrow."

Sam led the way down a path between palmetto bushes and thick brush. They stopped beside the creek about three city blocks from Bill's truck. The tide was high with just a few tips of marsh grass protruding above the ripples on the water.

"Winston," Bill asked, "why do you have a post on each side of this small creek?"

"We're going to anchor the net across this creek and we tie the ends off to the posts," Winston answered. "Providing that a big shark or a porpoise does not destroy our net, we should be able to catch a mess of seafood when the tide ebbs. This section of the creek is a sand bottom, exactly like the creek bank we're standing on. If the bottom here was mud, our lead lines would sink and pull part of the net to the bottom. When that happens, we can't catch anything because the cork lines would be under water and the fish could swim over the net."

"Sam," Winston said, "help Clyde push the bateau into the creek and don't lose the oars."

As soon as the boys had the boat in the water, Winston handed Bill the end of a rope and said, "Bill, we're going to run this net to be sure there are no turns or twists in it before we put it across this creek. You pull the cork line into the boat and I will run the lead line." Shortly they had the net in the stern of the bateau ready to put overboard.

Winston tied the cork line to the top of the post where they were standing, and Bill tied the lead line to its bottom. He and Sam seated themselves in the boat and Winston manned the oars, rowing slowly across the creek. Sam was in the stern of the boat, slowly feeding the net into the water, watching the lead line sink to the bottom and the cork line floating on the top. When they reached the far side of the creek, Winston pulled the bateau up into the marsh grass to hold it steady. Then he tied the cork and the lead lines to the other post before pulling the rest of the net in a pile.

When Winston and Sam returned with the bateau, Bill asked, "What do we do now?"

Winston looked at his pocket watch and then said, "We will

have to wait for the tide to ebb. About one hour from now, we will drop the rest of the net behind the piece we have in the river. By then, the first piece of net in the creek will be settled several inches into the sand. And, if we have an abundance of fish, crabs, shrimp, and other sea life trying to get through the net, their sheer weight will be trying to pull our cork lines under water. If we allow that to happen, the only thing we will catch is bottom fish. Bill, Sam, Cynthia, and I are going to hoe our winter garden and pick some cabbage and onions while we wait for the tide to ebb. You children bring the wagon and wheelbarrow."

"We will help you," Bill replied.

After working in the garden for an hour, Winston said, "Bill and I are going to return to the creek and drop the remainder of the net across it. Sam, you children carry some of the vegetables to each of our houses. You and Clyde unload the vegetables, then take this twenty cents and use the wheelbarrow and wagon to bring us four blocks of ice from the general store. We will be waiting for you beside the creek."

At the creek bank, Bill noticed the cork line bobbing up and down, caused by fish ramming the net, trying to escape. Winston said, "Bill, I'll row us across the creek, and you feed the net into the water after we retrieve it." Minutes later the last section of the net was across the creek.

"Winston," Bill asked, "how much longer will it be before we pull the net to the bank?"

"This small river will be dry in about an hour, but all creeks have potholes that hold water. We're not going to pull the net to the bank. We pick up the seafood we want to eat and then we'll retrieve the net." Winston packed his pipe and took a seat on a stump while Bill, fascinated, watched the fin of a small shark which was constantly ramming the net, causing the cork line to submerge momentarily.

By the time Clyde and Sam returned, the water level in the creek had dropped to less than one foot. Mona was ecstatic as she stood beside her father, pointing at the visible sea creatures floundering on the sandy bottom. "Clyde," Sam said, "pull the wagon behind that clump of palmettos and we'll unload the ice on our cleaning table."

Winston knocked the ashes from his pipe and handed everyone a pair of heavy gloves. He said, "The last of the water has gone so put on your boots and these gloves for protection."

Sam carried four baskets across the sand and placed them beside the pile of sea creatures.

Winston said, "Bill, you and your children pay attention to Sam."

Sam picked up a catfish in each hand by the head and he held it with his fingers laced against their sharp fins.

Winston continued, "Those heavy fins protruding from the back and sides of a catfish will go through clothing, boots, and gloves."

Sam threw the catfish into a pothole behind the seafood and then grabbed the tails of two 4-foot sharks and pulled them to the bank. The sharks were thrashing their heads from side to side, ready to bite anything they came in contact with.

Sam picked up a crab in each hand by their flippers and held them as Winston explained. "A crab's claws can pinch through a rubber glove or any part of your skin. When you pick up a crab, grab him from the backside by holding his flippers."

Sam dropped the crabs into a basket and picked up two stingrays by the holes near their eyes.

Winston continued, "Notice the long stinger on the tail of each stingray. If a stinger goes into your flesh, it will produce poisoning that will give you a world of hurt. In fact, it will hurt so badly, you might want me to put you out of your misery. Let's gather our catch."

Mona and Clyde were cautious and observant, watching Sam, Cynthia, and the men toss bass, trout, flounder, whiting, mullet, and crabs into the baskets, while throwing the trash fish and a few horseshoe crabs into potholes. They picked up the shrimp last. Mona said, "Mr. Johannsen, this is exciting! We have caught three bushels of crabs, four bushels of fish, and just over two bushels of shrimp."

"Yes, Mona, we have a fair catch," Winston said. "Let's carry our catch to the table and dress it. Sam, you and Clyde fill those four buckets with saltwater." Winston dumped the shrimp on the table and the fishermen started heading them. When they finished, Winston said, "We have over a hundred and fifty pounds of shrimp. Cynthia, wash the shrimp, and Sam can then put some ice on them."

Bill started to scale a flounder, but Winston said, "Hold it, Bill. Watch me fillet a fish." He grabbed a large trout and filleted the meat from each side of the backbone. He picked up the backbone, which was still attached to the head, tail, fins, intestines, and then tossed it into a waste bucket. He then sliced the skin from each slab of meat. "See, Bill, this method of cleaning fish is faster, and we won't waste time scaling or gutting it. But be extra careful, these filleting knives are extremely sharp."

After cleaning his sixth one, Bill became proficient at filleting fish.

"Sam," Winston said, "while we clean these fish, you and Clyde put the slabs in baskets and wash them. Then chip some more ice and distribute it throughout the meat."

"Winston," Bill asked, "what do we do with the scraps when we finish?"

Pointing, Winston said, "We put all of it in that hole over there. The wild hogs and coons will eat most of it in one or two days." Moments later Winston said, "Okay, let's get some ice on these last slabs of fish, load our bounty into the wagons, and go home. We still have to cook the crabs and put them on ice."

When the fishermen reached Winston's house, Betty and Gloria were waiting for them. Betty lit a fire under a large cast-iron pot while Clyde and Sam filled it with water. While waiting for the water to boil, the fish and shrimp were equally divided, and Clyde carried his family's portion home.

"Sam," Winston said, "put twelve slabs of fish and a few shrimp in the icebox. I'll put the rest of our seafood in the brine barrel."

Bill's family stood in awe as they watched Winston step under a shed and remove the lids from two wooden drums that had part of the tops cut off. He dumped his portion of fish into one and the shrimp into the other. "Winston, how long will that brine solution keep the seafood from spoiling?" Bill asked.

"Indefinitely, but if we don't eat it within three months, it will begin to lose its taste." He tore a piece of paper from a sack and wrote down the ingredients for the brine solution before saying, "Take this recipe for the brine solution and keep it. You don't have room for drums in your rolling home, but someday you'll get settled and this could help you."

"Winston, if we don't live close to the ocean, how will it help me?" Bill asked.

"We use the same formula in my brine solution for treating beef, pork, and wild game."

Bill was puffing on his pipe when Winston said, "The water has started to boil, so let's dump these crabs into the pot."

When the crabs went into the hot water, Bill noticed that many of them were snapping with their claws. "How long do we wait before we clean the crabs?"

"When the water comes back to a boil, we will wait thirteen minutes and then dip the crabs onto the worktable."

"Papa," Mona said, "the crabs are turning a reddish pink, and some of them are trying to crawl out of the pot. Mr. Johannsen has taught us a lot about catching and cleaning seafood, hasn't he?"

"Yes, Mona, he has, and I appreciate any information for survival that will help us, especially in these hard times."

Winston checked the time and began using a wire net to dip the crabs from the kettle onto the worktable. Steam and the aroma from the crabs filled the air. He put a glove on his left hand and picked up a crab before saying, "If you have never shucked a crab, watch me and I will give you a few pointers." He broke a joint claw from the crab and the end had a piece of reddish white meat protruding from it, so he handed it to Bill and said, "Sample this because you may not even like crab meat."

After eating it, Bill exclaimed, "That is delicious."

Winston had already separated the other claw joint and the legs from the body of the crab, and he handed Clyde and Mona some to eat. They both agreed with their dad about the taste.

"Mr. Johannsen," Mona said, "when we worked at the shrimp heading tables in Brunswick, Georgia, we watched the workers shucking crabs. We tried it a few times, but we never learned how to do it very quickly. Maybe our working on these will help us improve our speed on cleaning crabs."

"Mona, we have three bushels of crabs on the table," Winston said. "We're going to remove their claws, legs, and flippers before we do anything else. Then we'll back them, remove their devil fingers, rinse them, and put them on ice. We can remove the meat from the body anytime we want to." He moved Gloria near the table where she could sit and work with the families. Within two hours, the crabs were broken down, washed, divided, and put on ice. "Sam, you and Clyde bury the crab scraps, wash the table, hang up the seine, wash the hardware, and that will conclude this fishing trip."

"Winston, this fishing trip has been a great experience for us. You have certainly taught my family a few things," Bill said. "How often do you use the beach seine?"

"As you learned this morning, using the beach seine is slow work. And considering the time it takes to clean the catch the better part of a day is used up. So we usually use the seine only when we run out of seafood in the barrels. If we want a mess of fish for a meal or two, we use one of our cast-nets to catch what we need. If the weather is clear next weekend, Sam and I will teach you and Clyde how to use the seven- and five-foot cast-nets."

Bill returned to the fertilizer factory on Monday, grateful that his family was constantly experiencing new feats and had Christian neighbors. They loved the area, and he hated the idea about having to leave Fernandina Beach within a few months. Winston Johannsen and his daughter Gloria Sikes were friends who could be trusted, and Bill felt sorry for Gloria without an able-bodied man to love and support her and her two children.

Bill stepped from his trailer on Saturday morning to find Clyde, Sam, Cynthia, and Winston waiting for him. "Bill, the tide is high, so this is a good time for you to learn to use a cast-net," Winston said. After speaking, Bill noticed a net in the bucket Sam was carrying and another one in Clyde's. He followed them to the bank where they had used the beach seine last week.

To the men's surprise, Clyde said, "Watch this." Meticulously he attached the rope loop tight over his right wrist. He then folded the five-foot cast-net over his extended left arm and coiled the rope on top of it. He gripped a lead sinker and threw the net as hard and high as he could. Before it hit the water, the net was spread in a perfect three-hundred-sixty-degree circle. Clyde waited for the lead line to hit the sandy bottom hoping several fish were feeding beneath the net. Slowly, he began pulling the rope taut, slowly drawing the lead line closed, hopefully trapping the fish in the net. He continued dropping the casting rope at his feet as he pulled in the net.

When Clyde pulled the slip ring above the cast-net upward opening it, four trout and seven mullet fell into the bucket. Sam grinned and said, "Clyde and I have been practicing. Mr. Dykes, are you ready to try this?"

"Yes, I am, but remember, I've been working, not practicing." Bill picked up the larger seven-foot net and did exactly what Winston told him to do. However, each time he made a cast, the net became tangled and he did not catch anything.

Winston said, "Bill, when you cast the net again try tossing it higher above your head. When you release the lead line from your grip, try to keep your hand moving in a circular motion." Bill threw the net again and it spread perfectly before it hit the water. He pulled the net from the creek and dumped four trout, a bass, and eight mullet into the bucket.

Bill and Clyde kept casting and caught two buckets of fish before cleaning them and going home. That evening, the two families enjoyed some of the best seafood they had ever tasted.

While standing beside his trailer, Bill asked, "Winston, when is Gloria's baby due?"

"Within two weeks," Winston said. "It is possible that she could have a Christmas baby. Bill, your wife told Gloria that you have delivered several babies. If you would consider delivering another one, it would save me a five-dollar doctor's fee."

"Winston, I will do everything I can, but remember, I'm not a doctor."

"Thanks. I've been negotiating with a neighbor down the road, trying to buy a cow so we will have milk for the baby. Sam and I have been repairing a fence to keep livestock fenced in. We're also trying to grow a few more crops to feed animals. Today we're going to repair the roof over a stall for a cow. I have enough hay in the barn to feed one through the winter months, but I don't have money for the animal."

"Winston, how much does your neighbor want for his cow?"

"Fifteen dollars cash on the barrel head, and he won't go any lower. Any cow in these parts that gives an abundance of milk each day is worth more than beef on the hoof."

"Winston, you and your family have helped us more than most people would, and I'd like to reciprocate, if it won't offend you. Will you accept monetary help from me?" Bill said.

Winston took a seat on a stump, packed his pipe, lit it, and looked at Bill a short time before saying, "I have scratched out a scant living for my family my entire life and we have survived without charity. We were doing well selling vegetables until this recession engulfed everyone. Soon we will have an infant in the house, and I've been racking my brain about how to acquire money for the cow. Bill, I will accept your help on the condition that you are lending me money and I am obligated to repay it."

"Sure," Bill said, "let's go get the cow, and we will repair the stall when we get back."

They walked just over a mile and Winston purchased the cow from Mr. Gladwaller. They looped a rope around Daisy's neck and led her home. Winston put Daisy in his pasture and he, Bill, and the boys repaired the stall. Before sunset, Sam put Daisy in the stall where she had fresh water, hay, and a nonleaking stall to protect her from the wind and rain.

"Sam, Winston," Bill said, "I have an idea about how the two of you can make some money. You are proficient in catching and cleaning large amounts of seafood. In my opinion, if Sam set up a roadside stand near the service station on highway 17 on Wednesdays and Fridays, you could possibly sell between five to fifteen dollars' worth a week. However, Sam would need transportation to and fro for himself and his seafood."

Winston was silent a short time before saying, "That could be our answer for survival. We could also sell vegetables and a few other items. Lace Smith, my neighbor, passes here each morning going to his job at the machine shop. I feel sure he would give Sam a ride morning and evenings. Most of the locals living in this area catch their own seafood, but the transits driving up and down the main highway might purchase some. Bill, we will try your idea. If we are fortunate enough to take in a few dollars per week that would be a godsend."

"Grandpa," Sam said, "I think we should try selling some boiled shrimp and corn bread. There might be times when transits would want to eat on the spot. Boiled shrimp will sell for more money than the raw ones. Those people could always get something to drink at the station."

"Sam, let's make a sign to install beside the highway. Then we will check the tide chart and go fishing on Monday," Winston said. "Thanks, Bill, we will give the seafood business our best effort. If your idea pans out, I will buy Sam a bicycle with a trailer to transport seafood to the highway."

Bill waved at Clyde and his neighbors as he left for work on Monday morning. They had the seine, buckets, wheelbarrow, and wagon, heading for the creek. When he came home later in the day, Winston had the seine hanging between two pine trees. He was patching holes in the webbing using a net needle. "Winston," Bill asked, "did you have a good catch?"

"Yeah, we were lucky. We caught three bushels of shrimp, over two baskets of large fish, and we kept three bushels of crabs. We decided to sell boiled crabs along with the other seafood. My neighbor Lace said he would transport Sam and the seafood to and from the highway. Within two weeks we will know if your idea is worthwhile. The only cost for this business is ice and the seine for the seafood." Winston laughed and continued, "Sam and I also have to cut more firewood for cooking the shrimp and crabs."

"Winston, I'm going home to wash and get out of these fertilizer clothes. Betty won't let me keep them in the house until they're washed, and I don't blame her. I don't know how to sew nets, but if there is anything I can do to help, just ask."

"No, Bill, after I fix these holes, I'm going to rehang the

lead line. By Saturday evening I will know about the sales of seafood in this area."

Late Wednesday evening, Lace Smith stopped his truck on the shoulder of the road to pick up Sam, but he was gone. He looked at Sam's sign and a note was attached to it. The note read, "Mr. Smith, I have sold all my seafood and rode my bicycle home. See you Friday morning. Thanks, Sam."

Lace smiled and said, "Thank God." He drove away happy.

Bill and Clyde left their trailer Saturday and went over to Winston's backyard. Sam had an abundance of change, mostly pennies, on the worktable, counting it. Each time he counted a dollar, he handed it to Winston. When Sam finished, Bill said, "Good morning. How did the sales go?"

Sam's face was aglow as he said, "Mr. Dykes, we sold seventeen dollars and two cents worth of seafood. We spent twenty-five cents on ice, so we have a net profit of sixteen dollars and seventy-seven cents."

Gratitude beamed on Bill's face as he said, "Sam, I anticipated a few sales, but this is great news. In fact, you're doing much better than a man working by the hour. Did you make a few big sales or a lot of small ones?"

"Mr. Dykes, I made two sales a few minutes after I got to the highway. There is a road crew working in that area, and they bought all of the cooked seafood I had. We sell raw shrimp for two cents per pound, but we get five cents for boiled shrimp and crabs. I didn't think anyone would buy the boiled crabs or shrimp for five cents but they sold first. The good news is that next week, two state highway crews will start rebuilding two bridges within a half mile of my stand. Most of the cars that stopped by were from out of state, but many of the sales came from pulpwood people and the ones who chip pine trees for their tar."

"Bill, we're getting ready to build two more boxes to transport seafood to Sam's stand," Winston said. "The work will keep us in high gear, but Sam and I have decided to open the stand three days a week. Those bridge and road workers won't be in this vicinity very long, so we're going to try to sell every pound of seafood we can. Maybe by the time the workers leave, we will have a few local customers and tourists to sustain us. Tomorrow morning we're going to drop our net while the tide is flooding and ebbing. We need to catch more seafood to be ready for business on Monday."

On Sunday, Clyde and Bill helped their neighbors catch seafood, clean fish, head shrimp, cook it, and bury the scraps.

Betty and Mona spent all of their spare time at Winston's house cooking, cleaning, washing clothes, and assisting Gloria. Gloria was huge. Bending her body was almost impossible, and though she tried to work, her movements were slow. Mona and Cynthia had assumed the duties of feeding Daisy, milking her, and churning butter.

The following Saturday, Bill and Clyde visited their neighbors and watched Sam count money. Half of it was in small change, but when he finished, he said, "Grandpa, we have thirty-four dollars and fifty cents. But, next week is Christmas and the construction crews are laid off the entire seven days."

"That's okay, Sam," Winston said. "Next Tuesday is Christmas Day so we will also remain home, do our chores, and celebrate the birth of Jesus. Most of the people around here won't be buying seafood at this time of the year. We also need to stock up on firewood, stock some hay, and repair our chicken coop. Sam, I forgot to tell you but before Christmas, you will have a new bicycle and a small trailer to transport our seafood."

"Grandpa, you mentioned our chicken coop, but we don't have any chickens," Sam said.

"No, we don't, Sam. But now we have the money to buy a few laying hens," Winston answered. "Bill, what days are you off during Christmas?"

"The fertilizer plant will be shut down the entire week. What do you have in mind?"

"Betty is performing our household chores so my family wants to invite yours to our home for the holidays. I want to take you with me to gather some oysters. We use tongs to gather them and it will be good for you to learn. Today Clyde and Sam are going to cut a cedar tree, and our families can decorate it with ornaments on Christmas eve. This Saturday I'm going to the general store with Lace to pick up some baby items and supplies. You are welcome to come with us."

"Thanks, Winston, I would appreciate the ride, because I also need to purchase some coffee and a few other items," Bill said.

As Bill left the trailer Saturday morning to go with Winston, Betty said, "Darling, try to get everything on this shopping list. If you can find a gift for Gloria's expected baby, buy it."

Friendship and Hope

On Monday morning, the day before Christmas eve, Betty assisted Bill in delivering Gloria's baby. She was born at seven o'clock in one of Winston's bedrooms. The baby was healthy, loud, dark-complected with black hair, and estimated to weigh about seven pounds. Betty wiped sweat from Gloria's forehead as Bill cut the infant's umbilical cord and tied off the ends. Gently, he tapped the infant on her bottom and she cried. Immediately he began cleaning the newborn.

Barely audible, Gloria asked, "Bill, do I have a boy or a girl?"

"Gloria, you have a beautiful healthy girl who has all of her parts." He wrapped the child in a small white quilt and laid her next to her mother. He said, "As you can see, she's gorgeous, has bushy black hair, and a cute nose. Those two tiny pink marks on her little fat cheeks were caused by me when I pulled her from your womb. Her eyes are closed, but she already has black eyebrows. I'll leave the two of you for now and you can rest while Betty tidies up the room and you. Our families are in the next room, cutting and coloring decorations for the Christmas tree, but they are anxiously awaiting the news of this birth. What are you going to name the baby?"

Gloria smiled and said, "Christine Samantha Sikes. We will call her Christy."

As Bill entered the living room, Cynthia said, "Mr. Dykes, we heard a baby cry. Are Mama and the baby okay?"

"Yes, Cynthia, your mother and your new sister are resting. Your mother has named the baby Christine Samantha, two beautiful names." Bill noticed the decorations on the cedar tree. The children had used scissors to cut out designs of snowmen, Santa Claus, reindeer, sheep, goats, chickens, horses, cows, camels, angels, and snow sleds with reindeer. They had colored each design with crayons before attaching them to the tree. A star, which had been made from cardboard, tinfoil, and wire, was attached to the top of the tree. A candle mounted to the wall illuminated the different colors on the decorations.

"You children can hang these," Winston said. He handed them a box which contained different colored ribbons that Gloria had previously cut from old garments, and pinecones that he had dipped into different colors of paint. "Sam, the tide is low, so Bill and I are going to the creek and gather some oysters. Mrs. Dykes has offered to stay with us and take care of the household until Gloria is on her feet and able to handle the household chores. While I'm gone, you and Clyde continue cutting firewood until we have at least a cord on hand."

Winston and Bill took the wagon, wheelbarrow, three wire baskets, and a pair of oyster tongs and went down to the creek. After putting on their rubber boots, they picked up the tongs and baskets, and Bill followed Winston down the sandy bottom creek until they reached a pothole about one hundred by ten feet wide.

Winston opened the tongs, dropped them into the salty water, and then closed them. When he pulled the tongs from the water, he opened the jaws and dropped three clusters and six large single oysters on the sand. He said, "Bill, throw the clusters back into the water, but rinse the mud from the singles. We'll keep the large ones."

After they had gathered a bushel of oysters, Bill noticed that his old friend was breathing heavily. He said, "Winston, let me gather some because you are doing all the hard work."

When Bill took the tongs, he understood why Winston was tired. The tongs were extremely heavy. The long handles and grappling jaws were made of solid heavy metal. Bill did exactly what Winston told him. Drop the grapplers in one spot, push the long handles apart in order to close the jaws, retrieve the tongs, open the jaws and drop the oysters, move a few feet, and repeat the process. They gathered three and a half bushels of single oysters before going home.

When the tools were rinsed and put away, Winston said, "Bill, let's shuck two bushels of the oysters and put them on ice. Tomorrow we will have an oyster roast with the rest of them. Have you ever shucked oysters?"

Bill shook his head, indicating the negative.

"Take this glove and oyster knife. Put the glove on your left hand and watch me. I will shuck one for you to eat." He took an oyster knife and opened the shell of an eight-inch oyster by prying the narrow, pointed end open to separate the shells. He rinsed mud from the tip of the knife before cutting the tough muscle which was connected to the shell and fed the organ.

Bill laughed and asked, "Am I supposed to eat that slimy looking thing?"

"Bill, you're never going to know what you've been missing until you eat one," Winston said.

Bill tilted his head backward, opened his mouth, and Winston dropped the oyster between his teeth. After chewing and swallowing, Bill said, "Winston, that is one of the most delicious things I have ever tasted! I'm looking forward to the oyster roast. Let's get to work." When the two bushels were shucked, they put them on ice and disposed of the shells. They rinsed the remaining oysters, sprinkled some ice between and on top of them, covered them with a burlap bag, and put them under an oak tree in the backyard.

On Christmas eve morning, the temperature was forty-six degrees, with the wind howling in excess of twenty knots, blowing fog onto the mainland from the Atlantic Ocean. While she reclined beside the fireplace in a huge rocking chair, Gloria fed Christy with a bottle of milk. She smiled, amazed at the most activities she had ever seen in her father's home.

Betty said, "Clyde, when you and Sam finish filling the wood boxes, take the garbage out, wash your hands, and then peel these potatoes."

Cynthia and Mona were busy mixing the ingredients for two pecan and two sweet potato pies. "Mama, do we have any cinnamon?" Cynthia asked. "Mrs. Dyke's recipe calls for some."

"Yes, Cynthia. There's a box on the shelf to the left of the kitchen sink." Gloria was thankful to be useful and add something to the chores. Even the dog, Snuffy, had a piece of stove wood in his mouth, carrying it to the wood box. Betty was cutting onions, pecans, fruits, and celery on the opposite end of the worktable and Gloria said softly, "Hopefully, our girls won't mix any of those onions in the pie or fruitcake ingredients."

The hour was past one when the family members who were home sat down for a meal with hot tea. The wind had ceased, and the fog hung heavy over the coastal area, reducing visibility to less than twenty feet. While eating, four shotgun blasts startled the diners.

Cynthia grinned and said, "That's probably Mr. Dykes, Mr. Thornton, and Grandpa shooting ducks. Granddaddy told me we would have duck for Christmas dinner." They continued to eat while Snuffy growled each time the blasts broke the silence.

On the creek bank, Chuck Thornton, Winston's neighbor, said, "Here, boys, fetch them to me." Two golden retrievers, each with a duck in his mouth, swam from the creek, shook the water from his body, and laid the bounty at Chuck's feet. "Winston, Bill, we have twelve mallards and three teal. Do we keep shooting or call it a day?"

Winston saw the multitude of ducks flying in just above the water, already dropping their wings in preparation for landing. Some of them skidded across the surface of the water, while others disappeared in and around the acorn trees. With almost zero visibility and the high tide, the ducks would not feed offshore. The fog was a safety net for them while feeding in the woods, small creeks, and the farmers' dried-up fields.

Suddenly the honking of geese caught the hunters' attention as they turned their heads looking toward the sky. Nothing was visible, but the honking sounds grew louder. "Winston," Chuck asked, "do you have anything in your field for geese to eat?"

"Yes, there are a few acres of dried-up cornstalks with a few ears of corn on them. I don't want to waste food, but it has been a long time since I had a goose." The honking sounds grew nearer. "We have enough ducks for a meal," Winston continued, "so let's go to the edge of the cornfield." They put their game in burlap bags and quietly made their way to the field where they knelt down at the fence line and prepared to shoot.

Swishing, fluttering, and honking sounds occurred all around them. The hunters lay flat on the ground, watching the geese's heads in front of them extending up into the fog. Chuck whispered softly, "When I say now, let's shoot." After the soft sound of shotguns being cocked, a degree of silence settled over the area. Chuck whispered, "Now." Chuck fired his repeating Winchester three times as Bill and Winston, who had single-barreled guns, fired once.

As the flock of geese took flight, they caused a loud commotion similar to that of a herd of wild horses being chased by would-be horsemen. "Let's search the field and try to find what we killed," Chuck said. The hunters walked the field over and picked up six geese. "That's two geese each," Chuck continued. "Can you picture them as a centerpiece on our tables tomorrow? Let's clean our birds at the edge of the creek and go home."

Just past four o'clock, Betty went to the backyard to observe her first oyster roast. A fire was burning beneath a piece of roofing tin, which was supported by several bricks. A pile of oysters was on the hot tin, sizzling, with some of the oyster juice escaping from between the shells. The aroma from saltwater, oyster juice, and oak wood burning filled the air. Winston and Bill each wore a glove on his left hand to grasp the hot shells as they pried them open. Betty waited and watched as Bill dropped an oyster into Mona's mouth. She looked at the other children, with their heads tilted with their mouths wide open, and it reminded her of a mother duck feeding her young chicks.

"Bill," Betty said as she pulled a plate from her apron, "Gloria asked me to bring her four well-done oysters."

"Betty, how many do you want?" Winston asked.

"No, thank you, Winston, I'll pass," Betty quickly answered. "I'm looking forward to the fried duck and vegetables we're having for a late supper."

When Betty carried the oysters inside, Gloria asked, "Betty, would you put a little hot sauce on them and cut me a small piece of corn bread? And I'll have a cup of hot tea, if you don't mind?"

While Gloria snacked, Betty took Christy from her crib and changed her diaper. Christy was blessed with good health and always laughed when Betty cleaned her fanny and sprinkled her behind with baby powder before pinning on her diaper.

It was eight o'clock when the two families sat down to pray and eat a meal of fried duck, oyster stew with crackers, and vegetables. Later Bill put logs on the fire while Betty and the children cleaned the kitchen and put the remaining food away. "Winston," Bill asked, "what are all those folded sheets of papers attached to the Christmas tree?"

In a low tone, Winston explained, "Bill that was Gloria's idea. For the past several years, each member of our family, with the exception of the adults, has written a love letter to the family, expressing his or her love and gratitude for our existence and for one another. We do this in lieu of presents, which we cannot afford. Tomorrow each child will read his or her declarations. It is a good thing that helps bond our family together. Thanks to you and your family, this will be a bountiful celebration on Christ's birthday."

When Bill awoke the following morning, his family had already gone to Winston's house. Quickly he cleaned up and joined them, where the families were having breakfast. In unison they all said, "Merry Christmas and love to Christ on his birthday."

"And a merry Christmas to all of you," Bill replied. "Since I am the sleepyhead this morning, tell me, why is everyone up so early?"

"Papa," Mona answered, "we want to enjoy every minute of this special day because all of us have been blessed. Cynthia has already milked the cow, and the rest of us have completed the other chores. Mama will serve baked goose and the trimmings at two o'clock."

Bill took a seat at the table and inhaled the aroma of fruit cakes baking. He poured himself a cup of coffee as Betty set a plate of fried oysters, grits, butter, cheese biscuits, and jelly before him. After breakfast, Winston and Bill went to the stoop to smoke their pipes while the families cleaned the kitchen. Shortly, Cynthia opened the door and said, "Grandpa, it's time to come inside for the reading of our many blessings."

The men knocked the ashes from their pipes, went inside, and took seats with the families. Winston opened a Bible to the chapter of Luke and handed it to Gloria. After she read the scriptures describing the birth of Christ, she smiled and said, "And this is why we celebrate Christmas."

As Winston pulled several sheets of paper from the Christmas tree he said, "We will now receive our Christmas gifts—gifts of love expressed by words. Mona, will you be the first to read your love offering?"

She unfolded the paper and read, "First, I thank the Lord for life and for making our salvation possible. Second, I thank the Lord for my personal intellect, which makes it possible for me to express my love and appreciation for my fellow human beings. I deeply love and respect the Lord, my family, and our new friends, the Sikes family. Nightly I pray for the lost souls on this continent and for the ones who are hungry. And I wish Jesus a happy birthday on this special day. Thank you."

Sam blushed as he accepted his letter and read, "I just want to say thanks to the Dykes family for helping my family and allowing us to celebrate the Lord's birthday with them. I have come to love Mr. Dykes and his family, and I appreciate the many things they have taught me about survival and business, which helps my family. And I thank everyone who will always put the Lord first, not only on his birthday, but every day of the year."

Clyde took his letter and read, "Since hard times beset this nation, and our family left the coal mine, I have learned many things about survival—thanks to people like Mr. Johannsen and the Sikes family, who have shared their knowledge, wealth, and love. I sincerely love the Lord and everyone here. For me, the most important thing I have learned is to have faith in the Lord and he will guide us through hard times. Each night I pray for many people, especially the ones in this room."

Cynthia accepted two sheets of paper from Winston and read, "Many times in people's lives they will say, 'The Lord works in mysterious ways.' After this depression engulfed this country and Father left home, I asked Mother what would become of us. She answered, 'The Lord works in mysterious ways, and I have faith that He will provide for us.' One of the Lord's ways was to send us a Christian family, the Dykes, who has helped us through hard times. My family has come to love each member of the Dykes family, not only for helping us, but also for the compassion they bestow upon us and other people each day.

"As I look back at the lessons I have learned this past year, survival for my family was foremost on my mind, but praying each night with my mother has helped and has given me an inner peace," Cynthia continued. "At the moment, all of us are very fortunate, and our blessings are many. While praying each night, I ask the Lord to help the people in this country who are struggling to survive. The birth of Christy at Christmastime has put a gleam in all of our eyes and a spring in our steps. Not until Grandpa and Sam started selling vegetables from the garden and seafood from the creek, did I finally realize how much our Lord has given us. Our Lord is good to us and I will continue to love Him. Thank you."

The adults applauded and Winston raised his coffee cup as he said, "Let's drink a toast to the letter writers." After a prolonged toast, a horn sounded from outside. He said, "That will be Chuck Thornton and Lace Smith. They always stop by on Christmas morning. Bill, let's greet them and talk a spell."

As they put on their coats and left the room, Gloria picked up Christy and began rocking her to sleep. Betty looked through the window and said, "Gloria, the menfolk are leaving in a truck. Where are they going?"

Gloria answered, "They are going to the creek bank to drink a toast to Jesus and smoke their pipes. They will sit and talk about politics, their work, and their plans for the coming year. They will also warm their insides while they talk and make plans."

Betty was busy stuffing the two geese as she said, "Gloria, I don't understand. Winston and Bill left here with cups of hot coffee and a thermos bottle. Their insides should already be warm!"

Gloria stopped laughing and said, "Betty, both Lace and Chuck have a whiskey still in their backyards. They're not bootleggers, but both of them keep a supply of corn whiskey on hand to ward off the cold and for what they call medicinal purposes. There are times when men have to let the little boy come out of their systems. Papa joins them three times a year. Oh, I don't approve, but I've never objected to it openly. If a few drinks hurt him or this family, he wouldn't do it."

Betty was solemn and continued stuffing the geese as she thought about Bill drinking corn liquor for medical purposes, inwardly laughing.

The men were sitting on a log in front of a small fire when Chuck added corn whiskey to their coffee and said, "This juice should wake up our brains and stimulate us. Lace, you're the only one here who reads a daily newspaper. Have our politicians made any predictions about the economy getting better during the coming year?"

"Yes, many of them have, but all of it is bad, according to most of them," Lace answered. "This country will ship a minimum of goods overseas this year, but the people here will buy very little. We all know when big or small businesses don't have orders for their products, they close shop. Each week I read about several large corporations closing. The depression in some of the foreign countries is worse than it is here, which means they won't be placing many orders with our country. Bill," Lace continued, "since you left the coal mine, in your travels through the states, have you seen a posting for or heard of a permanent job?"

"No," Bill answered. "I have worked at jobs in North and South Carolina, Georgia, and here. Several of the jobs lasted less than half a day. The longest period of work I've found was on a plantation in South Carolina. When this depression started, my wife and I decided to become a mobile family. So far I've found work, but we have to keep moving. We won't know if we made the right decision until this depression ends."

"If you are feeding your family and keeping your head above water, you did the right thing by being mobile," Winston said. "Lace, is there any news about the stability of the machine shop where you work?"

"Yes. The company posted a bulletin two weeks ago, notifying us that we have orders for the next eight months," Lace said. "As you know, we're the only tool and die shop in this area. However, while they're still making money, we all have to take a cut in pay. Like everyone, I'm concerned about this economic mess, but worrying about it won't solve anything. Chuck, what about your business, are you secure for another year?"

Chuck laughed and said, "Financial security in this nation is becoming a joke. Anyone who believes that this nation is financially secure needs to talk to the Wall Street brokers, our bankers, the union leaders, traveling salesmen, and anyone associated with the trade commission. At this moment, the most secure people in this country are the small farmers, fishermen, or anyone who owns or works with food products, because they can feed themselves and their families."

"Chuck, how is business at your general store?" Lace asked.

"Our business is at a standstill," Chuck said. "We issue a fifty-dollar credit to anyone who lives in this area and has been trading with us for several years. Daily we have people we have never seen before come in wanting credit, and as hard as it is to do, we have to turn them away."

"Chuck, do you believe that all the credit you're posting to your books will be repaid?" Winston asked.

"I believe my creditors have good intentions, but I expect to lose some money. Four weeks ago, I started accepting guns, watches, ducks, chickens, grain, vehicles, tools, and tractors as barter. Last week I swapped two identical farm tractors I had on hand for a year-old large flatbed truck that I can use on my farm. My theory about accepting different types of barter for groceries and gas is, 'A bird in my hand is better than credit on the books.' But if I refused to barter, a lot of people would go hungry."

"Bill," Chuck asked, "what is your next destination when you leave here?"

"Chuck, my family loves this area and we would like to buy a house and live here. But if we have to travel to find work, we will leave. So far, we've traveled slowly and read the road signs, and that has enabled me to find part-time jobs. I plan to drive down the eastern coast to the southern tip of this state if necessary, but if I don't find work, I'll turn north. If I must, I will go across the Florida panhandle. If it is necessary, we will go through the Gulf states and I will look for work in the oil fields in Louisiana and Texas."

For two hours, the four men enjoyed the odors and the scenery around them, especially the burning wood, the salty creek, the cedar trees, and their hot liquid. Finally Lace said, "Winston, Chuck and I have been reluctant to tell you, but Jack was killed at the service station in Yulee last night. According to the sheriff, he broke the glass door and entered the station. He was filling a bag with auto parts when Matt Robbins was awakened by the noise.

He and Jack got into a scuffle and Jack tried to take his pistol from him. That's when Matt pumped three slugs into Jack's chest instantly killing him.

"The sheriff asked us to notify you because he didn't want to be the bearer of bad tidings at Christmastime, and I agree with him. The sheriff is holding Jack's body in a jail cell until you pick it up. If you and Gloria want us to," Lace continued, "Chuck and I will use my truck and move Jack's body to your family plot in the morning."

Winston was staring at the fire as he said, "Thanks, Lace. I have been expecting something like this for years. I won't tell my family about Jack until tomorrow morning and then we'll bury him. There's no point in spoiling this day because of Jack's exploits. We had better head for home. All of us have a feast waiting to be consumed, and I am looking forward to it." They kicked dirt on the fire, extinguishing it. At Winston's house, the men parted after wishing each other a Merry Christmas.

As Bill and Winston entered the house, they noticed the worktable had been brought in from the backyard and was put end to end against the one in the kitchen. Each table was covered with a red-and-white oil cloth with a checkerboard design. The tables held place settings for eight diners. Steam evaporated from two steaming platters that Betty had just set down. Each platter contained a goose and as Bill inhaled the aroma from the birds, he said, "If those geese taste as good as they smell, I'll try to shoot a few more."

Cynthia and Mona put mashed potatoes, gravy, candied yams, onions, corn bread, steamed cabbage, oyster dressing, and field peas on the table. Clyde and Sam placed two cakes, four pies, dessert plates, knives, and forks on a sideboard. "If everyone will be seated," Gloria said, "we will each say a silent blessing and thank the Lord before we eat."

The group took their seats, bowed their heads, and thanked the Lord for the bounty before them. All eyes were on Betty as she was the last one to finish praying. She opened her eyes and said, "Bill, would you and Winston each carve a goose? I cooked them by Gloria's recipe, and she assured me that the meat would be delicious and the oyster dressing superb."

The hour was past two o'clock and the group was hungry. As they stuffed themselves, Bill commented, "Winston, this is some of the best meat I have ever eaten. And this oyster dressing is by far the best yet. How did you cooks give this dressing a complete oyster taste?"

"Bill," Gloria said, "while the dressing was in the oven, Betty poured two cups of oyster juice over it every twenty minutes. You have probably noticed that the dressing cooked inside the geese has a different taste."

Bill gulped before dipping himself a second helping.

After the diners finished the main course and the children cleared the table, each one was served dessert with his or her beverage. Afterward, everyone helped put the food away and cleaned the kitchen.

Winston added logs to the fireplace before taking Christy from her pallet and rocking her. The group reclined, and humbly spoke of their good health and the things they planned to do in the coming weeks. The day ended, and the Dykes family was about to return to their trailer when Betty turned from the front door and said, "Winston, I want you, Gloria, and the children to know that this is the best Christmas our family has ever had. Thank you."

Shortly after Bill and his family entered the trailer, he said, "I have something to tell you, so please, all of you take a seat. Last night Gloria's husband, Jack, broke into a service station and was killed while trying to steal from the owner. Winston didn't want to spoil Christmas Day for his family, so he decided not to tell them the tragic news until tomorrow morning. Clyde, in the morning you and I will dig a grave at Winston's cemetery plot. Winston will move Jack's body to the gravesite in Lace's truck. Betty, you and Mona will need to comfort the bereaved family early tomorrow."

Everyone was shocked, but they went to bed to pray for Jack and his family.

The next morning when the family arose from their bunks and got dressed, Bill had dressed and had breakfast on the table. "Betty, has Gloria mentioned when she will be able to resume her household duties?" Bill asked.

"Yes, she thanked me and said that she could handle the chores in her home, starting today. But with this tragedy, I will need to stay near her for the next day or two."

While Bill and Clyde dug the grave that had previously been marked off, Winston, Lace, and Chuck washed Jack's body and dressed him in a suit with a white shirt and a tie. With the help of deputies, they put the corpse in a pine box which Chuck had delivered from his general store.

Winston said, "Sheriff, thanks for your candor in this senseless crime. Tell Matt Robbins I will stop by his station and pay for the damages."

"Winston," the sheriff said, "you didn't mention it, so I took the liberty of asking the young preacher, Simon Coles, to meet you at the burial plot and speak a few words."

Winston nodded and he and his friends drove away.

When Lace parked the truck at the small cemetery, Bill and Winston's families, Lace's family, Chuck's family, the preacher, Matt Robbins, and two deputies stood beside the grave. Four men put the open casket across two sawhorses. Simon Coles opened his Bible and said, "This morning we are gathered here to pay our final respects to Jack Sikes." He read from the book of Psalms about the comforts of life and the hereafter. He gave the eulogy in a low tone, trying to comfort Jack's family. After a prayer the preacher said, "Anyone who wants to have a last look at Jack should do so now."

The funeral procession walked slowly beside the casket for a last look at Jack. Gloria, Sam, and Cynthia each placed a flower on their loved one as they wiped tears from their cheeks. Minutes later, Winston and some of his friends accompanied the Sikes family to their home. Bill, Lace, Chuck, and Matt nailed the top on the coffin shut and lowered it into the ground before covering it with dirt and erecting a cross.

As the grave tenders left the cemetery plot, Matt said, "I've always been a friend to this family, and I'm truly sorry about this. Why did I have to be the one to stop Jack from committing his wicked ways?"

"Heavens, Matt, it's not your fault," Chuck said. "All of us are surprised that this didn't happen years ago. I'm also sorry for the family, but they will be better off without Jack's stealing, lying, and making trouble for everyone. This is one of those sad days in life that can't be avoided."

The men joined the group at Winston's home and conversed about happier times with one another until late in the evening. Within a few days, no one mentioned Jack's name. Even Gloria had said, "I tried to have a life with Jack, but everything he touched, with the exception of Sam, Cynthia, and Christy, failed."

Within two weeks, Winston and Sam were in high gear, catching and selling seafood to construction crews and patrons beside the highway. Gloria assumed her duties in the household and quickly realized that keeping busy was good for her. Bill returned to work and was happy to be saving a few coins again. However, he was notified that his job would end on the last day of January.

Bill was on the creek bank with Winston and the boys when

he told them he would be leaving in a few weeks, looking for another job. He said, “Winston, after I’m laid off, I’m going to remain here for a couple of weeks and eat my fill of oysters and shrimp. While I’m stuffing my belly, Clyde and I can help you replace the tin on your roof and those other jobs you need to do.”

“Bill, if you can spare the time, it will be greatly appreciated,” Winston said.

Seeking a Destination

Two weeks before Bill's job ended, he and Clyde made a list of the things they knew needed to be repaired on Winston's property. Bill said, "Clyde, since our family loves and cares about Winston and his family, we're going to stay here for a few days, eat our fill of seafood, and help Winston with the repairs. We're also going to help Winston catch, clean, and cook seafood in order to keep Sam selling the product beside the highway."

After Bill's job ended, he and Clyde helped Winston replace hinges on the exterior doors, install a wall in the barn, replace two windows in the house, repair fences, and replace the tin roof on the house. They were sitting on the apex of the roof, looking at Winston's land, when Bill suddenly asked, "Winston, who owns that land adjoining yours?"

"Lawrence Coleman's name is on the deed to secure debt, and the property is under foreclosure. It will be sold on the courthouse steps at ten a.m. next Wednesday. Lawrence left Florida six months ago looking for a job."

Bill gazed at the land and asked, "How many acres does Lawrence have down there?"

"About twenty-eight acres," Winston answered. "It is a beautiful piece of high and dry property and most of it joins the river."

"Winston, do you plan on bidding on that property?" Bill said.

"No, sir. I'm going to try to keep my own farm productive so my family can survive these hard times. Bill, land around here has been selling for twenty-five to seventy-five cents per acre. Land in this country is cheap and prices are dropping as we speak. Property is of no value to anyone unless he is living on it or else he's making money from farming. Many people in Florida are losing their land because they can't afford to pay the county and city taxes."

"Winston, when spring arrives, who will plow your fields?" Bill asked.

"I owned a mule until a year ago, but she died. Last year, Lace sent one of his hired hands with a tractor to plow my fields for me. He told me not to worry about plowing or planting this year because he would take care of it. Bill, thanks to you and a few other friends, my property is in the best condition it has ever been. After paying the bill for the building supplies, I have over nine hundred dollars in savings, and Sam is selling a lot of winter vegetables and seafood."

"Winston," Bill said, "I'm going to put on my rubber boots and walk over that land. My family and I would love living here beside the creek with your family for neighbors, provided I could make a living. If that property is as high and dry as it looks from here, I'm going to bid on it."

"Bill, if you are in a spending mood, there is also a small lot on the main street in Fernandina Beach that will also be sold next Wednesday. The owner of the lot was destitute when he left Florida two months ago. If you can afford to purchase the lot and hold it until the economy turns around, you should turn a huge profit in the years to come."

"Winston, if you will go with me Wednesday morning, we can have breakfast in Fernandina and then look at the lot. Then we could go to the courthouse and attend the auction."

"It's a long walk to town, Bill, so we will need to leave early. I will meet you in the yard at seven o'clock. I haven't been to town for six months, but I've heard a lot about businesses which have closed or about to close. Bill, remember the parcel of land next to me is number one hundred seven. The town lot is number twenty-four."

After supper Bill told his family that he was planning to bid on the two parcels of land. Betty was ecstatic and exclaimed, "That's wonderful! I hope you will be financially able to bid high enough to buy it. Living beside this creek with Gloria and her family for neighbors would be living a dream! Our children love it here and there's nothing that will match the taste of the seafood from the creek. The weather here is mild and it never snows. Darling, if we settled here for good, you and Clyde could build that boat you're always talking about."

On Wednesday morning Bill and Winston had walked about half a mile when they caught a ride to Fernandina. After eating a greasy breakfast, they walked down the street and Bill could see a huge river at the end of it where several large shrimp boats were moored. Four blocks from the river, Winston said, "This is the lot I spoke of. That sign reads one hundred twenty by two hundred feet. If you notice, the dry goods store on the left and the shoe store on the right have gone out of business. It is a sad time when half of the stores on the street are closed."

After pacing the lot off, Bill said, "The dimensions given seem to be correct. Winston, I'll make a bid on this lot, but the property I really want is next to you."

They went to the courthouse, took a seat on the steps, packed their pipes, and waited along with six other men. Minutes before the auction began, nine other men and two ladies joined them.

Shortly two men and a lady, carrying a small table, a chair, and a box containing several folders, exited the courthouse. The lady pulled a folder from the box, opened it, and handed the auctioneer several documents before sitting down at the table. The auctioneer opened the auction and quickly sold four properties. He then said, "We have twenty-eight acres of land, more or less, being sold for delinquent taxes. The parcel number is one hundred seven. This is a high and dry piece of land bordering a saltwater creek. Do I have a bid?"

A man wearing a trench coat said, "I will bid twelve cents per acre."

The auctioneer said, "I have a bid of twelve cents per acre. Are there any other bids?"

Bill motioned to the auctioneer and said, "I bid fourteen cents per acre."

Bill and the well-dressed man kept raising their bids until the price was twenty-eight cents. Bill was awarded the twenty-eight acres for seven dollars and eighty-four cents, plus the cost of stamps, and a recording fee.

The auctioneer pounded his gavel to get the bidders' attention. "Thank you. The last parcel of property for sale is a city lot and the minimum bid is twenty-five dollars. The dimensions of lot number twenty-four are one hundred twenty feet on a front street by two hundred feet deep. Do I have a bid?"

After the first bid of twenty-five dollars, four different men kept bidding against one another until the price reached one hundred fifty-five dollars. The auctioneer said, "I have a bid of one hundred fifty-five dollars going once, going twice."

As the auctioneer raised his mallet to finalize the bid, Bill said, "I will pay one hundred sixty dollars." After raising his bid a second time, Bill bought the lot for one hundred sixty-five dollars.

Bill had just paid the city employees and signed the documents for the properties, when the clerk asked, "Mr. Dykes, where do you want your tax bills mailed to?"

"I hope to be working out of state for a period of time," Bill replied. As he handed the clerk a slip of paper, he said, "Please mail the bills to Mr. Johannsen at this address. He has agreed to pay the taxes for me until I return."

As they walked home, Winston said, "Since the auctioneer awarded you that city lot, I've been thinking of what type of business would do well on it. At the moment, I can't think of anything. Bill, since you enjoy working with your hands, you do not strike me as being a storekeeper who would enjoy serving customers. And, at this time, even if you had a building on the lot, I don't think you could rent it to anyone. Your plan to wait for the economy to improve seems to be the right thing to do."

While father and son made the last repair on Winston's farm, Bill said, "Clyde, it has been over three weeks since I drew a paycheck. It is time for our family to be moving on."

On the following Sunday morning, Bill and his family stocked firewood, packed up the few items around their trailer, and prepared to go south. On Monday morning it was a sad occasion for everyone when Winston and his family said their farewell to the Dykes family before watching them drive away.

No one spoke until they were south of Jacksonville because each member of the Dykes family was thinking about friends and their beautiful piece of land facing the salty river. Finally Bill said, "The city of Jacksonville appears to be poverty stricken. More than half of the stores are closed and people are wandering about with helpless facial expressions." No one else commented on the closed business stores.

The hour was past three o'clock when Betty finally said, "Bill, we need to stop. All of us need to stretch and relieve ourselves. When you find a secluded area, pull over and stop."

Shortly Bill parked the truck on the shoulder of the road and unlocked the rear door to the trailer for his family to use the bathroom.

Mona said, "I'll take Snuffy into the woods."

While waiting for Mona, several transients walked by staring at the Dykes family. Three small barefoot children with bags slung over their shoulders walked around the truck, and a small boy was pulling a wagon with a little pale-face girl in it.

"Bill," Betty asked, "why do so many of the people walk on

the scorching hot highway?"

"Remember, Betty, the shoulders of the road are full of sandspurs. If they are not wearing shoes, they usually step off the highway until the vehicle passes, and then they get back on the road." When Bill drove away, he noticed Betty turned her head to avoid looking at the children's skinny faces.

Two hours later, Bill slowed the truck and cautiously parked about forty yards off the highway behind a stand of pine trees and palmetto bushes. Clyde quickly checked for snakes and cleared the underbrush at the rear of the truck. The weather was warm, so after dinner the family went outside to watch the setting sun. "Papa," Mona said, "there are twenty-one campfires behind us and people are gathered around them, cooking a meal. I counted fourteen fires on the other side of the highway."

The evening was interrupted by two blasts from a shotgun. Bill heard someone say, "Johnny, pick up those squirrels and carry them to the cook-pot. I think I see a fox squirrel in the distance."

Minutes later another blast erupted, and the shooter said to no one in particular, "This big devil will give us a good meal."

Bill watched the shooter carry the squirrels to the campfire, dress them, and drop the meat into a large pot hanging over the fire.

Just before sunset Betty said, "Bill, we're going inside to read and get ready for bed. Are you coming with us?"

"No, Betty. I want to talk with some of these people about work in central and south Florida. I'll be in shortly, but latch the door." Bill continued smoking his pipe, waiting for the people around the campfires to finish eating.

Minutes later Bill approached the squirrel shooter and said, "Good evening. I admire your shooting skills. Sir, my name is Bill Dykes. My family and I have never been to central or south Florida, but we are looking for work. Do you know if any jobs are available around here or further south?"

The huge young man extended his hand and said, "My name is George Cline. I will tell you what I know, but if you are headed south, it's a waste of time. My family and I worked on several farms for five different citrus growers, picking fruit and pruning trees until four months ago. When we were let go, we left south Florida. That area is overrun with people seeking piecework. It seems as if there's a family down there for each orange or grapefruit tree. To make matters worse, there's very little industry in Florida, with the exception of fishing. And even the commercial fishermen have a limit on how much they can sell each week."

Bill was dribbling pipe tobacco into the bowl of his pipe from a tin of Prince Albert when he asked, "George, do you smoke?"

George laughed and said, "There was a time when I did, but I can't afford tobacco anymore. I haven't had a smoke for fourteen months." Bill handed the man his tin of tobacco, and moments later they took a seat on a log, and enjoyed the tobacco and the cool evening.

"George, when you were laid off, did you look for any other type of work, other than picking fruit or farmwork?" Bill asked.

"Yes. By trade I'm a heavy equipment operator. I was fortunate to find two part-time jobs as a carpenter and one as a sharecropper. Bill, we've walked from the orange groves up to West Palm, to Fort Pierce, to Melbourne, then Daytona Beach, and St. Augustine. Not to mention the hundreds of other businesses where I tried to find work, I also tried the farms along the highway. The majority of the people who are still in business have signs posted in front of them reading 'No Jobs Available.' We have been living in that tent over there for over a month, eating squirrels, rabbits, possum, coon, deer, and alligator tail. Frankly, I don't know which direction to go.

"Most of the larger cities have set up soup kitchens," George continued. "They give away free bowls of soup at noon each day. I am thankful for the soup and shouldn't criticize it, but the quality and the quantity is poor. Also, it breaks my heart to have to subject my family to this type of life. If I could just find a job making five to ten dollars a week and a patch of woods with wild game, my family could survive this depression."

"George," Bill asked, "have those people sitting around those campfires had a meal today?"

George shook his head as he said, "Bill, the children who have not been abandoned get to eat after their guardians, but they have to eat the scraps providing there are some left. The most pitiful ones are those sitting around the six campfires near the highway. All of those children were abandoned by their parents shortly after the depression began."

Bill stood up and said, "George, wait for me a few minutes. I'll try to help the needy, but not the greedy." Bill laid the tin of tobacco on the log beside George and went to the trailer.

Shortly Bill returned, carrying two bushel baskets of food on his shoulders. He said, "George, if you will help me and show me the groups of children who have been abandoned, we will give them food." As they went to the children, several adults around the other campfires stood up to watch the proceedings.

When they reached the hungry children, George said, "Boys and girls, this man is Bill Dykes. Have any of you had supper tonight?" All of them shook their heads indicating no. "Well, Mr. Dykes has brought you some food." Quickly the children ran to their bundles and returned with a tin plate, spoon, and a tin can. George asked, "Do you want us to heat the food?"

All sixteen of the children answered in unison and said, "No, sir."

The children stood in a straight line as Bill ladled rice and field peas onto their plates, and George put a slice of ham and a piece of corn bread on each one. While the children ate, the two men filled their tin cups with milk. George said, "Bill, watching these children eat is a good and glorious sight, because people like us can only scratch the surface of the problem. One would think that President Hoover and his constituents could do something to alleviate this problem."

"Yes, one would think that a government who can raise money to fight wars and pay politicians huge salaries could find a way to feed hungry children during hard times," Bill said. "George, if you can meet me at the trailer early, I'll leave a few jars of peaches, peas, butterbeans, tomatoes, okra, and a few other items for your family and the children. After I do that, I'm going south as far as St. Augustine. But, if I can't find a job, I will take your advice and go across the Florida panhandle and keep going west. George, I don't pretend to know the situation here, but please be sure the children get the food I leave for them. Good night."

When Bill returned to the trailer, he told his family about what George had told him, and about the children he fed.

Betty said, "Darling, since we left the coal mine, we have been blessed and you have managed to save some money. You promised me that you would purchase a tent for some of the homeless children we see. I think the time to do it is now. The further south we travel, the children look worse in spite of their protruding cheekbones. I haven't seen one today who has any meat on his or her bones."

The following morning when Bill introduced his family to George, the children, with their possessions were waiting beside the bushes a short distance away. Their yellow sallow faces had a look of anticipation, but their bodies were gleaming white. Two of the smaller boys were shirtless and one could count their ribs.

Betty said, "Mr. Cline, those children are spotless. Where did they bathe?"

"There's an artesian well about one hundred yards north of here, near the edge of the woods. The one thing we have is plenty of water," George said.

"Mrs. Dykes, one of the older children said, 'We should look our best for the family who is willing to feed us.' Last night when I told them about your family donating food, each of them prayed for all of you."

Betty motioned for the children to come to the trailer. She said, "Please, all of you take a seat on the ground and we will give you breakfast." Betty and Mona filled the children's plates with fried potatoes, sausage, biscuits, jam, and canned plums. George filled their tin cups with sweet sassafras tea which he had boiled from roots.

While the children ate, Betty said, "George, with the exception of this box of staple goods and breakfast foods, I've packed four bushel baskets with jars of assorted foods that won't spoil. Bill said to leave them with you to distribute among your family and these children."

"Mama," Mona interrupted, "the red-headed girl over there has a bad cut on her heel and it looks infected. I'll get the first-aid kit, a basin of warm water, and some clean rags so you can treat it."

When the children finished breakfast, they scrubbed their utensils with sand. Then the little red-headed girl limped to the trailer with Mona.

Betty asked the injured child, "What is your name?"

"Helen Smith, Mrs. Dykes. Several days ago a truck was passing and I stepped off the highway and cut my heel on a broken piece of tin."

"Helen, let's wash your foot in this water and clean the cut before I apply some iodine and a bandage," Betty said. After washing and drying Helen's foot, she opened the bottle of iodine and said, "This will sting for a moment or two, but sit very still. I think this will stop the infection." Helen grimaced when Betty poured the liquid on the cut but she didn't move. As Betty bandaged the girl's foot, she said, "Mona, Helen's feet look to be about the same size as yours. Get me two pairs of white socks and your tennis shoes from the trailer. Helen, I will leave enough medical supplies with you so that Mr. Cline can change your bandage for several days."

After Helen put on the socks and shoes she said, "My

feet feel fine, and I can walk better. Thank you very much, Mrs. Dykes."

"George," Bill said, "my wife insists that I get you a couple of tents and a wagon to move the children from one location to another. Would you consider looking after them and trying to find a home for this group?"

Silence permeated the group before George finally answered, "Mr. Dykes, I will try for thirty days, but I'm stone broke and I also have to look for work. There's a general store about eight miles down the highway where I bought my tent and pegs for six dollars."

"I'll see what I can do," Bill said. "Betty, let's load up and go to the general store."

Bill pulled onto highway 17 and had gone about four miles when Clyde read a sign which was nailed to a fence post. "Forty-acre farm for sale, or will consider hiring a sharecropper. Farm can also be leased on a five-year contract. Anyone interested contact Moses McGrath at the address below." The address was written so small Clyde could not read it from the road.

Less than an eighth of a mile further down the highway, a man was nailing an identical sign to another fence post. Bill stopped the truck, backed up on the shoulder of the highway, and stepped out. As he walked toward the old man he noticed a bicycle leaning against the fence; no other vehicle was in sight.

"Good morning, sir," Bill said. "I noticed the sign you're nailing up, and there's another one like it down the highway. Are you the owner of these farms?"

"Yes, sir, I am. I'm Moses McGrath, and I have four small farms for sale. Four months ago I had a sharecropper working each of them. They thought they could do better by working in the city, so they left on short notice. Are you interested in buying a farm?"

"Maybe, but I doubt I can afford one," Bill said. "Sir, I'm an out-of-work coal miner. My name is Bill Dykes. Do you have the time to show me these farms?"

"Of course, I do. Follow me and we'll look at this one first." To Bill's surprise, when they entered the yard at the rear of the barn, Moses pulled a set of small binoculars from beneath the bib of his coveralls. He said, "Look through these and you can see the cultivated fields and what the tenant farmers left behind."

Bill put the binoculars to his eyes, adjusted the lens, and said, "My heavens, those sharecroppers left a roof over their heads, a well for water, and a winter garden in the field! I venture to say that by now they're in some city, standing in line for a bowl of soup and no place to sleep." For the next two hours, Moses showed Bill the four farms which were all facing the highway.

After revisiting the farm where they had started out, Bill asked, "Mr. McGrath, how much are you asking for this farm?"

"Mr. Dykes, for the past month I've quoted prices to several people who wanted to buy these farms, but very few of them have any money. Less than two years ago, I paid off the mortgage on my last farm but it broke me. I owe back taxes on all the farms, and unless I make a sale the county will shortly take them for delinquent taxes. I have cut the price on this one to three hundred dollars and that is as low as I can go."

Bill looked at the small pecan orchard, hog pens, buildings, corral, well, a patch of woods, and a thirty-acre cultivated field. He extended his hand and said, "Sir, it's a deal." After shaking Moses's hand, he asked, "Where do we have to go to finalize the transaction?"

"Mr. Webster's general store has a law office in it. It also has a post office, notary, county offices, small bar, lunch counter, barbershop, and a prescription department. The lawyer is in the process of trying to form a municipality for this area. The store is well stocked. In fact, it is the only place for miles around to purchase just about any item you need."

"Mr. McGrath, you can ride with me to the store, and we'll get this transaction started, providing the lawyer is in." After putting his bicycle over the fence, Moses got into the cab of the truck with Bill and Betty and the children got into the trailer. When Bill parked at the gas pump, he and his family were astonished at the size of the general store. It was everything Moses had said it was and more. There were two gas pumps and one for diesel fuel. Pens for livestock and fowl were visible at the rear along with a building stocked with feed for animals.

While Clyde filled the gas tank, a station attendant checked the oil and the water and cleaned the windshield. When Bill and the others entered the store, they were pleasantly surprised. The room was huge with independent shops located on the left side. Because they needed to replace the food they had given away, Betty and the children began picking up bags and boxes of groceries and putting them on the counter.

Bill followed Moses to an office where he was introduced to the lawyer, Mr. Herman Clark. Moses said, "Herman, Mr. Dykes is going to purchase one of my farms, parcel number sixty, for three hundred dollars. When can we close the sale?"

"Moses," the barrister said, "I can do a title search and have the paperwork ready by ten o'clock tomorrow morning."

"Thank you," Bill said. "If you have a plat of the property, I'd like to have one when I pick up the deed. We will see you in the morning."

While Bill paid for the gas and groceries, Moses introduced him to Cleat Webster, the owner of the store.

"Mr. Webster," Bill asked, "when you sell livestock, do you deliver the animals?"

"Yes, sir, the delivery is free providing it is no more than twenty-five miles from this store. After that distance, we charge three cents per mile."

"Thanks, we will see you in the morning. Betty, where are the groceries?" Bill asked.

"The clerks were kind enough to put them in the truck," Betty answered.

Bill remarked urgently, "If we're going to own a farm, we have to talk with George Cline and find out if he will operate it. We had better get going."

While driving to the farm, Bill recognized several transients walking beside the highway as those he had seen the night before. After Bill dropped Moses off to get his bicycle, he returned where George and the children were camped. George, watching and giving advice to four of the older boys who were cleaning two deer, turned and asked, "Bill, did you get the tents?"

"No, but I think I got something better. I purchased a small farm. It has a farmhouse, an excellent barn, water well, hog pens, a chicken coop, a thirty-acre cultivated field with about a four-acre winter garden, a corral, and good fences. The farmhouse has a fireplace with a large living room with an adjoining dining room and several pieces of furniture. It has three bedrooms and a huge kitchen with a cast-iron stove. There are two well-built outhouses located next to the barn. George, you told me that you had some farm experience. If I stock the farm with a mule, breeding hogs, chickens, tools, and the household items a family needs, will you operate it?

"I realize the house is not large enough for your family and the sixteen children," Bill continued, "but we could seal off one corner of the barn with two large rooms, one for the girls and one for the boys. We could floor the rooms and build a fireplace with an opening adjoining each room. We would have to build bunk beds and several shelves for the children. Do you think that you and your family want to take on the job?"

George grinned and said, "Bill, if you are doing all this to help people in need, and you know we're destitute, how can I refuse? After all, you're offering to feed my family. When will you own this farm?"

"The closing deal is set for tomorrow morning at ten. Do you think those boys can finish butchering those deer and look after the children while you and I take a ride?"

"Bill, those boys are hungry; they can handle the chore. What do you have in mind?" George asked.

Bill said, "I'm assuming that before noon tomorrow we will own a farm. We need to go over the farm and make a list of the items you will need to make it productive whereas you can feed everyone."

"Bill, let me speak to the boys and to my wife and I'll meet you at the truck."

Shortly, Bill parked in front of the farmhouse and they went inside. Bill led George to the largest bedroom and said, "George, if I miss anything you think we need, tell me while I write out this list." After going to all the rooms Bill said, "There are two bed frames in two of the bedrooms. I've noted that we need one bed, three mattresses, and shelves for each of them. The kitchen needs a stove, two safes, a worktable, and more shelves. Did you notice anything else I need to note?"

"Bill, the kitchen has a good cast-iron stove," George commented.

"Yes, it does," Bill said. "But during the canning season when your wife and the girls are canning food for sixteen children and your family of four, they will need two. We can build furniture for the dining and living rooms. Our wives can make a list of utensils, blankets, pillows, oil lamps, and the other household items needed. Let's go to the barn."

As they entered, George exclaimed, "Holy Toledo, that Studebaker wagon is almost new! I'm surprised the seller let you have it. And there's enough lumber stacked against the wall to build the furniture and frame part of the floor and walls in here."

"George, the wagon, lumber, and those nails aren't exactly a gift. I have to pay off the eight-dollar balance on those items at the closing tomorrow," Bill commented. "We will need some fire brick, common bricks, concrete, builder's sand, and mortar mix for the fireplace. George, will you go to the loft and count the bales of hay and anything else of value up there?"

Shortly George yelled, "There are fourteen bales of hay, three shovels, three hoes, two rakes, a large box filled with nails and fence staples, two hand saws, one crosscut saw, two levels, three claw hammers, six files, a ball of twine, two block planes, two folding rules, two hand drills, drill bits, a ball of twine, two rolls of rope, one roll of half-inch cable, and two sets of posthole diggers. I see a horse collar, trace chains, a single tree, saddle, and two bridles inside the wagon. There are two plows and four buckets behind the horse stall. Bill, do all these supplies come with the farm?"

"Everything," Bill said, "and there are several tools scattered about in the field." After packing their pipes, they went outside and Bill said, "Thank goodness the stock pens and watering containers are in good shape. You will need three sows, a boar, fifteen laying hens, a rooster, a mule, two milk cows, a few goats, several fryers until you can breed a few, and feed for the animals. Let's get a bite to eat."

While returning to the trailer, Bill said, "George, it will take two trips to do so, but before I go to the attorney's office in the morning, I would like to move everyone to the farm. Until we get the children's rooms built, it will be close quarters for all of you, but everyone will be out of the rain. After Mr. McGrath signs the deed, I'll buy the animals and the chickens and have them delivered. If your wife and Betty will have their supply list ready, I will pick those items up late tomorrow. George, what are you writing?"

"I'm making up a work schedule for my family and the children. I'm trying to get organized so each one will have a job he or she is capable of doing. We have my two teenage boys plus the seven others that I will assign jobs that will require the most stamina. The smaller children will be required to perform easier jobs and be supervised by my wife, Sara."

Bill was in deep thought but finally commented, "George, that is good planning. The thing that concerns me most is what you can produce and sell to make money for the basic essentials, such as staple goods, lamp oil, an occasional piece of hardware, clothes, and shoes for all of you. Other than beef, hogs, and fowl, there is not much of a demand for farm products. But don't concern yourself, I will think of something."

When Bill parked the truck, he said, "George, I will be ready to move the first group of children to the farm at seven in the morning."

"We will be ready," George replied.

Minutes later Bill heard George say, "Boys, strike the tent. We will sleep under the stars tonight."

Road of Disappointment

By nine o'clock the following morning, Bill and George had moved George's family, the children, and their meager belongings to the farm. After the group looked over the farmhouse and the outbuildings, George and his wife, Sara, put the children to work cleaning the house, sharpening tools, organizing tools in the barn, filling water troughs, cooking grits and green beans, gathering vegetables, and cutting firewood.

As Bill had requested, Betty gave him a sheet of paper and said, "This is a list of household items this group will need. These mattresses will probably have to be ordered, so don't forget them. It's almost nine-thirty; it's time for you to go see the lawyer."

Before ten-thirty, Bill had purchased the farm and had given to the barrister the address of Winston Johannsen at Fernandina Beach where his property tax bill should be mailed. He was about to leave the office when the attorney said, "Mr. Dykes, if you are interested, the six hundred acres of timberland adjoining your farm has also been foreclosed on. At the auction, no one came forward to pay the taxes, and it can be purchased for seven cents per acre. No trees have been cut off of it for at least three decades. Except for a small creek running through the property, the land is high and dry. I have fished in the creek many times and always had a good catch. If you would like to look it over, the boundary markers on the property are concrete and stand about a foot above the ground."

"Mr. Clark," Bill said, "I have looked across the fence at some of the timber and liked what I saw. I'll accept your word about the elevation of the property and will buy it as soon as the deed is ready. Thanks. If it's convenient for you, I will see you tomorrow."

Bill pulled the supply list from his pocket and left the office to speak with the owner of the store. "Good morning. Mr. Webster,

I have made a list of items we need for the farm. Do you have the time to price them for me?"

Mr. Webster smiled as he said, "I'll take the time." He took the papers and began writing the price beside the name of each item. Bill packed his pipe and looked at stock items while he waited.

Shortly Mr. Webster said, "Mr. Dykes, I have everything you want except four of the mattresses. I will have to order those. Look over these prices and see if you agree with them."

Bill looked at the list and was amazed at how prices had dropped. He said, "These prices are okay, but I would like to look at the livestock before you total up my list of supplies."

"Follow me," Mr. Webster said. At the stock pens, he explained, "These mules are about three years old. The four cows are almost four years of age. The goats are less than two. The hogs vary in age from six months to four years. All the livestock is in good shape and have been fed well."

With Mr. Webster's help, Bill cautiously picked out the animals he wanted to buy. The last purchases he made were the chickens and feed for the animals. He asked, "Mr. Webster, when will you deliver all of this?"

"Mr. Dykes, we will deliver two truckloads today and the rest of it in the morning. You said earlier that you wanted to hire Steve Wiggins, the brick mason. When do you want him to go to work?"

"Sir, if you deliver the material for the fireplace in the morning, we will pour a foundation for it tomorrow. If Steve can be on the job the day after tomorrow, he can go to work," Bill answered.

As Bill paid for his order, Mr. Webster said, "Mr. Dykes, one thing I forgot to mention is that when we make a delivery, we unload our own trucks. In the past, we have had customers who would try to unload the animals and some of them were injured in the process, so we will put them in your barn, field, corral, or wherever you want them."

Bill returned to the farm and he and his family set up a temporary homesite. Bill and Clyde were filling their water barrel when George approached them and said, "Well, Bill, I assume you are in the farming business. When will the supplies get here?"

"Mr. Webster assured me that everything except four of the

mattresses will be here before two o'clock tomorrow." Pointing, Bill continued, "George, I'm going to buy the six hundred acres of timberland adjoining this farm. That will be your source for poles, timber, fence posts, and firewood. The lawyer said that several foot-high concrete posts mark the boundary lines. According to the barrister, there is a small creek running through it with plenty of fish."

"That is good news," George said. "Tomorrow my crew will build a gate between the field and the timberland. The quicker we can get the mule and wagon in there, the quicker we can get the wood we will need. My boys and I have been discussing the fact that we need more land to raise grain for the animals and to help feed the children. As soon as we complete the chores we have planned, with your permission, I would like to clear another fifty acres of land."

"George, you have many formidable tasks to accomplish, so operate this farm at your discretion. When the supplies are here and secure, I know you will be assigning jobs, and the children will have many things to learn. I've already told my family to report to you for work in the morning. Tomorrow, assign one boy to help me install the vent pipe and stove in the kitchen. When we finish that job, we'll install the pitcher pump over the well and construct a barrier over and around it so no one can fall in. The day after the brick mason finishes the fireplace, we will close in one corner of the barn and build the bunks, shelves, and a small sitting room."

The hour was past noon when two trucks arrived and the drivers unloaded the animals, feed, fireplace material, a woodstove with vents, four windows, and several boxes of hardware and kitchen equipment. George gave the drivers instructions about where to put everything.

When Bill's family came from the trailer two mornings later, the children were getting their instructions for the workday. George said, "Today my sons will work with the brick mason. Max, you and Melvin will help Mr. Dykes build furniture. Carson, David, Sonny, and Calvin, you are to hitch the mule to the wagon and continue cutting firewood and gathering fat lighter knots. Continue unloading it beside the barn. Peggy, Darlene, and Mary, you will feed the animals, gather eggs, fill the water troughs, and then report to my wife." George continued reading his list, making sure everyone had a job and understood how to do it.

"Darling," Betty asked, "why doesn't George assign the children their chores on a permanent basis instead of changing their work schedule daily?"

"Betty, until the construction and repair work is completed, George will have to issue new instructions each morning. A perfect example is when the fireplace is completed his sons will be free to work on another job. I think you noticed that he assigned every child a job he or she is capable of performing. And George has been very careful at rotating children on all jobs to be certain that at least two of them will become knowledgeable in the performance of different jobs. It's time for us to go to work."

Three weeks after Bill purchased the farm, the additions and repairs to the house and barn were complete. The following morning, a sow gave birth to a litter of piglets. After supper everyone on the farm stood beside the hog pen, gazing at the newborns and giving each a name.

George said, "Children, if we can continue raising hogs and chickens, we will soon have something besides venison, squirrels, rabbits, possums, and quail to go with our rice and beans. Mr. Dykes and my boys built us a nice smokehouse to keep meat from spoiling, and it is our job to see that it is filled to capacity and the meat is cured properly."

The following day, a Sunday, Bill and George walked around the farm, checking to be sure that everything was in order. Finally George said, "Bill, I wish you would stop worrying. You are leaving us with a good farmhouse, solid barn, good corral, new fence wire around the chicken coop, strong hog pens, one old and two new outhouses, excellent stock, a large smokehouse, a creek full of fish, and the tools necessary for clearing the land needed before the spring planting. The formula you gave me for curing and preserving meat is perfect. Within two years, I hope to be planting at least two hundred acres of corn for livestock."

"George, I truly hope you obtain your goals," Bill said. "We will be leaving early in the morning. Betty will write to Sara occasionally and keep you posted as to our whereabouts. If you should need something for the farm, be sure to let us know as soon as we settle in one place for a few weeks. I won't make any suggestions about how you should handle the farm business because you know more about it than I do, and you are aware of the state of affairs in the country. Besides your family, you have sixteen children who are willing to work. You also have four unoccupied bunks in the barn, should you decide to adopt more children."

Saying farewell the following morning was time consuming for both families, including the children, because Betty had to talk with and hug each child. After Bill drove away from the farm, he surprised his family when he stopped at Mr. Webster's general store and said, "Clyde, fill the gas tank." He gave Betty some money and continued, "You and Mona go inside and purchase high-top shoes, socks, two shirts, undergarments, two pairs of coveralls, caps, and a coat for each person at the farm. And, ask Mr. Webster to deliver the items."

After Betty paid Mr. Webster and they drove away, she said, "Darling, that was a good deed you did. Everyone on the farm needs those items. Do you think George and the children will be successful at farming?"

"Betty, I believe that crew will survive, but I don't expect them to make any real money. Most of the food they produce will be consumed by themselves and the animals. The only way they might make any cash money will be to sell some hogs, chicken eggs, selling drums of pine tar they collect from chipping pine trees, or they might also get money from hiring out as part-time laborers. However, the farming children do have a place to sleep, and if all goes well, they will be able to feed themselves and keep warm.

"And speaking of money," Bill continued. "When we left the coal mine, we had two thousand two hundred sixteen dollars. I was lucky at finding work and within a short span of time we saved another three thousand dollars. After buying the two parcels of land in Fernandina and purchasing this farm and supplies, we still have three thousand ten dollars. We have been fortunate because we have been able to save most of the money I have made, but unless we encounter a catastrophe, our charity work is over until I find a job. I need to have some money on hand for taxes on the land we've purchased, truck repairs, groceries, and other necessities."

The following evening, Bill parked the truck a few miles outside of St. Augustine in a patch of woods. By nightfall, campfires were visible on both sides of the highway, and people were commenting about the herbs, frogs, and other wildlife they were cooking. However, many transients were still going in both directions on the highway, trying to escape the heat of day.

Clyde said, "Mama, the pathetic scenes beside the highway never change. The transients are sad, disgruntled, hungry, and pathetic looking. I noticed the adults around the campfires always eat before the children are fed. Why don't they all eat together?"

"Clyde, that eating arrangement was established in many households long before the depression swept this country. Since the adults are the breadwinners of the family, the common consensus is that an adult must eat well and stay healthy."

A light rain began to fall, adding to the misery of the transients.

Bill parked the truck in downtown St. Augustine the following morning beside the bay and for two hours his family walked the streets of the oldest city in the United States. St. Augustine was a replica of every town they had seen. Foreclosure or "Gone Out of Business" notices were posted on the front windows of banks, warehouses, credit unions, vendors, and many of the retail shops. At noon the family walked around a corner and immediately came to a stop because there was a line of people six blocks long. Each person had a bowl, plate, and a spoon in his hand waiting for the soup kitchen to open.

Bill and his family crossed the street and took a seat on a bench facing the temporary soup kitchen. Shortly, four women began ladling soup into the transients' containers while four teenage girls handed each a piece of bread. The line of transients moved quickly and once a person had his or her food, they crossed the street and sat on the curb to eat.

Mona noticed a sign at the entrance to the soup kitchen and read, "Free soup once each day at noon. If you don't have a bowl and a spoon, the price is five cents."

When there were fewer than twenty people in the soup line, Bill said, "Let's eat. A bowl of that soup might make us think about how fortunate we have been, and make us thankful for what we do have."

After crossing the street, Bill approached a server and said, "We don't have any utensils with us, so I'll pay the twenty cents." The server nodded and filled four soup bowls. Bill noticed that the money container where the server dropped the coins into contained only his twenty cents.

Bill's family returned to the bench and tasted their soup. When Betty tasted hers, she exclaimed, "This is colored water and not fit for a hog, much less human consumption! My bowl of water has two slivers of potato peelings and a bone from a chicken. Even the bread is tasteless!"

The family sat looking at Bill, but no one ate. He turned to four pathetic-looking children who were barefoot and asked, "Would you care for some more soup?" The children nodded their heads, so Bill and his family poured their soup into their containers and gave them their bread.

After returning the soup bowls and utensils, the family

drove away. A few minutes later, Betty said, "Sara told me about the pathetic plight the people in south Florida are facing and I'm glad you are going to take George's advice and go west."

A week passed as Bill looked for work in the small cities and towns, but he found nothing but poverty. Two weeks later he was offered a job in Tallahassee, but he declined it; because twenty cents per hour was too little for him to accept. While they were going through Tallahassee, Betty posted letters to Winston Johannsen and George Cline.

A few days later, Bill found a job and worked at a boatyard in Mobile, Alabama, for two weeks. When the job ended, he and his family traveled slowly west, looking for work in every town or hamlet they passed. Daily they read newspapers, searching for work but nothing pertaining to a job was advertised.

Bill and his family were parked outside of Lake Charles, Louisiana, along with other transients, when Clyde said, "Papa, you and Mama have cautioned me about not getting concerned with the economics in this country. To me the situation looks almost hopeless. Could it be that there are no jobs to be found anywhere? Since we left Fernandina Beach, I have heard people talking about looking for work all over the country, and all of them are of the same opinion as they say, 'There are no jobs and no one is starting new projects to create any.'"

"Clyde," Betty replied, "when we left the coal mine, your father was extremely blessed at finding jobs. However, he knew the development of events in the future would probably change. The events that happen to a person in the future is called his destiny. Our Lord has a plan for this family, so stop worrying and place your trust in him."

Bill and his family spent a month looking for work in Pascagoula, Biloxi, Gulfport, and New Orleans, along with many of the people in those cities. A common theory about pessimism was stated by anyone who turned away people who were looking for work. The Gulf states were devastated and overshadowed by gloom, despair, hunger, and lost hope.

A week after leaving Baton Rouge, Bill applied for a job at an oil company outside Morgan City, Louisiana. Mr. Steve Herman, the owner of the company, was impressed with Bill's qualifications. He said, "Mr. Dykes, I have three wells that are producing oil. I'm going to gamble and sink a fourth well, but if it fails, I will have to let you go because I already have a full crew for my operations. However, if the well should produce a substantial yield, and you can perform the work, I will keep you on the payroll. I will see you at the job site Monday morning."

In order to be near fresh water, the Dykes family set up a homesite several hundred yards from the oil rigs. The land was flat and barren looking. Standing water, potholes, garbage cans, scraps from construction work, and oil spills decorated the area. To complete the blight on nature, abandoned oil derricks that failed to produce oil were scattered about.

Betty said, "Darling, I don't mean to grumble, but of all the many places we have lived, this area is the most unsightly. If those wildflowers were not in bloom, the place would have a complete look of devastation."

Bill went to the job site Monday morning, and Mr. Herman introduced him to the crew with whom he would be working. Pointing, he said, "This is the Smith brothers, George and Sam. Sam is my fastest employee and these men are Morgan Jones and Case Mack, our oldest man. Case came from Colorado and has been with us for seven months. As badly as we hate to see him go, he will be leaving us in a few weeks. Bill, today you will be working with Case inside the tent, unless Morgan needs you. I will check with you at the end of the day." The crew went to work, and Mr. Herman drove away in his truck.

After rolling up the edges of the tent in order to let the sunlight in, Case said, "Bill, you can start rebuilding those pumps on that table. The new parts and tools are in the boxes underneath it. I will be helping the other men sink drilling rods into the earth for a short time. If you can't find a tool or a part you need, just yell out."

Bill pulled a pump to the edge of the table and started disassembling it. The work was easy because many times at the coal mine, he had rebuilt pumps that were identical to that one. While working, he occasionally glanced at the men working under the derrick and decided that the crew was multicraft workers because they all of performed any type of work at hand.

For two weeks, Bill worked on pumps, drive belts, and chains. He welded metal shafts together, spliced cable on heavy rigging, ran wire for lights, ran errands, cut timbers, and made repairs on the wood structure surrounding the oil rig.

The work was dirty and oily, but Bill liked it much better than he did working at the fertilizer factory. He worked closely with Case Mack, who was friendly, and they immediately became good friends. While they were rebuilding a small Perkins diesel engine, Bill asked, "Case, when you lived in Colorado, for whom did you work?"

"Bill, during the spring and summer, I would go down to the lowlands and work at herding sheep and cattle. When I returned to the mountains, I worked at prospecting for gold, but I was not successful. My parents were killed in an avalanche, and I inherited seven thousand acres of land on a mountainside close to Colorado Springs. My land is covered with boulders, rocks, trees, snow, wildlife, and caves. During my six years of prospecting, on eight different occasions, I found small pockets of gold, but the yield from the largest pocket was less than thirteen hundred dollars.

"That was a lot of money," Case continued, "but it was thirteen months before I found another one. I didn't have any experience at using dynamite, but I set off charges in two different caves, but my blasts were unsuccessful. I tried to blast holes in the caves to go a few yards horizontally, but each time I blew the roof on the floor of each one. Bill, have you ever used dynamite?"

Bill grinned and said, "Yes, for many years I was a dynamiter for a coal-mining company. One of my jobs was to drill holes and set dynamite charges in different mining shafts each day."

"Bill, that sounds like a secure position. Why did you leave such a good job?" Case asked.

"Case, just after this depression hit this country, the coal mine closed. I bought a truck and built a traveling trailer on it for my family. Since that time, we have been moving from one state to another, looking for work. For almost two years, I've worked at several temporary jobs, but I have not found a permanent one. If they don't find oil in this well, I will be on the road again, searching for another job. Case, do you live near this oil field?"

The old man laughed, pointed, and said, "That tent about two hundred yards behind us is my living quarters. In Colorado, I left two well-built log cabins. One of them was where my parents lived and the other one was for me and my wife. When I left Colorado, I asked my best friend, an old Indian named Chikata, to look after my property until I return."

"Case, do you plan to look for gold when you return to Colorado?"

"Bill, I don't have the gold fever, but I would like to set off a few charges of dynamite in some of the caves. If I do set off a few blasts, and don't find a sufficient amount of gold, I can walk away from gold mining, knowing that I gave prospecting my best effort. But, I won't be satisfied until I try the dynamite again."

Bill and his family associated with Case and his wife on a frequent basis. On many weekends they fished in a pond, hunted rabbits, quail, and enjoyed cookouts. Case was a huge fifty-eight-year-old man with blond hair, blue eyes, and Mona and Clyde took to him like a second father. Case taught Clyde how to snare rabbits and trap wild game, and he taught Mona how to paint pictures. Case's wife, Myrna, and Betty quickly became friends, and they shared the same interests, with God being first.

On Tuesday morning, Case said to Bill, "Next Sunday I'm going to the store to pick up some supplies. Morgan mentioned that a barnstormer with a biplane will be in the field in front of the store offering rides to the public for fifty cents. Would you and your family like to come along?"

"Thanks, Case, we do need a few staples, and a plane ride for Betty might break the monotony for her. It might even blow the curls out of her hair."

When Bill told his family about the barnstormer, Clyde and Mona started counting their pennies, looking forward to Sunday.

However, Betty said, "No one is going to get me in a flying machine that is partially made of canvas, speeding hundreds of feet above the earth. Bill, we will have to rise early Sunday in order to worship before we go to the store." She began checking the shelves and making a list of needed supplies.

When the families arrived at the store Sunday morning, a group of about fifty people were watching as the pilot poured gasoline into the tank of the biplane. Shortly an old man strapped himself into the seat behind the pilot, and the aircraft raced across the field and they left the earth. The group watched the aircraft climb almost out of sight, racing toward the heavens. And then they heard the engine stall. Suddenly the aircraft tilted forward and plunged toward the earth, startling the onlookers. They heard the engine cough and then the biplane came diving toward them.

Slowly the aircraft came out of the dive and passed barely above the pedestrians' heads. Some of the people stood firm while others fell to the ground. The pilot executed two barrel rolls and then landed to pick up another paying customer.

"Papa, do you know who the pilot is?" Mona asked.

Bill shook his head and Mona said, "That is One Arm Harrigan!"

The air show was very entertaining. However, four of the paying customers who had delusions of grandeur about their daredevil skills, kissed the ground when they returned to earth.

After Mona and Clyde had taken their ride, they assisted One Arm with his cans of gasoline.

When another customer was airborne, Clyde said, “Mama, when I told One Arm that Papa worked for his family in South Carolina, he returned my and Mona’s money and gave us an extra dime.”

The air show ended as the group watched the biplane execute two figure eights before flying out of sight.

Five weeks and three days later, Mr. Herman’s oil well yielded nothing except small rocks and muddy water. He said to Bill, “I’ve wasted some money on this well, but I’m not the first man to fail trying to find oil. Bill, you are an excellent worker with many skills, and I hate to lose you, but I have to let you go. Bill, where will you go next?”

“Mr. Herman, we plan to go southeast along the Texas coast line.”

“Bill, take my advice and forget about finding a job in the valley of Texas,” Mr. Herman said. “The farmers there use immigrant workers. In fact, the majority of those jobs are filled with immigrants. I don’t know if Case mentioned it to you, but he is returning to Colorado. If I had not hired a replacement for him months ago, you could have filled his position.”

Bill shook Mr. Herman’s hand and said, “I appreciated the job, and I truly hope you find oil when you sink another well. We will be gone in the morning.”

While returning to the trailer, Bill was thinking about which direction he should go to find another job. In the distance, he could see Case and Myrna striking their tent and folding it up. Within an hour, both families were ready to hit the road the next morning. “Darling,” Betty said, “I invited Case and Myrna to eat supper with us before we part ways.”

“What are you serving for dinner?”

“Clyde and Mona’s favorite food, fried frog legs with mash potatoes, gravy, string beans, and ice tea,” she answered. “Bill, where are we going tomorrow?”

“Betty, I’ve been contemplating traveling along the Gulf Coast, but the truth is I don’t know where to go. There are two large construction crews who build boats in Galveston, but I have reservations about whether or not they are hiring anyone. I will pray and then decide in the morning.”

Case and Myrna arrived, and the adults quickly set up a table, benches, and chairs in the yard. While they ate, Bill noticed how his children attached themselves to the older couple and bombarded them with questions about Colorado. Then it dawned on him that other than their own parents, these were the only friends the children had to talk with and learn about new adventures and places in life.

Betty had just served dessert when Case asked, "Bill, would you and your family consider going to the mountains with us and let's search for gold?"

A piece of pie slipped from Betty's fork and dropped to her plate. Gasping, she stammered, "Prospecting for gold?"

Bill was smiling, but he said, "Case, this is the first offer we've ever had to search the mountains, and hope to make a living from gold. Tell me, other than frigid weather, avalanches, snowdrifts, and isolation in the mountains for months, what do you think we will find? To my knowledge, the banking world has never set an exact price for gold. Case, tell us the details of your offer."

"Bill, if you and your family will go with us to Colorado, you can live in the large log cabin my parents left me. And I will pay you forty percent of everything we find. But before we go up toward Pikes Peak, we would need to stop at a general store and stock up on the necessary supplies such as food, clothing, tobacco, gun shells, medical supplies, hand tools, snowshoes, dynamite, traps, and lamp oil. When the heavy snows come, a vehicle is useless on the trails. As you can see, I'm not trying to make it sound easy and fun, because you already know that mining is hard work, and it can be extremely dangerous."

Silence permeated the group for a short span of time. Bill finally broke the silence, saying, "Okay, family, we have a job offer of harsh conditions, hard work, solitude, no guarantee of making a penny, or a chance to become rich. A few years ago, I told you we wouldn't return to the snow country, but I'm having second thoughts. Let's take a vote about which direction we want to go, southeast or northwest. Remember, just one dissenting vote and we go southeast. Anyone who wants to go to the snow country, raise his hand."

Quickly Clyde and Mona raised their right hands, and Betty, with a concerned look on her face, raised hers. Bill said, "I also want to try prospecting." He stood and continued, "Case, it is unanimous, so you have four partners." As the two men shook hands, Bill asked, "Case, what time do we leave in the morning?"

"I think seven o'clock will be early enough. After all, we're not in a great hurry. Who knows, we may find a job or two while traveling."

"Mr. Mack," Mona said, "tonight I will pray for a safe and prosperous expedition. If the Lord wills it, you and Papa will find gold."

"Mona, you could be right. In the past while I was searching for large quantities of gold, I tried everything except prayer, and I appreciate you reminding me about the right thing to do," Case said.

At seven a.m., Bill had the trailer rolling at forty-five miles per hour, following Case's pickup truck. "Darling," Betty said, "if for any reason you should lose sight of Case's truck, do you know which highways to take?"

Bill handed Betty a map and said, "Yes. Case marked this map for us." He pointed as he continued, "We're leaving Morgan City on the Gulf Coast, heading for Baton Rouge, then Vicksburg, Mississippi, and then to Little Rock, Arkansas. From there we go to Springfield, Missouri, and then proceed on to the outskirts of Kansas City, Kansas. Then we go to Omaha, Nebraska, before stopping outside of Colorado Springs, Colorado. Betty, we will stock up on supplies before going up to Case's property. This is going to be a very long, rigorous trip. And, if for any reason I lose Case, I will meet him in front of the post office in Colorado Springs. "

Three days after leaving the Gulf Coast, the travelers passed fewer transients beside the highway, and Case made frequent stops for Snuffy and the families. On the fifth day, they remained camped beside the highway because torrential rains drenched the area. Two days later the scenery north was beautiful as they rolled by cowhands and cows south of Kansas City. Since leaving Morgan City, Clyde and Mona had taken turns riding in the cab of Case's truck.

Several days later, the travelers parked at a large general store just north of Colorado Springs. Snow-capped mountains shone like beacons in the distance. As the children stood in awe gazing up, Case said, "Clyde, you and Mona take a good look at those peaks. Your new home is very close to them."

After two hours of shopping, the two families had purchased the supplies they needed to survive in the wilderness. Meticulously, Bill strapped the dynamite and cans of gas and lamp oil to shelves in the trailer before the clerks loaded their other supplies into their trucks.

Case said, "Bill, Myrna and I would like to treat your family to dinner, and then we will spend the night at the lodge before going into the high country in the morning. Do you think that would be agreeable with your family?"

"That would be perfect," Betty said. "I need to stop by the post office and mail two letters and a money order. Now that we will have a permanent address, we should have mail to pick up after winter passes."

After stopping at the post office, Case led the way to the only diner close by.

While the families were seating themselves, Case and Myrna spoke to several people. Bill's family noticed that the people were dressed in different types of western attire. Most of them wore the typical cowboy hats, jeans, and boots, while a few resembled prospectors. Seated in a booth near them were three burly-looking men who resembled trappers. Their garments were made from buffalo hides, cowhides, and leather from other animals. They wore leggings and shoes tied down with leather straps.

Softly Mona whispered, "Beards must be the fashion here, because every man except Papa and Mr. Mack has one."

To the delight of Bill's family, they ate their first buffalo steak with all the trimmings. Afterward, they rented rooms at the only lodge in town and took hot baths and quickly changed clothes because they wanted to go window shopping. As the families walked past a bank building, Bill stopped and said, "Case, this is the first bank I've ever seen that has a sign reading 'Bank and Assay Office.'"

"Bill, many of the larger banks out west provide the service of weighing, pricing, and buying precious metals from customers. Usually if a person has a large amount of metal or stones to sell, he or she will telephone a large bank in another city in order to find out the true market value of that product. A few banks have been known to take advantage of miners."

The families continued walking and looking in windows at the western attire, tools, and the latest devices for ranching, farming, and mining. Before dark they returned to the lodge for the night.

An hour after daybreak, the families had eaten and were on the road again, with Bill following Case's truck. He noticed a few ranches with cattle grazing and windmills turning, but he was most conscious of the winding road that gradually kept going higher. Shortly the pavement ended, and Case slowed down to twenty-five miles per hour. They went around a curve and all they could see on their left was a huge mountain.

"Papa," Mona said, "we had better hope a boulder doesn't roll down, because from here, I can't see the top of the mountain on our left."

Case slowed down even more, and moments later, Bill hit a big pothole.

After going around another curve, Betty said, "Darling, the drop-off on this side of the truck is at least a mile. I'm glad you keep good tires on the truck. A blowout could send us right over the cliff or off the road."

Except for seeing less foliage and more mountains, the scenery was much the same. Occasionally they would see deer feeding high up on the winding trails.

"Papa," Mona said, "since we left town, we've only passed seven houses and all of them are log cabins. Why don't they build their houses like the rest of the people in this country?"

Bill shifted gears because the incline of the road was a gradual sharp degree upward. His truck had four forward gears and before he reached the apex, Bill had the vehicle in first gear and both hands on the steering wheel.

The road leveled out, and Bill answered Mona's question. "Mona, in order to withstand the wind and the heavy snows in these mountains, shelters must be very strong. Many times during the winter, the roof has to support up to six feet of snow. All of the cabins we have passed have several large posts inside of them to help support the roof. Three 55-gallon containers of snow is equivalent to one drum of water. One drum of water weighs approximately four hundred forty pounds.

"Case warned us that we won't have electricity, telephones, or running water," Bill continued. "Our water supply will come from a small stream from a waterfall in the rear of the cabins. During the winter we will keep four drums of snow inside for fresh water, because once in a while a blizzard will freeze the stream and waterfall in back of the cabins. All of us need to pay close attention to what Case and Myrna tell us about these mountains, especially anything about safety and survival."

Rounding a curve beside a mountain, Bill quickly put his foot on the brake because the road ran down hill for about a half mile. He said, "This is the first drop on this road since we left Colorado Springs."

Approximately two hours after leaving Colorado Springs, Bill pulled about one hundred feet off the dirt trail and parked beside Case's truck in front of two log cabins. As the families stepped from the trucks, Case said, "Bill, the largest cabin is your family's home."

When they moved toward the front door, a huge Indian stepped from the corner of the cabin. He dipped his bloody hands in a bucket of water, scrubbed, and then dried them. Case grasped the Indian by the shoulders and he and Myrna greeted him.

Myrna said, "Chikata, this is Bill and Betty Dykes and their children, Clyde and Mona. This family has come to live and work with us." Snuffy was sniffing Chikata's feet so Myrna said, "And this is their dog Snuffy."

The Indian shook hands with the family and said, "Welcome to my ancestors' mountains. You will enjoy living here." Chikata turned toward the cabin, made a grunting sound, and a huge dog of mixed breeding came running to him. He said, "This is Onox. He is a hunting and work dog who will enjoy having Snuffy as a companion. Mr. Mack, I was cleaning a bear when you drove up. As soon as I finish, I will unload the trucks."

Case opened the thick front door, and the group entered a large room. The scene the Dykes family encountered consisted of heavy-duty homemade chairs, couches, bookshelves filled with books, oil lamps, gun racks with numerous firearms, furniture, pillows, bear rugs in front of the fireplace, and large posts helping support the roof.

"This is unbelievable!" Betty exclaimed. "It is so spacious

and is completely furnished. Everything is so clean. Bill, the kitchen and dining rooms are large enough to serve twenty people. The kitchen has three safes, two stoves, a large wood box, and ample pots, pans, plates, and silverware for several families. This home is a ladies' paradise."

"Betty," Myrna said, "come look at the three bedrooms. The furnishings in them are also homemade. There are no closets, but the shelving is more than adequate for clothing and other supplies."

"Myrna, what are the mattresses stuffed with?" Betty asked.

"Chikata stuffed them with feathers from ducks, geese, chickens, turkeys, and quail. All of you come with me to the worktables beside the fireplace." When Myrna had their attention, she continued, "These tables are where the menfolk work at cleaning guns, repairing traps and fishing equipment, sharpening small knives, cutting pieces of animal hides, and sewing boots, belts, clothing, sacks, straps for tying things together, and many other things to work with."

The families went through the back door into a narrow room that contained two aluminum tubs for bathing, a stand holding two wash pans, a mirror, towels, and a clothesline. Several bags of lime for treating human waste were stacked on the floor.

"Mrs. Mack," Mona asked, "why do you have a clothesline inside?"

"Mona, we have another clothesline out back, but during the winter months, garments won't dry—they just freeze. When the temperature drops below freezing, we have to dry clothes in here or beside the fireplace."

"Case, speaking of the four-foot fireplace," Bill said, "I noticed a brass knob mounted in front of the stone facing. Is that a screw device to open and close the large damper without burning or getting your hands dirty?"

"Exactly, and it's efficient and easy," Case said. "We built this cabin with huge logs which we ran through two saw blades in order to give us a flat surface on each side. Before one log was placed on top of another, we coated the flat edges with tar which had been heated. Then we drilled holes and drove wooden dowels through the logs to join them together. I don't want to brag, but at bedtime, if you will bank the fire, and close the damper about halfway, and keep the shutters covering the glass windows closed, this cabin is tight and holds heat well. Let's go out back."

When the families were in the backyard, Clyde said, "I see Chikata hanging the bear meat in the log smokehouse." As they looked around, they saw two outhouses, a wire pen, the remains of a summer garden, a large stream, a beautiful waterfall flowing through a hole in the mountain, and at least a three-acre fenced-in yard.

"Mr. Mack," Clyde asked, "what is the large building joining each cabin used for?"

"Come with me and I'll show you." The group followed Case as he went through a rear door and watched as he opened two huge swinging doors on the front side. At the rear end of the huge room were a chicken pen, a duck pen, a goat stall, and three other stalls for horses.

"As you can see," Case continued, "this is our tool, fowl, and wood storage building. We let the fowl and goats graze in the backyard during the daylight hours. We use the small diesel tractor for the garden and for pulling sleds of wood and for anything else that is heavy. Those horse stalls over there were for a mule or two until I bought the tractor."

"Mr. Mack," Clyde asked, "how many cords of wood are in here?"

"Clyde, there's between three or four, but our first big chore will be to get at least four more moved in here before winter sets in. We keep our wood supply inside and each house has a door adjacent to this building. While I've been working in the oil field, Chikata has been cutting wood and stacking it on the mountainside. We will use the tractor and sled to move the wood in here as quickly as possible."

"Papa, take a look at the mining tools, snowshoes, skis, and snow sleds hanging on the wall," Mona blurted out. "Mr. Mack, are the snow sleds for play?"

Case laughed and said, "Mona, you and Clyde can use them to slide down a small embankment, but never try to use a sled to traverse a mountain. When the snows come, we will use the sleds to move slain animals to the smokehouse. Bill, I see Chikata unloading our supplies, let's go to work."

Chikata and Myrna unloaded the trucks while the others carried part of the supplies into the cabins and some of the boxes and cans into the storage shed. Two hours later after the families had stored their goods, Betty said, "Everyone take a seat at the table, and we'll have ham sandwiches with tea."

When the meal was over, Case said, "Bill, you and I need to winterize the trucks and put them out of our way. This time of the year we don't have many days when anyone can drive on these trails."

They moved the vehicles beside the storage shed and jacked them up before putting timbers under the axels. They drained the radiators and completely filled each one with antifreeze. They then started the engines and let them run for five minutes. When the time was up, they checked the level on the reservoir again.

"Mr. Mack," Clyde remarked, "I noticed a bunk and some personal belongings in the storage shed. Who owns them?"

"Oh, I forgot to tell you," Case said. "Although we have spare bedrooms, Chikata prefers to sleep in the shed with the goats, ducks, and chickens. He believes a warm house is bad for one's health. However, at dusk each day, he looks forward to performing chores beside the fireplace. Bill, if Betty doesn't mind, Chikata will take his meals with your family because he wants to learn new things from all of you."

"He is welcome," Bill said. "He can educate us about this big mountain range and what to expect this winter."

Case continued, "Clyde, in the months to come, Chikata will teach you and Mona many things about nature, tracking, wild game, leatherwork, making and stringing a longbow, avalanches, snowdrifts, and he has no equal when it comes to maintaining and using knives. Bill, tomorrow we will finish stocking the wood and then I will also show you four of the mines. Let's call it a day."

When Bill entered the cabin, Betty and Mona were fixing supper. The date was August 31, and they had the windows and shutters open, airing out the cabin. Bill went to his bedroom to look it over and to check on his shotgun. When he exited the room, Chikata and Clyde were at the work-table scrapping taler from a bear skin.

"It's time to wash and eat," Mona said.

Shortly the group sat down to eat at a worktable in the kitchen. When Chikata saw his friends join hands, he extended his to Betty and Mona. After Bill gave a short prayer, they released hands and Clyde, in succession, passed the mash potatoes, gravy, roast beef, string beans, and biscuits to Chikata first, because he was their house guest.

"Mr. Bill," Chikata asked, "you just said a prayer to your God. Why did you thank God for what nature provides?"

"Chikata, God provided this world for his people. Everything on it, including nature, was created by God. Even the air and stones are his creation. Man has invented many things by using what God put on this earth, but no man has ever created anything. Everyone should thank God for his many gifts, including nature."

The group began eating, but Chikata was still looking at

Bill in deep concentration.

"Mr. Bill," Chikata said, "Case and Myrna taught me to read from the Holy Book that they gave me, but I don't understand many of the words. When you have the time, would you help me to understand the Book and its meaning?"

"Yes, Chikata, my entire family will help you to learn about our God."

When the meal was over, Clyde went with Chikata and watched him open the rear door of the storage shed and put food and water in containers for the fowl and the goats. Before he finished, the animals were in a single file, going to their pens.

After Clyde closed the gates, he said, "Chikata, I've already filled the wood box for the stove, and tomorrow I will assume this chore. When do you milk the goats?"

"Early each morning I milk the goats, gather eggs, and clean out the pens. Do you wish to help me?"

Clyde nodded, so Chikata said, "I'll wake you at sunrise. Let's go finish scrapping the bear hide and then carry the waste outside." At dusk the families turned off the lanterns and went to bed.

At first daybreak, Chikata shook Clyde and said, "Get dressed and come to the storage shed." When Clyde entered the shed, he noticed a basket of eggs and an empty bucket on the floor, and Chikata was milking a goat. He said, "Clyde, take that bucket and milk those two goats."

When Bill's family exited their rooms, Chikata was serving eggs, biscuits, and bear meat for breakfast and Clyde was pouring milk and coffee. "Mom, breakfast is ready," Clyde announced.

The family prayed and as they ate, Bill asked, "What is inside those backpacks beside the door?"

"Dad," Clyde answered, "Chikata packed ropes, matches, water, food, old coats, knives, chipping hammers, chisels, and flashlights for us. While he is using the tractor today, he is going to load the sled with those supplies and take them to one of the caves. On the way back, he is going to pull the sled with firewood and store it in the barn. In that way we save time."

Shortly, Bill and Clyde were following Case up a mountainside while Chikata pulled the sled with the tractor. When they were about two hundred yards up the mountain, they unloaded their supplies and quickly loaded the first stack of cut wood onto the sled. Clyde stepped on the rear of the tractor and said, "I'm going with Chikata and help unload the sled."

"Bill," Case said, "there are four more stacks of wood up there behind that clump of brush. And one of the mines is just above the wood, so let's take a look at it while we're waiting." At the entrance to the mine, they got flashlights and chipping hammers from the packs and went inside. "Bill, this mine is where I found the most gold, but I have yet to discover a vein."

When Bill switched on his flashlight, several bats flew outside. He said, "This shaft is about eighty feet deep by twenty feet wide. We could set off two charges before shoring would be necessary." Bill went to the far end of the mine and used a hammer to chip away several pieces of rock. "Case, I don't claim to be a geologist, but I would suggest blasting here. This wall facing is not limestone, sand, or slag. Are the other three caves about the same size as this one?"

"Two of them are, but the one higher up the mountain is twice this size," Case said. "The large cave is where Chikata found eight small nuggets, but remember, all we have done so far is just chip away at the walls."

"Case, did Chikata pack some dynamite?"

"Yes, twelve sticks," Case said.

"I hear the tractor returning, so if you agree, after we load the sled, we'll chisel some holes and set off three charges later today," Bill said.

Clyde was standing behind Chikata, who had parked the tractor beside the wood pile, and jokingly said, "Dad, we saw you coming from a mine. Did you find any gold?"

"Not yet, son, but give us a little time."

After loading the sled, Bill and Case returned to the cave and started chiseling holes. The granite was hard, and the work was slow. Before they finished opening three holes, all of the wood had been moved and Chikata and Clyde had returned to the mine to lend a helping hand.

Bill slid a dynamite stick into each hole, attached the fuses, and said, "Gather the tools and get out of here before I set this off." Bill noticed Chikata said something to his dog, Onox, and he left the mine. After Bill lit the fuses, he quickly joined the others outside. Simultaneously, the dynamite erupted and dust and small particles spewed through the mine entrance.

"Mama, I thought the men were going to move wood, not dynamite for gold," Mona said. "The unexpected noise startled me."

"So did I, but you know your father, he doesn't waste time while working. Mona, I see a fox on the mountainside. He seems to be watching the chickens. Remind me to tell Chikata about him. We don't want him eating them."

When the dust settled, Case said, "Okay, let's check the rocks for gold before we remove them from the mine." Inside, Case lit two lanterns and continued, "Clyde, gold is yellow or yellowish brown in color, so be careful and don't throw away any nuggets."

They went to work picking up large rocks and carefully inspecting each one before tossing it into one of three wheelbarrows. As soon as the wheelbarrows were full, Clyde and Chikata rolled them outside and discarded the waste a short distance from the mine entrance. Case used a sledgehammer to break a large boulder into pieces. When he picked up the pieces, Onox growled furiously and began digging where the boulder had been removed.

The workers watched as Onox pawed up a nugget of gold half as big as a child's fist and clenched it between his teeth. He walked straight to his master and deposited the nugget on the floor in front of him. Chikata wiped the nugget clean and handed it to Case so all of them could inspect it.

"Onox must have seen a glimmer of the nugget to know where to dig," Case said.

Snuffy began digging in the same spot where Onox had found his nugget. The dried earth around Sunffy's feet revealed four nuggets about a third the size of the one Onox had found. Case said, "Clyde, while we move these stones, you scoot down to the storage shed and bring us two yard rakes. We will rake this floor clean and then dig to see if there is any gold beneath us." The miners quickly inspected and removed the last of the stones just prior to Clyde's return.

"It's past one o'clock, let's stop for lunch," Case said.

The workers sat down on a log to eat sandwiches and drink coffee. "Mr. Case," Clyde asked, "how many dollars' worth of gold do you think we have found this morning?"

"Clyde, I don't know exactly. But the amount in that bag is at least ten times as much as the gold I sold for thirteen hundred dollars. I'm hoping there's a lot more under the dirt in that mine." The group was anxious to dig, so they ate in a hurry and returned to the mine shaft.

"Bill, let's start digging at the far end of the shaft and work our way to the entrance," Case said. "When we've dug up about four feet across the floor, Chikata and Clyde can sift through the dirt while we remove it. Then we will replace the dirt and dig another few feet. We will check the dirt again for gold a second time while filling the hole. Then we will dig another four feet if you agree."

Sweat dripped from the miners because the work was hard and the cave was hot. An hour later, Bill threw a shovel of dirt against the wall and Onox and Snuffy growled—the workers froze. Before the miners could bend over, the dogs each had a gold nugget between his teeth, carrying it to Chikata. He cleaned the nuggets and handed them to Case. Case held one in each palm and said, "They are as wide as a silver dollar and five times as heavy. Bill, I'm thinking of all the time we wasted in the oil field when we should have been mining."

Bill laughed and said, "That could be true, but who knows, this may be all we find."

Two hours before dark, the miners found three large and four small nuggets. Bill said, "Case, another four more feet of digging and we will be finished on this floor."

"You're right, Bill, but thanks to our dogs, this has been a profitable day." Case looked at his pocket watch and continued. "It's less than two hours before dark, so we had better head for home and take care of the chores."

After making their way down the mountainside, they approached Betty and Myrna, who were taking clothes off the line. Myrna said, "Men, there are four tubs of hot water and clean clothes waiting for you in the back rooms. Betty, Mona, and I have already filled the wood boxes and taken care of the chores. We brought the fowl in and the goats early because Betty saw a fox stalking them this afternoon. Chikata, I think you will need to set out a cage before dark. After all of you finish bathing, supper will be on the table."

Clyde took his bath in a hurry and rushed to the storage shed where the wire cages were. Anxious to catch a fox, he quickly took a cage to the backyard. When supper was over, Clyde watched Chikata hang two pieces of meat inside the cage and set the trap door. He said, "Clyde, in the morning, we could have ourselves a fox."

"What will we do with him?" Clyde asked.

"If we catch a small fox, we can try to make a pet out of him and then try to catch another one of the opposite sex. We could raise foxes and sell the furs," Chikata said.

"What would we do with the meat?" Clyde asked.

"We would eat it; it is delicious. Clyde, foxes are not a lot of trouble if you keep them caged and they have room to romp."

At Case's request, Bill followed him to hide their gold. Case stopped behind the smokehouse and moved a piece of flagstone before digging a hole. He placed the pouch of gold in the ground, replaced the dirt, and pushed the flagstone over the loose earth. He said, "As you know, gold can bring out atrocious acts in so many men. Bill, at different times of the year, miners, hunters, and trappers will stop here to spend the night. It is a courtesy that mountain people grant to one another—a meal and lodging. Remember to warn your family about never telling anyone what we have found, because many a miner has disappeared in these mountains."

At daybreak Chikata woke Clyde to help with the chores. "Have you checked the cage?" Clyde asked.

Chikata smiled and said, "Yes, I put our fox in a wire pen with a tin roof over it."

"Can't the fox dig out and escape?"

"Clyde, the pen has a flagstone floor and small wire mesh around it. I've already left food and water for the animal. Let's milk the goats and fix breakfast."

When the meal was prepared, Clyde quickly inhaled his food; he wanted to look at the fox before going to work.

The miners returned to the mine and it was eleven o'clock before they found two small nuggets. By two p.m., they finished digging and covering the mine floor, which yielded nothing else.

"Bill," Case said, "do you think we should go to another mine or keep blasting in this one?"

"Well, I think we should dig up the entrance to this mine before shoring up and dynamiting deeper into the mountain. I believe we should exhaust our efforts on this shaft before moving on."

The miners went to work, excavating an area about twelve square yards by two feet deep.

"It is a pleasure digging out here in the cool breeze," Clyde said. As he threw a shovel of dirt to the side, everyone stopped working. Three large nuggets were visible on the pile of dirt. Clyde continued digging in that spot and found four more nuggets. By quitting time the miners had covered the last hole.

While going down the mountain, Case said, "Bill, the next

time you have an idea about digging in a certain spot, blurt it out. Some men are born with a certain destiny, while others have natural luck. I'm certain we'll find a cache of gold when you blast further into the mine."

Bill and Chikata were laughing, so Case continued. "You two laugh all you want to, but while you're on a lucky streak, we need to stick with your ideas until we exhaust them or find out you are wrong."

When they reached the cabins, Clyde went straight to the pen to find Mona talking to the fox. "What have you named him?" Clyde asked.

"Scrambo, and he's a she. Mrs. Myrna said that she's about two years old. She needs a male playmate for companionship. If we could raise some baby foxes, we could train them."

"Saturday I'm going deer hunting with the men," Clyde boasted. "Chikata said that while we're in the woods, we'll set out two traps. Have the chores been taken care of?"

Mona nodded and replied, "Yes, everything has been taken care of."

After supper Betty was working in the kitchen, enjoying a moment of silence as she watched and listened to her family. They were working with leather and at the same time, answering Chikata's questions about the Lord. Each night the group gathered at the worktables to share the details of their daily work, make plans for tomorrow, and learn from one another. They always went to bed early because they needed the rest for another day of grueling labor in the mountain.

For safety reasons, the miners spent the next two days cutting timbers and shoring up the mine. At quitting time, Case said, "Monday morning we can chisel some holes and blast away. Let's go home and ready ourselves for a good hunt tomorrow."

"Mr. Mack," Clyde said, "everywhere I've looked in these mountains, I've seen deer roaming up and down game trails. Where will we hunt?"

"Clyde, our stock of venison in the smokehouse is about depleted. So in the morning, Chikata will check the direction of the wind, because we want it blowing in our faces. He will pick a game trail on the side of a mountain where we will have a chance to kill several animals. He will also pick a spot where we can use the tractor and sled to transport our kill to the cabins. Remember, we don't kill small deer, just grown ones."

"Mr. Mack, will I get to shoot?" Clyde asked.

"Yes, your father has given me permission to let you use a

single-shot thirty-thirty rifle."

Chikata had breakfast ready and everyone was up two hours before daybreak. Before the sun rose, he had dispersed the hunters above a game trail with a light breeze in their faces. Just after sunrise, a single line of deer walked in a path going down the mountainside. Everyone knew that once the shooting started, the deer had three directions in which to go—forward, backward, or over the side of the mountain to a certain death.

Chikata crouched with a lever-action Winchester rifle and watched four small deer pass within a few yards of him. He knew the moment he fired, the others would also shoot and the remaining animals on the narrow trail would be trapped. Chikata took aim at a buck's head and pulled the trigger. Almost simultaneously, Case fired and moments later Bill and Clyde shot their weapons. They kept shooting until twelve deer lay motionless on the game trail.

While Bill, Case, and Clyde were looking at their kill, Chikata parked the tractor and the wooden sled a few feet from the game trail. Quickly they hung four deer to tree limbs and gutted, skinned, and cut the meat into pieces before placing it in tubs. After making short work of cleaning their kill, Chikata put the twelve deer hides along with the tubs, on the sled, and the hunters headed for the smokehouse.

Before noon the venison had been washed, treated with a brine solution, and was hanging in the smokehouse. Chikata said, "Clyde, watch and help me stretch the hides out to dry, so we can use them for bindings later." Shortly they had the hides tightly stretched between trees to dry and cure.

While the hunters were washing and getting ready for lunch, Chikata pointed and said, "A storm will be here shortly; let's eat and do our chores before it hits this area."

"Case," Bill said, "this is a beautiful September day and the sky is clear. What makes him think a storm is coming?"

"Bill, look behind Pikes Peak at the bluish-purple sky lining. The wind is blowing toward us, and within a short time we're going to see rain, high winds, and possibly some hail or snow."

Lacota

While completing their chores, Clyde and Chikata were moving the fowl and goats inside when the sky began rumbling and lightning started flashing. It seemed to be striking everywhere. The wind increased and blew from several directions. Small pellets of hail blanketed the land, followed by heavy rain. Within three hours, the temperature had dropped below forty degrees and the rain increased.

Bill said, "I'll start a fire and take the damp chill out of the air." He opened the damper above the firebox and lit the wood it contained. Within minutes, the cabin was warmer, and Bill thought about Case's remarks about how the cabin had been built. Darkness set in early due to an overcast sky.

The men were rigging fishing equipment, cleaning their guns, and putting away their hunting equipment when Mona announced, "Supper is on the table; let's eat."

After the meal was finished, Betty and Mona quickly cleaned the kitchen and joined the others at the worktables. As they sat working, Chikata said, "It will probably snow tonight so we will need to dress heavier tomorrow." The Dykes family was startled, but they said nothing. Chikata continued, "Clyde, after our worship service in the morning, we will tie a guide rope from the corner of the cabin up to the caves and look for game tracks."

"We know the way to and from the mines, so why do we need a guide rope?" Clyde asked.

"Yes, Clyde, we know the trail when it's visible, but if a blizzard should hit while we are working in the mines, it could be difficult to find the cabins, because visibility could be less than two feet. Many people have frozen to death in these mountains because they could not find their way."

While Betty enjoyed the family's lifestyle and the

comfortable home, she was immensely pleased with the conversations her family had with Chikata about the Bible each evening while they sat and worked at various activities. Chikata never ran out of questions about the Book and many times her family had to think, contemplate, read, and search the scriptures before they could answer him.

The following morning when Clyde and Chikata went out to tend to the fowl and milk the goats, the mountains were blanketed with snow. After taking care of the chores, eating breakfast, and participating in the worship service, they put coils of rope over their shoulders, attached one end to the corner of the cabin, and headed up the mountain. Occasionally, Chikata would stop, pull the slack out of the rope, wrap it around a pine tree, and then move on.

"Chikata," Clyde asked, "I noticed that you brought your rifle, as well as a longbow and arrows. Why do you need both weapons?"

"Well, for two reasons. Late yesterday I heard several elk off in the distance. If we can spot two or more of them within shooting range, we might drop one with the bow and another one with the rifle. If we use the rifle first, any game nearby would be alerted and leave the area before I could get off a second shot. There's always a few of them combing this area, pawing the ground looking for a meal."

When they finished tying off the guide ropes, Clyde followed his friend up the mountainside.

As he looked through binoculars, Chikata said, "I can see animal tracks near the bottom of the ravine. Let's take a seat on that log with the bushes in front of it where we will have a clear view of the slope below. And the breeze will be in our faces here. The elk are always feeding through this area."

They sat on the log, drank coffee, and Clyde shivered. Shortly, the silence was broken by the sounds of an elk.

Clyde kept glancing at Chikata, who seemed to be made of stone as he sat motionless, staring between the bushes. Silently, he gripped Clyde by the shoulder, and they eased to a standing position. Chikata leaned his rifle against a limb before stringing an arrow onto the longbow. They could see two elk pawing the snow away and feeding slowly toward them. Clyde estimated that one elk was about sixty yards from them and the other about seventy. Chikata shot an arrow into the elk nearest them and quickly used his rifle to shoot the second one.

As they bogged through the snow toward the elk, Clyde

said, "Now I understand why you used the longbow—the weapon is almost noiseless. Had you used the rifle first, we wouldn't have but one animal to eat. Do you want me to get a sled so we can move all this meat to the smokehouse?"

"Yes," Chikata said, "that will be a big help, but we'll need both sleds for the job. I'll start cleaning the animals and cutting them into pieces." Chikata opened his supply sack and retrieved his game sacks, short saw, hatchet, leather straps, and two filleting knives while Clyde went down the mountainside.

Chikata was in the process of cleaning the second elk when Clyde returned with the sleds and Bill and Case.

"That's a lot of meat," Bill said. "The luck we're always craving seems to have been with the hunters this morning."

Case assisted Chikata while Bill and Clyde put the sacks of meat onto the sleds and tied them down. Within two hours they had returned home, cut the animals into smaller pieces, treated the elk with brine solution, and hung the meat in the smokehouse.

"Case," Bill asked, "does it always snow up here this early in the year?"

"Yes. Winter always starts no later than September. Anyone going into these mountains in the early fall should carry heavy clothing and weapons because nature can be very unforgiving. Tomorrow morning you won't see any sweat while we're working in the cave. Clyde, take these elk scraps and give Scrambo, the fox, Snuffy, and Onox some meat and bones to chew on."

The miners went to work the following morning and every day for the next several weeks. They blasted, shoveled, dug, and moved tons of rock outside the caves. During those grueling weeks, they found only eight small nuggets, but no one let on that he was discouraged. They had not yet worked in the largest caves. And each had his own ideas and hopes about what they might find. At the end of a working day, Case said, "Tomorrow morning, December the fourth, we'll start in the last cave on this ridge. Don't ask me what it means, but Chikata believes that it contains very strong spirits and echoes from the past."

Bill set off the first dynamite charge the following morning, and when the dust cleared, the miners entered the cave and Bill said, "There's a faint light in here. There has to be a shaft somewhere above going to the surface of the mountain."

After lighting a lantern, Clyde, Onox, and Snuffy went through a small opening in the rear of the cave. "Hurry, come in here!" Clyde yelled. "It's not dark, but lanterns will help. I think we've found a burial ground."

After hanging their lanterns on rock edges, the miners stood in awe. Chikata finally said, "So this is where Lacota dwelled and held his private rituals! We have just found the great mystery that has puzzled the Nez Perce Indian tribes for decades." Quickly, Chikata built a small fire with rotten leather, kneeled before it, and pulled the smoke to his body while chanting for several minutes. Respectfully, the miners stood silently, waiting for Chikata to finish communicating with his ancestors.

Finally Chikata stood, looked around, pointed, and continued, "I see eighteen metal Spanish hats stacked on top of one another like cordwood. I count thirty-two rifles leaning against the wall and twelve pistols. I see tomahawks, knives, bows, arrows, and several bags that probably contain powder and shot neatly stacked. Over in the corner are stacks of bones.

"From here, I can't tell if they are animal or human. The skeleton leaning against the wall, dressed in Indian attire with a peace pipe and sacks of magic powder in his hands, is the great legendary Lacota. The skeleton at Lacota's feet with his hands bound behind his back and his feet tied was probably his last victim."

"Chikata, how can you be sure the skeleton against the wall is Lacota?" Case asked. "I, too, have heard many legendary tales about the great warrior and medicine man, but I have not heard of anyone who has left a legend about an ancestor who has seen him."

Pointing, Chikata said, "All of you look at the headdress, necklace, medallion, arm- and wristbands, the belt on the skeleton, and the maraca Lacota used to wave like a baton and spread his magic powder. All of it is solid gold, embodied with leather, which Lacota was known for. Before he sat down to join the Great Spirit, he dressed himself as no other Indian has been known to do. He also executed his last enemy and placed him at his feet before he transcended to the Great Spirit. Many traditional stories have been handed down for decades about the journey of life that no medicine man except Lacota completely understood.

"The markings on the gold chain and medallion are the key to the trails of life that mark the way for all the tribes to join the Great Spirit, according to Lacota," Chikata continued. "Many tribes and their chiefs have seen the ornaments, but no one has been permitted to touch or study them, and that includes the headdress, maraca, and other sacred pieces. Look at the golden shield with markings and paintings across it resting against Lacota's skeleton. Notice the paintings of the white pigeons resting beneath the eagle's wings. They were treated with waxberry. Those are signs of a true warrior being transported to the Great Spirit."

Clyde had been busy pulling rocks away from another opening where Onox and Snuffy were pawing at the small boulders. He moved a few and yelled, "All of you look through this hole! I can see stacks of skeletons, several skeletons tied to posts, weapons, dozens of sacks containing something, and many other metallic items!"

The miners quickly moved small rocks and boulders away and made a passageway large enough to walk through. After retrieving two lanterns and entering the chamber, they stood silently. Each was shocked at what he saw.

Finally Case said, "This room is at least thirty by thirty feet. There are at least forty skeletons against the wall, stacked in a crisscross fashion like cordwood. I count eight skeletons all dressed in old Spanish uniforms and they are lashed to posts. The skeleton supported by the wooden frame with four posts was once a prominent Indian woman. I can tell by the faded white leather and gold jewelry that adorns her and by the crafty weejuns embedded with gold on her feet. She could have been Lacota's sister, wife, or daughter. Bill, see what is in those old leather bags."

"We all need to be very careful," Chikata said. "We don't want to reach into something and grab a poisonous spider, scorpion, snake, or magic powder that could kill us."

After picking up six rotten leather bags and discarding them, Bill said, "Those probably contained water because each one is moldy inside." He reached with both hands to grab a large bag that was obviously full of something. The rotten leather of which the bag was made tore apart and spilled gold nuggets on the floor. Bill used his knife and quickly slashed open the tops of fourteen other bags. They too were filled with gold nuggets. "Case, I count fifteen bags of gold. You are a rich man!"

Case said, "No, my friends, all of us are rich. Chikata, what should we do with Lacota's personal articles in these rooms?"

"It is obvious that Lacota killed the Spaniards who came to these mountains and committed mayhem in order to steal Indians' gold," Chikata said. "I'm sure many of these bones are the skeletons of Indians, but we will never know how many, or why they were killed, unless we accept Lacota's legend about them being evil. Case, you and Bill take the sacks of yellow iron, remove the ornaments from the skeletons, all the weapons, and use all of it to support yourselves and the hungry people you have spoken of."

Chikata hesitated a moment and then said, "The skeletons and some of the ornaments Lacota and his loved one are wearing should be buried separately in the outer chamber away from these other skeletons. We should keep the gold shield, medallion, and chain for prosperity. After we finish doing that, if it's all right with you, Case, Bill could use dynamite and close this evil chamber with boulders forever. And then Bill could use dynamite and close the entrance to Lacota's tomb." After searching the faces of the group, Chikata continued, "Everything we have found, except the gold, should remain a secret within this group until we think about the harm and mayhem that could possibly take place about what any of us say about this treasure to anyone."

Bill said, "I will abide by this group's agreement. Lacota's secret will go with me to my grave unless Chikata changes his mind."

Clyde said, "I agree, because Lacota could have been justified in doing what took place in these mountains. His secret will remain safe with me."

Case said, "I agree, and Lacota's secret will be with me or whatever this group decides. Clyde, bring us the sleds, several more leather bags, and a few more tie straps from the barn."

When Clyde returned the men quickly tied the rifles, lances, and the bags containing tomahawks, pistols, and bags of shot to a sled. After putting the gold into smaller freshly treated leather bags and then securing them within larger bags, they strapped each to a sled. "Case," Bill asked, "after we bury the gold and put these weapons in the shed, do we search this cave again before honoring Chikata's request?"

"Bill, I think we should search both chambers thoroughly before closing them," Case said. "After we finish, we will help Chikata clean up and rearrange the skeletons as he sees fit. Whether or not Lacota transcended the Indians with whom he lived, may or may not be known to Chikata. Perhaps in the months ahead, he will explain to us Lacota's teachings and actions."

A heavy snow was falling when the miners pulled the sleds down the mountain leaving the cave. "This is perfect weather in which to bury our gold," Case said. "No one going up or coming down the mountain can see us."

After the gold was buried and the dirt and flagstone were replaced, they went to the barn and cleaned and oiled the weapons, before storing them in wooden boxes.

As the miners entered the cabin, Mona said, "Mr. Mack,

you and Mrs. Myrna are going to eat with us tonight. Supper is on the table." After Betty said a short prayer the group began eating.

During their small talk, Mona said, "For the past several months, you miners haven't been doing very well. Has your luck changed?"

"Mona," Bill quickly answered, "you are right about our mining, but today our luck did change and we found some gold. But I'll repeat what I have told you before. Never tell anyone about our activities, because gold brings out the worst in some people. One loose word or a careless statement by any of us about gold and this land could be filled with murderers, thieves, and evil doers."

After the meal, the males went to the worktables and packed their pipes for a smoke while Clyde honed his pocket knife on a stone. "Chikata," Case asked, "would you tell us what you know about Lacota?"

"I will tell you what my father and grandfather told me, but remember their information was handed down by word of mouth and a few pictures on rock faces. But, keep in mind that the only physical proof I have is what I saw today. According to legend, Lacota was the oldest son of a chief and a beautiful princess. As a child he was swift, quick to learn Indian customs, a boy who questioned everything, loyal to his parents and tribe, but even in his youth, he was a loner, who often disappeared into the mountains. He was large for his age, and when he was still a young boy, he passed the rigorous ritual to become a warrior after he challenged what he considered an evil medicine man and defeated him in a knife fight.

"After three more medicine men visited Lacota's tribe to issue their proclamations and sprinkle their magic dust to ward off evil spirits, they left the village and were never seen again. Later the medicine men's statements proved to be false. By the time Lacota became a young man, Indians of all tribes feared and respected him for being a true medicine man who was endowed with knowledge from the Great Spirit.

"When Lacota approached other tribes, they remained silent and listened to his words, because his proclamations were always accurate. Life for the tribes was good until the invaders with the iron hats came from the South.

"When the Spanish army came to these mountains, slaughtering Indians with their long guns and stealing gold, the tribal leaders assembled for a powwow to decide on which mountain they would take refuge. Out of the darkness, Lacota appeared for the first time in many moons. Lacota explained, 'Tonight our enemies sleep on the snow in tents at the bottom of buffalo valley. In the morning while they are enjoying their food and campfires, we will destroy most of them.'

"Maschi, an old Indian chief, said, 'Lacota, your words have always been true. But our weapons are no match for the Spaniard's long guns. How can we possibly destroy these invaders?'"

"Lacota raised his arms toward the sky and said, 'Maschi, the Great Spirit has told me to use nature against the Spaniards and destroy him and his weapons by starting two avalanches at one time. All of you are aware of the high peaks on each side of buffalo valley, and they are capped with deep snow this time of the year. As we speak, sixteen warriors, armed with Spanish muskets, loaded with shot and powder, are trudging through the snow, making their way to the ridges beside the high peaks at buffalo valley. At sunrise in the morning, they will shoot the muskets they stole into the banks of snow, starting two tremendous avalanches. The only ones who will escape are the leaders who sleep in large tents at the edge of the woods at the far end of the valley.'"

"Hodak, a fierce warrior, said, 'Let me and my brothers confront those invaders at the edge of the woods.' 'No,' Lacota said, 'until it is over, you and this tribe will be hidden behind the trees on each side of the valley, away from the avalanche. Then collect any horses, muskets, shot, powder, or anything else that our tribes can use.'

"'What about any surviving prisoners?' Hodak asked.

"'There will be no prisoners!' Lacota shouted. 'The only ones you rescue will be Indians! All Spaniards are to be killed on the spot!' The tribe left the meeting with Lacota's sacred demands sealed within their minds and souls because anyone refusing to obey his orders would certainly die.

"Daybreak the following morning was cold, clear, and the sky was blue," Chikata continued. "The Spaniards had built up their cook fires and were enjoying a big breakfast. As the sun peaked over the tips of the mountains, they heard eight shots being fired high up in the peaks. Quickly eight more shots echoed down the valley from the other side of the highest peak. The arrogant soldiers, laughing about the echoes, stood up and watched the crows take flight squawking at one another.

"Seconds later, the Spaniards were stunned at the eerie cracking noises they heard. A noise and cracks caused by the ice and snow separating at the summit occurred, which was visible for miles. Then the soldiers watched the surface ice separate into deep crevices which ran across the high snowbanks and downward in slow motion. Many horses whinnied, broke free, and escaped into the timberland. A grounded thunder came from the peaks as millions of tons of snow and ice began shifting away from its location, rolling toward the valley, picking up momentum with each moment.

"The horrified Spaniards were cursing and screaming as they ran for safety. Death was certain for the soldiers, because in past years, an avalanche had occurred from one side or the other of the mountain, but never both sides at once—because there was no safe place to hide on the valley floor. The mammoth weight and speed of the gigantic avalanche sent rocks, boulders, trees, huge balls of snow, clumps of ice, and stumps hurtling into the valley at a horrifying speed. The lucky Spaniards were killed instantly, and the unlucky ones were buried beneath fifteen to twenty feet of snow and suffocated to death.

"The Indians who witnessed the avalanche waited high up in the tree lines on each side of the valley until the catastrophe ended and the power of nature calmed down. The Indians caught horses, gathered Spanish supplies, and quickly ended the lives of one hundred thirty-two injured soldiers. From a distance, Lacota, Maschi, and two young braves watched the Spanish chiefs and several of his subordinates retreat into the forest.

"'Maschi,' Lacota said, 'return to the village and continue to serve and lead our people. I will have a reckoning with those Spanish leaders.'"

Chikata took a sip of coffee and continued. "What you have just heard was told to me by my ancestors. Many of the stories came not only from Lacota, but also from chiefs and warriors. Until today, no Indian has heard or seen the bones of the Spanish soldiers who safely retreated into the forest. There is no doubt in my mind that the skeletons inside the cave and the ones in uniform who are strapped to posts were captured and died at the hands of Lacota. And the treasure that was being stolen was also captured.

"After the avalanches, at every Indian gathering, the chiefs always spoke of the great medicine man, Lacota, the one who created the grounded thunder to seek justice for his people. I could recant several more stories about Lacota's appearing at the council fires at the right time, and he always predicted what was about to happen, and always speaking the truth. After the grounded thunder incident, he was never seen more than twice a year by anyone. Many search parties were sent out to try to find his dwelling place, but they failed. At this time that is all I have to say, unless you have a question."

"That is an astounding story," Bill said. "It's a shame that the whole country can't hear it for prosperity."

"Chikata, was there any mention of the corpses and dead horses found in the valley after the snow melted the following spring?" Case asked.

"Yes, the following spring after the snow melted in the valley, the bodies of almost four hundred Spanish corpses and two hundred horses were found. The wild animals and different types of fowl feasted on them. It's getting late; let's go to bed."

The families were about to eat breakfast the following morning when a voice shouted, "Hello inside the house, is anybody home?" Bill and his family went outside as Case and Myrna were greeting two large men who were standing in front of three mules loaded with furs, hides, and supplies.

Pointing, Case said, "These are the brothers, Bob and Carson Cartwright. They're miners, trappers, mountain men, and my very good friends. This is Bill and Betty Dykes and their children, Clyde and Mona. Come inside and join us for breakfast. Clyde, help Chikata take the mules to the barn and unload them. Feed them well because our friends will spend the night with us."

The brothers were huge old men with long hair and thick beards. With the exception of their shirts, their clothing was made from animal skins. Before seating themselves, they removed their heavy belts, which exposed two pistols and a long knife attached to them.

After eating, Bob said, "That was a delicious meal. Mrs. Mack, those were the first chicken eggs we have eaten in over a year. Chicken eggs are one of the things I miss most about being away from civilization. Case, let's fill our coffee cups and go to the barn, I want to show you and Bill something." Inside the barn Chikata and Clyde had separated the pelts by species. There were bear, fox, cougar, deer, elk, beaver, wolf, buffalo, and bobcat. Two snow-white cougar pelts were on top of one of the piles.

"Those are the first white cougar pelts I've ever seen," Case said. "I didn't know there were albino cougars in this mountain range."

"We didn't either," Carson said, "until we entered a cave near Hanson's Cove. We wanted to stay in the same cave that the cougar wanted to live in. But he was there first and didn't want to leave, so I had to kill him. A few days later, we killed the second one who returned to the cave.

"Bill, Case knows we don't mine for gold, but when we see a few nuggets on the ground, we pick them up. Last year when we sold our pelts and several ounces of gold, we heard stories about the economic conditions that part of the population in this country is on the verge of starvation. Have things changed for the better?" Carson asked.

"No, Carson," Case said, "the conditions have grown worst, especially in the populated areas. The government does not seem to have a plan to improve the economy or feed the masses. And from the newspapers I read, the cities with larger populations also have the largest crime rate."

Carson continued, "Well, I'm ashamed to say it, but we have the same crimes up here. Several months ago we found Hope McDougal's body face down in the ashes at his campsite. Hope had been shot twice in the back. Hope always saw the good in everyone, and he trusted everybody. But getting back to this depression, there's enough food in these mountains to feed thousands of hungry people, but unless they are mountain wise, they could freeze to death."

The day was spent with the Cartwright brothers sharing many episodes about their lives in the mountains and the few men they had encountered the past year. At nightfall the old men accompanied Chikata to the barn for a night's sleep. A light snow was falling the next morning when Clyde led the brothers' mules from the barn. The animals were packed with their pelts and supplies and were ready to travel.

"Carson, if we didn't have this snow on the road, I could use the truck and run you down the trail to town," Case said.

"No, my friend, the Lord gave me two feet and legs, and I'm not getting into one of those truck contraptions and go racing down a mountain," Carson said. "This light snow and cool weather is perfect for travel. We won't sweat today." The families watched the brothers slowly disappear on the tram road.

"Case," Bill said, "I respect men like that, but I don't understand them. I can see why they would want to live in the mountains and commune with nature for a span of time, but why devote their entire lives to it?"

"First of all," Case said, "they love the mountains and they respect the animals that depend on nature for their food. By their admission, they prefer to live in seclusion and not be connected with people they don't know or trust. I can tell you a little about those two. As a small boy, I knew them and their parents—very astute people who loved and treasured these mountains. When Carson and Bob came home from the Great War, their personality had changed. They were still courteous, humble, and caring, but the once-friendly expression in their eyes had been erased. Within two to three days, they will stop by and pay their respects. Unless there is a blizzard blowing, they will move on and we will not see them again until next year, unless we encounter them in the mountains. Did you notice that they didn't inquire about our work or anything else we were doing—just if we were healthy?"

From the backyard Mona yelled, "We have caught Scrambo a playmate."

After the men moved the cage to the fox pen and put the fox in it, Mona asked, "Chikata, is it a female?"

"No, he's a half-grown male. Within a few months you will be in the fox business. We're going to work, but tonight remind me and I will tell you a few things about foxes and how to raise them," Chikata said.

The miners went back to the large cave and helped Chikata arrange the outer chamber as a tomb. They moved the skeleton at Lacota's feet to the next room and placed it on top of the other cadavers. They then placed the female skeleton in a sitting position beside Lacota. They picked up the Spanish helmets, bones, and several pieces of discarded wood and leather and carried the items to the outer chamber. Meticulously, Chikata wiped the dust from Lacota's peace pipe, armbands, moccasins, headdress, and belt before reverently replacing them.

"Chikata," Case asked, "what about Lacota's medallion, necklace, and golden shield?"

"We can't leave those items here," Chikata said. "They should be sent to a museum for future generations to study. I realize a solid gold shield is valuable, but the markings upon it represent knowledge and wisdom, which are worth much more than money. Many of the inscriptions they contain are the answers to the Great Spirit. Case, I think this room is ready to be closed, but all of you search or dig around for anything we might have missed."

After a thorough search and some digging, the miners found four nuggets and a bag containing nineteen golden Spanish rings, six armbands, and six bracelets. "Okay," Chikata said, "let's go to the outer room."

The miners cut the eight Spanish skeletons from the posts

and piled them on top of the others. "Since this chamber will be filled with boulders," Case said, "let's finish our search for gold and end this business."

The miners found another bag containing eight rings, four necklaces, nine coins, and four armbands, all of which were gold. Then they dug around on the floor, but found nothing.

"Let's chisel some holes for the dynamite and we'll seal this tomb forever," Case said. "Bill, where do you want the holes?"

Approximately two hours later, Bill inserted dynamite into the holes and ran a fuse to the outer chamber. He said, "Let's cover the opening to prevent dust from blowing into Lacota's and his loved one's tomb." Shortly Bill lit the fuse, and the novice miners were impressed after the explosion occurred.

"I wouldn't have believed it," Case said. "No dust or rocks came into this outer chamber." He tore the blanket away from the door opening and said, "Those boulders that are blocking this doorway look as if we stacked them on top of each other. When we dynamite the entrance to Lacota's tomb, we will be finished with these caves."

"Not quite," Bill said. "After we seal the entrance, we have to close the shaft that lets the sunlight into Lacota's tomb."

"Bill, we don't know where the shaft is located," Case said.

"I think I do," Bill said. "Let's get to work." When the entrance to the tomb was sealed with tons of boulders and trees lying on top of them, Bill said, "Follow me."

They followed Bill up the mountainside until he stopped. Suddenly Case said, "You're right, here it is." Using his flashlight, he looked into the shaft and said, "Anyone can see a short distance in there, but there is a turn in the shaft which prevents one from seeing the tomb."

Bill said, "Let's push a few of these small boulders into the shaft and close the hole." When they finished the heavy chore, Bill dropped two sticks of dynamite into the opening of the shaft and the miners headed for home as the loud boom echoed behind them.

The High Country

After the families had eaten breakfast and had their worship service the following Sunday morning, they all went out to the fox pen and watched Scrambo and his playmate frolic around, taking turns rolling a five-gallon can around in their pen. Onox and Snuffy, looking toward the front yard, growled, and the hair on their backs stood up.

"Someone is in the front yard," Chikata said.

The families went to investigate and were greeted by Carson and Bob Cartwright. "I'll put the pack animals in the barn," Clyde said.

"Thanks, Clyde, but no," Carson said. "We're only going to stay a few minutes and then use this daylight to travel. Mrs. Dykes, here are some letters and all of them are from Florida. Two of them are for Bill and they are marked special delivery. We also brought you several newspapers from Colorado Springs about the trouble in this country."

"Well, you at least have time to come inside and have a cup of coffee and tell us what you learned about the economic situation and what our politicians are doing in this country," Myrna said.

When everyone was seated at the worktables, Bob said, "While we were in Colorado Springs, we talked extensively with hardware clerks, bankers, a lodge owner, a corral operator, a fur trader, and two store owners.

"According to them, the only way the economy can get worse is for the government to go out of business. However, the federal government has started a few relief programs in some states that will pay workers less than one dollar per day. The newspaper Carson gave you describes one federal project called the WPA. In some states, the work program is called by different names."

Carson gulped the last of his coffee and said, "We're going to move on because we're anxious to leave civilization and check on our dogs. Bill, the invitation I extended to all of you to visit us still stands. Mrs. Mack, Mrs. Dykes, thanks for your hospitality."

Shortly the Cartwright brothers put on their snowshoes, led the pack mules out of the yard, and disappeared as they made their way up the mountain.

Anxious to hear how their friends were doing, the families went inside and took seats. Betty opened a letter and said, "This one is from Gloria Sikes and her family in Fernandina Beach, Florida, and it says,

"Dear Betty and family,

"First, Winston, Sam, Cynthia, and Christy send their love and each of us pray for you and your safety every night. Betty, after receiving your letters, we were astounded about Bill's working at so many different places on different jobs. We look with joy to the day when all of you can return here and build a home next door to us—we miss you.

"Winston and Sam are still doing well with the seafood and vegetable business beside the highway. In fact, they employ a helper on a full-time basis because sales have exceeded their expectations. Bill, thanks again for your ideas about commercial sales. And Christine, my daughter whom Bill delivered, is healthy, fat, loud, and beautiful.

"At night we often sit and talk about the quality time, Christmas, and the many chores we shared with the Dykes family and the Lord. Sam and Cynthia still quote verbatim the words and prayer Betty and others spoke to our Lord.

"We were delighted, but not shocked to learn that you bought a farm in order to help feed and provide for hungry children—God bless you. I would have to write many books to be able to ask all the questions we have for you, so we'll hold them until you return.

"Lace, Chuck, Mr. Thornton, and others are always inquiring as to where you are. We had a fish fry in the yard last month and Winston summed it up when a group of adults were inquiring about the Dykes family. He said, 'Regardless where the trails of life take them, some families have a destiny, and that one is blessed, and they will fulfill each cubicle of their life's mission to its fullest.'

"I have enclosed the receipts for your tax returns, but we wish you were living beside us and filing them. Winston laughed when I read about your going to the snow country. Sam said, 'If there is anything in those mountains worth finding, Mr. Dykes will find it, because the Master will help him.' We realize that you are snowbound, but at least you have a permanent address where I can write. Betty, bless you and please hug each member of your family, and remind them that we love all of you.

"Sincerely,

"Gloria Sikes.

"Post Script. Sam said to tell Mr. Dykes that he has been shooting squirrels and rabbits and catching seafood from the creek on his many acres of land."

Myrna filled the coffee cups and said, "Betty, Case and I are amazed at the many episodes that have taken place in your family. You certainly stay busy helping people."

Betty blushed and continued, "This letter is from George, Sara Cline, her boys, and the adopted children who are farming south of Jacksonville, Florida.

"Dear Betty and family,

"So much has happened since you have been gone I don't know where to begin, so I'll start with numbers. While the economic situation around us is bad, we seem to flourish because the Lord has blessed us. We now live with twenty adopted children and our two sons, and we're all healthy. The children work hard and never create problems. George and the older boys have cleared two hundred more acres of land, so the crops should increase again this year.

"Last year we planted a tobacco crop which turned out to be a small money maker. George knows that Bill worries about our being strapped for cash, so he wants him to stop worrying. George said to tell Bill that we made money from hogs, eggs, tobacco, peaches, pears, plums, pecans, animal hides, barrels of gum tar, and the older boys are performing contract labor, harvesting crops for other farmers, and working part time at a lumber mill.

"It was a big decision for him, but George purchased the farm next to us. He bought the farm and three hundred acres of pine trees behind it for two hundred eighty dollars at the auction held outside Mr. Webster's general store. The deed is in Bill's name and it is enclosed with the tax receipts in the large envelope marked special delivery. Your new property has a farmhouse, privy, water well, barn, forty acres of cultivated land, and stock pens. We believe the yield of gum tar from chipping boxes will pay for the farm within one year.

"I don't mean to brag, but the number of hogs, chickens, ducks, goats, and cows has increased. That is enough about numbers but, Bill, stop worrying and rest assured we are not lacking for anything.

"Several months ago, we built a small chapel between the two large oak trees. It is facing the highway. We had been holding church services in the barn but the children requested a place to worship. So for three months when anyone had some spare time, he worked on the chapel and it is now finished. By using Bill's timber, nails, and hardware, we did not have to spend a penny on the building.

"On different occasions, George tried to hire two different out-of-work ministers as our preacher, but each of them wanted thirty dollars per week, plus room and board. We can't afford that, so we will keep looking.

"Betty, one item that Bill and George forgot to mention was that children grow up and want to get married. Unless you forbid us to do so, we plan to use the chapel for a wedding next year. Mark Wilson, the eighteen-year-old boy who helped Bill in the kitchen, has our permission to marry Martha Sermons next year. She is seventeen, a Christian, and dedicated to our Lord, her work, and all of us.

"When Mark and Martha are in the same room, they can't keep their eyes off of each other. Our plan is to let them marry in the chapel when Martha is eighteen. If Bill doesn't object, they will occupy the newly acquired farmhouse. Mark has taken over the hog operation, which is by far our biggest money maker. When the number of hogs surpassed one hundred fifty, Mark said, 'As long as we can convert corn to pork, we should make money.' I must admit, these abandoned children are a close-knit group and they love, help, and protect each other. Betty, they never forget to include you and your family in their prayers.

"I'll close for now. Everyone has told me something to tell all of you and it is a general consensus that they all love you and your family and appreciate what all of you have done for all of us. Take care of yourselves and we pray for the time when we will see your family again.

"Sincerely, and love to all of you,

"Sara, George, our boys, and all of the children."

"Well," Case said, "we knew the Dykes family are worthwhile people who have covered a lot of miles, but we didn't know about land beside a river and a farm as well. It seems that you have accomplished some good work. Those letters from your friends disclose smart decisions, hard work, and excellent people."

"Case, many of those decisions turned out to be pure luck," Bill said.

"While all of us are here together," Case said, "Bill, Chikata, Clyde, and I have decided to let you know what has happened these past few months and what we have planned."

Everyone sat erect and eagerly awaited his explanation.

"These past few months, we found and mined an enormous amount of gold," Case continued. "If we get the same amount of money for it as I got for the few nuggets I sold earlier, we will be rich families. At this time we are not going down to a local bank, because if a blizzard hit this area, we would have a hard time returning home. And, too, a large sale of gold draws the attention of greedy men. When we do sell some gold, it will be a town far away from here.

"During the months ahead," Case continued, "we plan to go higher up into the mountains and continue mining, but we're in no hurry, and we won't take chances. But, we will be working farther away from home and we can't return here each night. So when we leave, we will be gone for a week or longer. Clyde, while we continue mining, you and Snuffy will remain here and look after the womenfolk and be responsible for the chores."

"When will you be leaving?" Myrna asked.

"We plan to leave the first of next week," Case answered. "Until then, we will work around here and then get our snow sleds loaded with our supplies and mining equipment. One last reminder—never let on to any outsider that gold is buried on these premises. If anyone should stop here for the night, do not tell them where we have gone or how long we will be away. If you encounter any strangers, just say we have gone hunting, but do not say what we are hunting for."

Three days later, it started snowing and continued for two days and nights, blanketing the mountains with three feet of snow. Early the following day, the miners left the cabins with Bill pulling one sled and Chikata the other one. The wearing of snowshoes and shoulder harnesses made their travel slow. They passed the caves they had previously worked and made their way to the top of the mountain by noon. An hour before sunset, they had descended the mountain and were halfway to the top of another one.

"Over there behind that clump of trees is a small cave," Case said. "Let's camp there tonight and mine it first. I know where seven other caves are and Chikata knows the whereabouts of two more we can also work." Prior to their entering the cave,

Case said, “Get out your flashlights and weapons and let’s make sure this one is not occupied with a cougar or a bear.” Slowly, they entered the cave and found it to be empty. Case continued, “So if you two agree, let’s camp behind those boulders beside the cave. There’s a ledge overhanging that spot and it will keep us dry. If we set up camp inside the cave, we will have to move our equipment tomorrow before we use the dynamite.”

A pitch-black night set in with a hard wind blowing and the temperature dropped drastically. After supper, Chikata banked the fire with logs and refilled everyone’s coffee cup. He said, “Very soon the rock facing will reflect the heat from the fire and our sleeping area will be warmer. This is bear and cougar country, so keep your pistol handy. Bill, Case and I found four small nuggets in this cave about a year ago, but we didn’t use dynamite, just chipping hammers.”

After breakfast, the miners lit their lanterns and slowly moved into the cave, examining the rock facings. Bill said, “I can see where you used hammers on the wall to my right. Do you remember where you found the nuggets?”

Pointing, Chikata said, “That’s where they were.”

“Good, let’s hollow out two holes about ten feet apart and set off our dynamite here,” Bill said, “then we will go further into this cave.”

They worked for two hours, using hammers and chisels to penetrate the hard surface. Bill pushed a stick of dynamite into each hole, joined the fuses, lit them, and the miners exited the cave. After the dynamite exploded, sediment and heavy dust funneled through the cave entrance. They sifted through the rock and searched the ground, but found nothing. The miners followed the same procedures for four more days, but failed to find any gold. Bill said, “Let’s go home and when we get back, let’s try another cave.”

Due to inclement weather, bad luck, shoring up the cave, and bear trouble, the miners’ productivity yielded only twenty-eight small nuggets for several days of hard labor. They kept to the schedule of mining four days and then trudging through the deep snow to return home for three days. They worked a grueling schedule and each one lost weight because he was totally exhausted.

During the month of December, the miners were returning home when Case said, “If it’s all right with you two, let’s rest for a week before we try again. I still believe there’s a vein of gold somewhere, just waiting for us. Bill, where do you think we should try our luck when we return?"

"Case, I suggest we try the largest cave, because I believe millions of years ago Mother Nature poured out her hottest deposits to form those mountains. By the way, I've heard of people having gold fever, but never vein fever." Chikata burst with laughter.

For a week the miners helped with the chores, smoked their pipes, played chess, and watched Clyde. Under Chikata's supervision he built a small house for the new foxes, who were about to be born. Mona continued to question Chikata about how to care for the expectant baby foxes.

Eight days later they left home, pulling one sled loaded with supplies. They arrived at the large cave and set up a shelter because there were no overhanging rock ledges to get under. At daybreak, they entered the cave and started chiseling holes to place dynamite.

Three hours later, three sticks of dynamite exploded, sending sediment, dust, and pebbles through the cave entrance. The miners, using their lanterns, were inspecting the rubble when Chikata said, "Here is a small vein about ten inches long. After we move this pile of rock we can see where it leads." They went to work removing rocks from the cave while Onox checked the stones. They then chiseled the vein from the rock face which yielded about two hundred ounces of gold. "So far, this is a good payday," Chikata said. "But where is Case's large vein?"

"If a large vein is here, it has to be deeper into the rock facing," Bill said. "I think we should set off two more charges of dynamite along this wall."

Without speaking a word, Case and Chikata started chiseling into the wall. The job took three hours because the solid granite was extremely hard, and the miners were exhausted from the constant swinging of the heavy hammers against the chisels. "Let's eat a bite before we collapse," Bill said.

After a meal of coffee, canned beans, hoe cakes, and elk meat, the miners set off two more charges. When they entered the mine and hung their lanterns on jagged ends of rock, they stood in awe. They knew the sight before them was extremely rare! Each was aware that he was joining the few men who had had the privilege of seeing a vein of pure gold at least three feet wide and nine feet high.

"Holy Moses, Bill was right!" Case said. "I wonder how thick it is?"

"It's our job to find out," Bill said. "There's enough gold

here to feed those thousands of abandoned hungry children that I have passed along the highways over the past few years. If we blast the gold from the wall, we will lose part of it, so we will have to chisel it away." They started chiseling at the bottom of the vein and discovered it to be three to four inches thick. The miners filled five large leather bags before sundown.

When Case looked at his pocket watch, Chikata said, "I'm going to move our campsite just inside the cave entrance. Since we can't use dynamite and we can't leave this cave unguarded, I will stay here while the two of you take a load home. Let's eat before we move our supplies."

After eating and moving their equipment, the miners gathered firewood until dark set in. Bill said, "I estimate it will take us at least two to three weeks to extract the gold." Chikata was tacking a heavy canvas across the entrance to the cave and Bill continued, "I know the canvas will keep some of the cold out, but do we really need it?"

"A snowstorm will hit this area tonight," Chikata said. "Come morning, the cave entrance will have at least four feet of snow in front of it." Two hours later, a blizzard engulfed the mountains with a heavy snow falling and the wind howling in excess of forty knots.

"Case," Bill asked, "is this cave on your property?"

"Yes, in fact, I own the land to the top of the next mountain."

Case had been leaning against the rock wall with a cup of coffee, thinking about his meeting Bill and Chikata, their friendships, and this gold expedition. He said, "Today we encountered a tremendous view that few men ever see. My desire to find a vein of gold was granted. But what we do with what we retrieve is what counts." Case believed he was about to ask Chikata a question that few men ever had the opportunity to answer. "Chikata, what will you do with your third of the gold?"

The scene was rare, but Chikata smiled and said, "You know I care nothing for most material items, but I would like to purchase two knives, a pair of those fancy lined cowboy boots, a new Winchester rifle, a shotgun, and two cases of ammunition. I've said nothing about the hungry people that I've heard you talk so much about, but I would like to help them. If Bill would take my share and use it to help feed the hungry, I would appreciate him taking on the job."

"Chikata, you need to think long and hard before you give away all of your fortune," Bill said. "Remember what the Lord referred to, 'we will always have the hungry and the poor people.'"

Promptly Chikata replied, "Bill, there's nothing to think about. I do not need wealth, because the Great Spirit has endowed me with good health, a good life, and true friends. The Book has taught me that no man needs a material treasure to pass through the gates for eternal life. I have been very fortunate to have lived among brothers and sisters who have treated me with honor. Since we found Lacota's solid-gold shield, I've been thinking about what to do with it, and I have finally come up with an answer."

"Chikata, I thought the shield was sacred to you," Case responded. "Are you contemplating parting with it?"

"Yes, Case, I will part with it. I understand some of the markings on the shield, but not all of them. With the exception of the Great Spirit, there is no one living who can explain the journey that is recorded on the shield.

"Two inscriptions on it are similar to three passages in the book of Revelation—a mystery to the living. If I gave the shield to some small gallery or institution, it would be stolen for its value in gold. The shield will become similar to Lincoln's Gettysburg Address. Men will debate the meaning of the shield's inscriptions exactly as they do about what Mr. Lincoln meant when he wrote his document. But they will not agree with each other.

"Bill," Chikata continued, "I'm asking you to take the shield with you when you leave these mountains. See that it is put in a large institution where the inhabitants of this country can study it. That shield is far too valuable a relic to be hidden away to gather dust. Do not tell anyone where the shield came from or where it was found. For your own privacy and protection, the best thing for you to do is to mail the shield from a town you do not live in and no one knows you."

"Chikata," Bill said, "I will do what you ask, on one condition. When your gold has been sold, I want you to keep part of the money for yourself."

Silence permeated the cave. Finally Chikata smiled and said, "All right, but I really don't need the paper money."

After breakfast the following morning, the miners shoveled about four feet of snow from the cave entrance before beginning their work. Three days later, the two sleds were piled high with bags of gold and strapped down on the sleds.

Case said, "Bill, early in the morning, we'll go home. Yesterday while Chikata was gathering wood, he came upon some cougar tracks so he is looking forward to staying here. I told him to hunt and rest, but he will probably have several sacks filled before we return. Bill, you know we can't make it home in one day with the load we have on the sleds."

"Yes, I have thought about the night we'll be spending in the snow. And when we start up the other mountainside, it will take both of us to pull one sled to the top, but it has to be done."

At daybreak, Case and Bill tied ropes to the snow sleds before starting out. The weight of the gold on the sleds required the miners to hold back on the ropes as they descended the mountain. However, they reached the bottom in record time, but both of them were winded. "Now the hard work begins," Bill said. "Let's have a cup of coffee before we start up the next mountain."

While Case drank his coffee, he said, "Bill, the last thing we want to do is pull one sled all the way to the top of this mountain and spend the night up there while leaving the other sled down here. I think we should go up to a spot where we wish to make camp and then return for the other sled." Bill nodded and they looped the ropes around their chests and started pulling. The miners bent forward and trudged through the snow with the dead weight cutting the ropes into their coats. The work was rigorous, causing the miners to sweat as they lunged ahead.

Three hours later, they stopped the sled and propped it against two pine trees so it could not slip down the mountainside. After descending the mountain, they rested before retrieving the other sled and pulling it uphill and putting it beside the first one. They were exhausted, but Bill said, "We had better gather some firewood; it is almost dark. Case, we should have brought the small tent with us and pitched it here. We will have to spend several nights at this campsite before we get all the gold to the cabin."

After eating and warming themselves, they dug two shallow trenches about two feet wide by twelve inches deep. Then they shoveled hot coals into the holes before spreading a few inches of dirt on top of it. They then placed their bedrolls over the fresh warm dirt and lay down for the night.

The wind increased and a light snow began falling. A short distance away, the cry of a wolf echoed through the canyon that enhanced the mountains' way of life for prowling predators.

The following morning when the miners reached the top of the mountain, Bill said, "Thank goodness, the rest of the way is downhill. Our families are probably frantic because we have been gone for over a week." Just past noon they pulled the sleds behind the barn and were greeted by their loved ones.

Mona asked, "Where is Chikata?"

"He wanted to stay at our cave and guard our equipment, and too, he saw a cougar's tracks and wanted to hunt him," Bill answered.

"Bill, if it's all right with you," Case said, "I thought we could bury this cache of gold in this soft dirt just outside the rear of the barn."

"Case, do you mean that all those bags contain gold?" Myrna asked in disbelief.

"Yes, dear, they do," Case said, "Bill found the mother lode. Its grueling work bringing it here and we should have at least four more loads as large as this one."

"Why don't you use the tractor and the sled to transport the gold?" Betty asked.

"Betty, the mountainside is too steep for the tractor and sled, not to mention the trees and boulders we wouldn't be able to go around." Case said. "This is one of those times when a horse or a mule would be superior to a machine."

Clyde and Bill were busy digging, so Case pitched in and within the hour, their gold was buried, and pieces of flagstone covered the area concealing the soft earth. After their menfolk bathed and shaved, Betty served lunch. While eating, and as a way of explanation, Case said, "You may as well know, Bill used dynamite and found the vein of gold I've been hoping for several years that I would find."

Case looked into the faces at the table and continued. "If we can get a fair price for our metal, all of us will be very rich. But, we still have a lot of hard strenuous work ahead of us before we reach that status. As always, secrecy from everyone about our fortune is of the utmost importance. Betty, Myrna and I have always believed the Lord intervened and sent your Christian family among us. I will ask you to pray and ask his help in guiding us to use our fortune properly."

After the group bowed their heads, Betty prayed.

"Dear Lord, thank you for another day, our families, our good health, our substance, your advent, and the atoning work you accomplished on this vessel. We thank you for sacrificing yourself in order for us to have everlasting life and to someday join you in paradise. Lord, if we receive wealth for this gold, we ask your guidance in distributing it among your people for their welfare.

"Lord, at this time, I ask that you bestow merciful wisdom into the minds and hearts of Bill, Chikata, and Case. I pray that each of them will do your bidding with the fortune that you have graciously permitted them to find. Thank you for keeping all of us safe and permitting us to do your will.

"In the name of Jesus, I submit this prayer.

"Amen."

Bill said, "Case asked me to explain the rest of our plan about the wealth we have discovered. The gold will be divided equally in three ways, and Chikata has asked me to take his share and use it to help feed the hungry people in this country. His share will be an enormous unselfish generous gift. He also has a solid-gold shield hidden inside the barn with markings and paintings inscribed on it. We found the shield in another cave several weeks ago, along with several bags of gold. The shield is about three feet long by two feet wide and it's about one-half of an inch thick. The gold shield is worth a fortune, but according to Chikata, the markings on it are more valuable because it has a history of the tribes who once lived in these mountains which he believes is one of a kind.

"Chikata told us that the shield once belonged to a medicine man by the name of Lacota," Bill continued. "He asked me to send the shield to a museum so that future generations can study and learn from it. I will do this, but when I send it, there will be no return address on the package so the authorities will not know who mailed it. If the people who study Indian culture learned where the shield or our gold came from, these mountains would be saturated with geologists, scientists, miners, thieves, con men, and murderers. In a nutshell, that is what has transpired recently and what we pray will happen."

"Papa," Mona said, "judging from what you have told us, this means that I can make out a long shopping list for our family in Florida."

Bill smiled and said, "Mona, our truck is not adequate to haul the amount of gold we will be leaving with. Come spring, we plan to go down to a town and sell a small amount of gold. We could purchase several new trucks with huge trailers to move the gold, but we don't want all of the gold in one place while we're traveling to Florida. However, on our way back, your mother will get her wish and buy gifts for everyone. We will stop and feed the hungry transients along the way. Case and I will be leaving before daylight in the morning and try to reach the cave within two days. We shouldn't be gone more than four or five days, unless we encounter a blizzard."

At five o'clock the following morning, Bill went outside to find Case pulling the sleds toward the front yard. "Good morning,

Case. Have we forgotten anything?"

"I don't think so. I packed the coffee and other food items, our weapons, the tent, leather bags, and Chikata's longbow and arrows." While putting on their snowshoes, Case continued. "According to the thermometer, the temperature is twenty-two degrees below zero. There's no wind and we have a clear sky with a full moon. Let's move."

They were traveling light, and the weather was perfect for traveling over the high mountains in the dead of winter. The sun was setting the following day when Chikata greeted them outside the cave and handed each a cup of coffee. "How are the families?" he asked.

"Just fine, I see you have stocked firewood and killed a cougar. That is a fine skin you have stretched out to cure." After looking around, Case continued. "Bill, while we've been gone, Chikata has filled enough bags for us to load the sleds again."

"Case, on certain areas of the wall, the gold separated easily from the rock facing," Chikata said. "Half of those bags contain chunks of gold twice as big as your fists. Let's load the sleds with bags and tie them down."

Chikata finished tying the bags to the sleds and secured the small tent on top of them.

Bill said, "We forgot the tent on the last trip and spent a cold night where we made camp about halfway up on the side of a mountain. Since we will be making several trips and stopping at the same area, we will leave the tent there." The following morning Bill and Case moved out again, heading home. The miners continued the grueling schedule, moving and securing their fortune to the cabin. Chikata had stopped moving the snow from the front of the cave, and except for a small path, only the top of the cave was open.

All three miners left the cave on December the nineteenth, planning to remain home and celebrate Christmas. They were within sight of the cabins when a blizzard hit the mountains. "This snow will seal the entrance to the cave and hide it completely," Chikata said. "When we return to the cave, our first job will be to shovel snow."

With Chikata to help transport their load of gold, they got home in record time. After burying the gold and watching the snow cover the flagstone, Case said, "Let's put the sleds and equipment away and celebrate the Lord's birthday."

Blessed Gifts

At dusk the following day, the two families were sitting around the worktables when Chikata came from the barn carrying the gold shield, a chain, and a medallion. As he placed the objects on a table, he said, "You will probably want to study and examine these, and if you want me to, I can explain some of the paintings and a few of the markings on them."

"Please do," Clyde and Mona said in unison.

"As you can tell from the rough surface on both sides of the shield, it was not made in a metal shop—it appears to have been hammered by someone trying to obtain a smooth surface," Chikata said. He turned the shield over and continued, "Notice the wide leather strap that was used to carry it. The strap has a painting on it, signifying a great hunter who was in distress. Look at the small holes with colored designs at the edges on both sides of the shield. Unfortunately, I have no idea what those markings signify."

"Chikata," Clyde begged, "there are many inscriptions on each object, so would you please point out the markings you know about and explain them to us. That would save us many questions."

For two hours the families asked Chikata about particular inscriptions the objects contained and listened as he elaborated about the lives of Indians and the different tribes. "Chikata, you omitted the small painting of the twelve arrows in the sky, going toward the sun," Clyde said. "What is their meaning?"

"Notice the different colored dots on each arrow. They signify the twelve tribes leaving the earth to join the Great Spirit. This large painting of twelve Indians and horse soldiers is about the time when the tribes were forced to go on the white man's reservations." Chikata picked up the chain and medallion and said, "It's getting late, do you wish me to continue or wait until tomorrow to explain the medallion?"

Betty quickly answered. "Chikata, this lesson on Indian culture is extraordinary, and we will never have this opportunity again." She picked up a magnifying glass and said, "Please, please continue."

Chikata pulled his knife from its scabbard and used it as a point to indicate the small detailed markings on the medallion. Methodically he explained which of the twelve tribes each represented, what duties each tribe performed, with which allies each tribe associated, and what each tribe accepted as truth to be held sacred.

Chikata laid the knife point on a tiny arrow which was barely visible, but one could tell that it was pointing to the center of the medallion. He explained, "This center piece which represents the sky or home to the Great Spirit was accepted by all the tribes. It means the Great Spirit is the one who provides nature such as the moon, sun, stars, food such as the Tonka, Mother Earth, and true leaders such as the chiefs or a medicine man."

The families went to bed late, but Betty was thinking about Chikata and his ancestors. She said to Bill, "Darling, our white race destroyed the Indians' culture, killed their main source of food, stole their land, gave them alcohol, imprisoned them on unfertile land, and did very little to indoctrinate them in the way of our Lord. In my opinion, some people will have a lot to answer for on judgment day."

"I agree," Bill said, "but all we can do now is vote and continue to practice Christian principles and be true and humane in our treatment of the people we encounter. Chikata is a healthy old Indian, but he has been blessed with wisdom. When I think of the things he has seen and many of the works he has done, I stand in awe of him. He has a pure heart and he covets nothing from anyone. I've never heard him speak of a wife or a girlfriend, and usually I have no interest in such matters, but in his case, I would like to know. Good night."

The following morning, the families stayed busy, performing different chores. But later in the day, Betty was beneath the snow-laden branches of the fruit trees, broadcasting bread crumbs for the birds, when Mona asked, "Mama, why do you feed the birds in the winter and not in the summer?"

"During the spring and summer season the birds have insects, berries, nectar, and many other things to feed on, so they don't need my help. But during the harsh winter months, those foods are not available to them so I try to help them."

"Mama, here come the menfolk with a tall Christmas tree! We've got to get busy decorating!"

After the men nailed a base to the tree, they put it in a corner beside the worktables and secured it to the wall. Mona and Clyde went to their trailer and got two small boxes of decorations. Mona explained, "These are homemade decorations, but they are gorgeous."

Case and Chikata went to the barn and returned with two baskets of pinecones that had been dipped into different colors of paint. Case said, "These cones have wires attached to them so you children can hang them on the tree. Bill, while the children and our wives decorate the tree, would you come to the barn with Chikata and me?"

Inside the barn, Case gave a short speech that had been well thought out. "Bill, Myrna and I have decided to entrust to you most of our gold. We love these mountains and we have no plans to settle anywhere else. Chikata and I are both getting old, so we have decided we will keep only a small portion of the gold for our retirement. We realize that you will have a tremendous job selling gold, dispersing money for food, shelter, clothes, medicine, and other items to help people, but you are young, honest, and a shrewd businessman. Will you take the job?"

Bill, deep in thought, took a long pull on his pipe and finally answered, "Yes, although I've never cared for big business. But, we have another big decision to address. First, I can't haul that amount of gold in my truck. Second, no one manufactures a truck large enough to haul the amount of gold we have mined. Third, if I purchased a larger truck to haul a large part of the gold, I could have a wreck or there is a possibility of losing the gold to thieves. Fourth, if we should sell all the gold in this or an adjoining state, this area would be crawling with people."

"Bill," Chikata said, "why don't we build sturdy boxes and ship most of the gold by train to your friends in Florida. According to what you have told us, Winston Johannsen is a trustworthy man who would store or hide the boxes for you. In that way, most of the wealth would not be in one place. Or you could ship the boxes to one of those holding companies to store and hold for you at a certain location. There are plenty of sturdy old boards in the corner of the barn that could be used for the job of shipping and storing, strong solid containers."

"That is a good plan, if Bill agrees," Case said. "But I think we should build two boxes to hold the gold. We should place smaller boxes inside the larger ones just in case they get dropped or damaged while being shipped. The question is, how much gold do we need to sell for Bill to have an adequate amount of money to stop in different towns and help feed hungry people on his return trip to Florida?"

Case and Chikata were looking at Bill.

"Let's build the boxes tomorrow morning," Bill said. "Then we will move the rest of the gold from the cave, after which we will begin selling part of it. Case, where would be the best place to sell part of the gold?"

"A Denver bank is about fifty miles away, and they have a reputation for honest dealings. After we finish mining, the first fair weather that will permit us to travel, we will make a few trips. Getting down these mountains is easy, but returning could be a problem. Chikata, I see someone leading two mules down the mountain."

Chikata squinted and said, "That's my old friend Hail Andrews. He's making his annual Christmas pilgrimage to sell some items and visit his deceased relatives in the Colorado Springs graveyard." Chikata laughed and, turning to Bill, said, "Bill, Hail is ninety-four years old, and he makes this trip every year to conduct business in Colorado Springs, such as selling gold nuggets, pelts, purchasing supplies, and then he delivers a hellfire and brimstone sermon to his deceased relatives in the graveyard. The one sermon I heard would have been great for the living, but in my opinion, his words were too late for his audience."

The ladies and children exited the cabin with Betty carrying a tray with cups and a pot of coffee. After introductions were made, Hail said, "Bill, Carson and Bob Cartwright spoke of you and your family and were impressed with all of you. For sound reasons, those two don't befriend or accept many strangers but they loved your family."

Hail went to one of the mules, untied two leather bags, handed them to Betty, and said, "Bob told me that all of you would celebrate Christ's birthday around a tree. The brothers sent these gifts as a token of their belief about the advent we celebrate."

Betty opened the bags and handed Mona and Clyde figurines that had been carved by the Cartwright brothers. The eighteen items were carvings of Mary, Joseph, baby Jesus asleep on a pile of hay, two sheep, three goats, two cows, a donkey, and a manger scene with seven shepherds standing outside of it.

"These are fantastic!" Betty exclaimed. "It is unbelievable to think that anyone could carve these with a knife. Mona, when

Mr. Andrews returns to his friends, we must send a card thanking them for these precious gifts."

Clyde said, "Mr. Andrews, I will put your mules in stalls and feed and water them."

"Clyde, wait just a moment," Hail said. "While the sun is shining, I will be moving on. The sooner I conclude my business among those civilized people and get back to these mountains where I belong, the better it will be for everyone. Besides, I would appreciate spending Christmas among Christian people like yourselves."

After Hail disappeared on the tram road, Case said, "Men, let's go hunting." For several days, Clyde and the men shot ducks, squirrels, rabbits, geese, and other types of birds. Other than taking care of chores, they built several large boxes to be used for shipping gold.

On Christmas eve morning, Hail returned and Clyde helped him store his supplies in the barn and take care of his animals. As the men entered the large cabin, Hail said, "That is the most beautiful tree and setting I have ever seen."

It was decorated with strips of newspapers for tinsel and pinecones that reflected different colors when the lantern light shone on them. Beneath the tree, a folded gray blanket with the manger scene on it exemplified the central focus point about the advent of history. A podium, made from logs, supported a Bible, which was opened to the second chapter of Luke.

The families and Hail spent the holidays in a humble, joyful, holy spirit, enjoying their Savior's birthday, the season, and one another. To everyone's delight, Hail remained with them for three days, because he had always cared for Chikata, Case, and Myrna. However, he was taken with Mona and Clyde, and he especially enjoyed conversing with Bill each night about coal mining and politicians.

The morning Hail left, the families bundled up and watched as he slowly made his way up the mountainside during a heavy snow. Mona said, "The other day Hail pointed to the mountaintop where he lived. He said, 'Mona, I live so close to heaven that I'm already cradled in our Lord's arms.'"

"Chikata," Bill asked, "at his age, how many more years do you think he can survive up there in the wilderness?"

"Bill, very few people would understand it, but when Hail expires, he wants to be alone, he has been ready to go for a long time. He would never be a burden to anyone if he could prevent it. Late last night while we sat on our cots talking, he told me about many things he had encountered during his life. He told me about episodes that happened in the past that I am sworn not to disclose until he is gone. That is one remarkable old man who looks forward to meeting his Maker. But, like the Cartwright brothers, he lost his trust in most of mankind many years ago in the Great War."

One week later, the miners returned to the cave and labored for three weeks, moving gold and burying it behind the cabins. Four days later, when they returned to the cave and filled ten sacks, Case said, "I think this job is finally finished, so we can rake the floors, gather our tools, and go home."

"Hold your horses," Bill said. "From what little I have learned about mining, there should be a deposit in the ground beneath that vein of gold we just removed from the wall. Chikata, hand me a shovel." Bill stomped the pointed end of the shovel into the ground and the miners heard a low metallic sound. Quickly Case and Chikata started digging at the opposite end of the wall. They discovered a slab of gold about twelve feet long by twelve inches wide.

"Bill," Chikata asked, "how did you know there would be a large chunk of gold down there?"

"I didn't know for sure, but it stands to reasons that millions of years ago there was a violent upheaval on the earth's surface that formed the rock formations in these mountains," Bill said. "When the gold vein was deposited here, it was in a molted state. I'm surmising that some of the gold settled in crevices and ran downhill on the granite sides of the cave. Common logic tells me that some of the gold settled on the floor.

"Let's dig at different intervals on the outside of the gold in order to find how thick it is," Bill continued. The miners dug at three different places and found the layer of gold to extend almost eight inches down into the ground. "Case, I think we should extract just enough gold to load the sleds. We can cover the holes and then take one load home. It will take us a few more weeks to finish this job."

The miners finished loading the sleds and covered the unmined gold before starting for home in brutal weather. Because of the inclement weather, six days passed before they returned to the cave at sundown. The following morning, the miners quickly moved the earth off the gold. Bill said, "Extracting this gold will be easy if we chisel a few holes between the gold and the rock facing, because that is the only place it is bonded to anything. Then we can chisel holes into the top of the vein about twelve inches apart and use crowbars to pry it loose."

Four nights later the miners were reclining, drinking coffee, and listening to the wind howl outside the cave when Case said, "Looking at those huge chunks of gold stacked neatly reminds me of the firewood at the cabins, waiting to be burned. Chikata, unless Bill finds another vein, the only job we have to do is to move it and our tools to the cabins. All of us have lost weight since we started mining, and I for one need some rest." However, Bill found gold underneath the floors in four other places.

During the first week of March, the miners finished their work at the caves and had moved the chunks and leather bags of gold into the barn. After some much-needed rest, they finished building the sturdy wooden boxes using screws to secure the planks on each one. They placed a box inside a larger one in order to keep them from being destroyed and to help support the heavy weight while being shipped.

After they filled the inside boxes with gold and secured the tops, Case said, "Mona and Myrna cut a two-inch stencil from cardboard with Winston Johannsen's name and address." He used a paintbrush and black paint to label the address on each box. Then he stenciled the word "tools"_on the top and each end of the boxes before covering them with a canvas. The job for digging up and packaging most of the gold took nine days.

"Bill," Case said, "we need to replace the wheels on the truck and be ready to go to Denver when the weather permits."

They replaced the wheels on the truck and applied chains to each tire before removing the chocks and lowering it to the ground. "Bill, check the emergency brake on the truck," Case said. "With the extra weight we are going to load inside this truck, you will hardly have to use the gas peddle while going down the mountains."

The following day the miners loaded Bill's truck with bags of gold, preparing to go to Denver. Bill cranked the truck and let it idle as he had been doing twice a month to keep the battery charged. Case looked at his pocket watch, removed a radio from a bag, and connected a wire to the truck battery. He kept turning a knob until he found a news station. Minutes later the announcer gave the weather report. He said, "For several days, the weather will be in the teens but no snow. We will have high winds and sunshine."

"That is exactly what we need," Case said. "We will leave at four o'clock tomorrow morning and hopefully be in Denver before one. Let's don't forget our hot coffee, lunches, and most of all, our pistols. Bill, be sure to tell Betty that we could be gone between two to three days because having gold assayed takes time. And, too, before we leave the cities, you said that you want to go to the post office, and all of us need to pick up some supplies and our mail."

Early the next morning, Bill checked the lock on the rear of the trailer and noticed the truck bed was sitting low. Minutes later the miners were rolling over the tram road, going downhill at fifteen miles per hour. Bill had to constantly use the brake pedal and the emergency brake to slow the truck down. When they entered Colorado Springs, Bill said, "Case, I don't pretend to know these roads, but if we could remove the snow chains, we could save some time."

"Oh, no, there will be snow on the highway all the way to Denver and they will be slick," Case said. "If we can average thirty-five to forty miles per hour, we will be at the bank with time to spare. Bill, when we enter the bank, for obvious reasons, look over my shortcomings because when I sell gold, I never put my given name or my correct address on their form sheet."

Chikata laughed and Bill asked, "Case, I know you detest lying, but what name do you write down for the bank?"

"John Smith, and I give the Rocky Mountains for my address."

Bill and Chikata laughed aloud.

The trio made one stop to use a restroom and purchase pipe tobacco. They entered Denver and passed two banks that had gone out of business before parking on a side entrance to a huge bank in the downtown area. Case went to a pay telephone and called a gold exchange in New York City to inquire about the price of gold. He returned to the truck and said, "Since I last sold gold, the price has gone up. Bill, let's go inside and see if they want to make a deal."

They entered the bank and Case introduced himself as John Smith to the head assayer, Mr. Sow. Case never called Bill by name, but referred to him as "My friend." After they agreed on a price per ounce for the gold, Case said, "Mr. Sow, we need two of your rolling carts and two of your clerks to help move our gold inside. While we're doing this, we don't want crowds of people or newsmen gawking or standing around."

"I understand," Mr. Sow said, "I will send two men to help you."

When Bill unlocked the door to the trailer, Chikata had already stacked some of the bags of gold near the door, so the men quickly loaded the carts and carried them into the bank. Three tables, each with scales, an assayer, a recording clerk, labor personnel, and a cart stood ready to weigh, price, and store the gold into the bank vault.

Mr. Sow said, "If Mr. Smith is ready, let's begin weighing the gold."

Case said, "With all due respect to everyone, let me check the accuracy of the three scales." He pulled an object from his coat, unwrapped it, and placed the piece of iron in the first tray. After he had put the iron in the other trays, he said, "Each scale recorded a reading of twenty-five ounces and that is exactly what this piece of iron weighs. Let's get to work."

The bankers each poured bags of gold into the pan and the assayer checked the content and then stated in a very loud voice the exact weight of each bag, which the clerk and Case recorded. As the process continued, everyone was precise, efficient, and everyone ceased making small talk. When a cart of gold had been weighed, Chikata and the clerks had another cart waiting. The time was five p.m. and the bank doors were locked when each bag of gold had been processed, finishing the weighing job.

Moments later Mr. Sow handed Case the bank's tally sheets and said, "Mr. Smith, according to our calculations, this is the weight of your gold and the price due you. How do these numbers compare with yours?"

Case looked at the sheets and said, "I've recorded one ounce less than your assayers, so I probably made a mistake with my adding. Mr. Sow, if you will, deduct one ounce from your count we will be in agreement."

Mr. Sow nodded and asked, "Mr. Smith, do you prefer a deposit slip, a check, a cashier's check, or cash?"

"Sir," Case said, "we prefer cash if it's not a burden on you. Chikata, would you get the suitcases out of the truck?"

The hour was approaching seven when the miners finished counting their money and storing twenty million, seven hundred forty-two thousand dollars inside the truck. As the miners drove away from Denver, Bill said, "Case, it is already dark and with no moon, Colorado Springs will be pitch black and the post office will be closed. Where do you suggest we spend the night?"

"Let's stay at the same lodge we did before. It is close to a grocery store, café, and the general store. And tomorrow, let's don't forget to buy more satchels for money storage." They entered Colorado Springs, ate, and went to the lodge to sleep. However, Chikata preferred to sleep in the trailer.

Before nine the following morning they had purchased their groceries and stored them in the trailer. Bill parked the truck in front of the general store and said, "While the two of you shop, I'm going across the street to the post office." He picked up his and Case's mail and purchased two money orders. He put one in an envelope for Winston Johannsen and the other in one for George Cline, along with letters from Betty. He mailed the envelopes by special delivery before returning to the general store.

Case and Chikata had put four cases of ammunition and six boxes in the rear of the trailer beside two new shotguns and three rifles. As they drove away, Chikata admired the two 12-inch hunting knives and a honing stone he had bought. Case started laughing and said, "Bill, you won't believe this but Chikata also bought a factory-made bow with several arrows. Can you believe an old Indian who has been successfully using his homemade bows and arrows all of his life would try something different?"

"Bill, that is not all we have to laugh about," Chikata said. "Case bought you a double-rigged shoulder holster with two top break forty-five caliber pistols and a case of ammunition. He said that you might need them while traveling with all that money. I truly hope that doesn't happen."

"I've been racking my brain as to the best way to distribute food to the needy, and not the greedy," Bill said. "I've been thinking of several ways and have come to the conclusion that setting up kitchens in warehouses in the larger cities is the best possible solution to feed the most people. In this country, there are thousands of empty warehouses that can be leased for a song. I could buy tents, but on a large scale, that would be a waste. The real problem is to find competent people to operate feeding centers."

When Bill parked the truck, the families greeted them and helped unload the trailer. "These four boxes are for our wives and the children," Case said. He handed Bill a box and continued, "This is the hardware Chikata spoke of."

After hiding their money, the men entered the large cabin and found their wives and children adorning new clothes, shoes, hats, and admiring kitchen hardware. Clyde was looking down the barrel of a single-barrel shotgun. He said, "Mr. Case, thanks to you, this is my first gun. Did you think to buy me some shells?"

"Yes, Clyde, but you can't have them until you get some instructions on gun safety from your father."

"Mr. Case, judging by all these gifts," Mona said, "we assume you got a fair price for the gold. Am I correct?"

"Yes, Mona, we did. And if your father's plan works, thousands of people will soon stop going to bed without their stomachs growling," Case answered.

After supper, the men again checked the tires and engine on the truck and loaded the trailer with sacks of gold. Before daylight, they entered Colorado Springs and proceeded to Denver. The weather was clear, and they sold another load without any trouble. Nine days later, on their fifth trip, they sold most of the sacks except a few that would be shipped to Winston. They had been home two days when a blizzard engulfed the Rockies so the men began loading boxes of gold, checking the labels on the boxes, and getting ready to ship them from the railroad station in Colorado Springs.

Bill looked at the bed of the truck and the tires which were embedded in the snow and said, "If we were going to Denver, this load would be too much. But we should be able to make a few trips downhill."

Four days later the snow was slowly melting, so they went to town and shipped the first load of boxes. Within three weeks, they shipped twenty-nine more loads, which finished their work shipping the gold to Florida.

When Bill told Case, Chikata, and Myrna that his family would be leaving within a week, Case said, "We truly hate to see you go, but we understand the critical situation. Bill, let's clean up the muskets, rings, bracelets, and the other ornaments. Chikata and I will build boxes and you can ship or sell them for something whenever you are ready. If they remain here, they won't help anybody. A few of the muskets were made in England, and they will sell for enough money to feed a few people. We will build a smaller box for the shield so you can mail it on your return trip."

After completing that task, their last project was the division of their cash money, which totaled one hundred forty-four million, two hundred twenty-six thousand dollars. Case and Chikata kept one million dollars each, and Bill stored most of what was left inside the secret compartments that were built into the trailer walls on the truck.

The following morning Bill said, "Let's start packing to leave here within two days; we have much work to do." Their friends helped load the trailer and it was a solemn experience.

When the group sat down for supper, Mona said, "Papa, everywhere we stop and find wonderful people and make friends, we always end up leaving. Will we ever settle down and remain in one place we can call home?"

"Mona," Bill answered, "unless our family has a catastrophe or a setback, after we make numerous stops to help the needy, I plan to build a house on the riverbank at Fernandina Beach, next door to Winston Johannsen. And, my plan is to remain beside that creek and grow old, while you and Clyde go to school. After our home is completed, Case, Chikata, Onox, and Myrna will come and stay with us for months at a time. That is when I hope to give them an excellent report about the many people they are responsible for helping and keeping them alive."

Mona's and Clyde's faces were radiant, and Mona asked, "Papa, who will look after these cabins and the foxes?"

"Mona, they are going to ask Mr. Andrews to stay here and look after everything, including the foxes and the other animals," Betty said. "Mr. Andrews is getting up in age and they're going to try to persuade him to live with them and hopefully he will write his memoirs."

Later in the night, Bill was sitting beside the fireplace making notes when Betty approached with a tray of coffee and raisin bread. She asked, "Darling, no one has asked or said how much money we will be leaving here with, but I need to know in order to help the transients along the highway."

Bill continued writing and didn't look up as he said, "Not counting the money we already had, there is more than one hundred forty-two million, two hundred twenty-six thousand dollars stored in the trailer."

Betty dropped the tray, creating a loud noise, as she exclaimed, "Do you mean that all that money is in cash and stored in the trailer?"

"Yes, dear, it is and that does not include most of the gold waiting for us on Winston's property, not to mention the items I told you about stored in the trailer. Betty, you and I have a huge responsibility to distribute a lot of money. We do not know the exact amount all the gold is worth, but I estimate somewhere around twenty-five to thirty billion dollars."

She picked up Bill's notes and said, "I see you are recording the names of cities where we can stop at and help feed the needy. What about the transients we will be passing beside the highway?"

"Time is of the essence, but when we pass transients, I plan to stop and you and the children can give them one-dollar bills. But, our first priority is to set up food kitchens and support the ones in the warehouses where we can help feed the most hungry people," Bill said.

"Why don't we donate food to the different churches in the

cities and give them the responsibility of feeding the hungry?"

"Betty, Case and I talked about that, but most churches are not set up to accommodate and feed thousands of people. However, I'm open to any suggestion you have that will help the most people who really need it."

Betty reclined, thinking, and then prayed, asking the Lord for his help.

Mercy Trip

Early, two mornings later, the Dykes family said their farewells to their friends, and Bill secured a promise from them that they would visit his family in Florida. For the first time in her life, Betty saw Bill hug two men and a lady, and whisper something to them before departing. Shortly the trailer was rolling over the tram road, heading toward Colorado Springs.

Bill stopped at a railway depot and shipped the six boxes of ornaments to Winston before heading for Nebraska. After leaving the depot, he said, "Betty, one of the satchels on the floor contains money. You and the children count out fifty thousand dollars and put it in one of the empty satchels." Bill drove carefully while his family counted money.

Later in the day they drove up to Boys Town, Nebraska. Clean cared-for buildings were visible, cultivated fields were abundant, and hundreds of boys were working with crops and livestock. Mona asked, "Papa, why don't they call this place Boys and Girls Town?"

"Mona, Case told me that this institution was established exclusively for orphaned boys, not girls. A boy who is accepted here cannot have any money or living relatives, and he is released from here at the age of eighteen. According to Case, this is a well-run institution."

Bill parked, took a slip of paper from the glove compartment, picked up a bag, and said, "Wait here, I'll return in a few minutes."

Shortly Bill exited the building and they drove away. He said, "Betty, Case had told me about the integrity and principles of Father Grannigan, who operates Boys Town. The man accepted the money with tears in his eyes and immediately prayed, thanking God and the instruments that provided the gift. Betty, he gave me the names of eight people in different cities where each is trying to raise money and feed the hungry from warehouses. That information should make our job a little easier in this area.

"Betty, don't put away your note pad because when we get settled, it will be your job to keep in touch with the head person of each charity we help. You will need not only the name of the institution, but also the address of each. In time they will need more money. After I asked, the Father answered my questions and reluctantly gave me some worthwhile advice."

"Darling, what advice did you need from the Father about how to give away money or buy food?" Betty quickly asked.

"After I told Father Grannigan of our plan to help as many charities as possible, he said, 'When any country goes through bad times, large amounts of money create a tendency for theft.' According to him, we should have a contract which binds a wholesale food supplier to make weekly deliveries to the warehouse kitchens, providing they are honest businessmen. He looked me in the eyes and said, 'Mr. Dykes, when you are spending fifty thousand dollars at one time for groceries, you possess a huge bargaining chip for prices.' Tonight, you and I will draw up a simple contract and have copies made. We will leave the suppliers' names vacant until we sign a contract with each wholesaler. Our money will be paid to food warehouses, and the recipients who distribute the food will know how much they are supposed to receive each week in order to feed hungry people."

The following day the family stopped on the Kansas state line at a small bank, and Bill had the contracts typed and copies made. While he was doing that, Betty exchanged large bills for 50,000 one-dollar bills. As they drove away, Betty recorded the Boys Town information in a ledger. Shortly Bill turned onto a highway that would carry them to Kansas City, Kansas.

Approaching twelve transients beside the road, Bill stopped and Betty and the children handed each of them 10 one-dollar bills and wished them Godspeed. The family spent the night at a lodge where Bill got directions to a charity warehouse. The following morning he drove to the warehouse and found two elderly ladies, Mrs. Jones and Mrs. Smart, along with four helpers, working in a corner kitchen. Before noon, soup and bread was served to eight hundred homeless people.

When the homeless had finished eating, Bill introduced his family to the operators of the kitchen. He explained to the ladies the purpose for his visit, and said, "Mrs. Jones, while I pick up a few supplies for my family, will you get the man you spoke of, Mr. Gibson, who operates the wholesale food warehouse, to meet us here at two o'clock?"

"Mr. Dykes, when he hears about the size of the cash sale you're speaking of, I'm sure he will be here," she quickly responded.

By three o'clock, Bill and Mr. Gibson had signed a contract which stated the amount of food to be delivered weekly for the homeless. Bill paid for a six-month supply in cash, and he accepted the receipt from Mr. Gibson and handed it to Betty. Shaking hands, Bill said, "It has been a pleasure meeting all of you, and either my wife or I will keep in contact with you for your needs in the future."

"Mr. Dykes," Mrs. Smart said, "our thanks and prayers go out to everyone who provided this gift. And thank you for adding the resources to provide the bag lunches for an evening meal. The fortunate people who have food have no idea what a peanut-butter-and-jelly sandwich with a piece of fruit means to homeless people at the end of the day. We look forward to seeing or hearing from you again."

As Bill drove away, he said, "Our destination is St. Louis, Missouri."

"Darling," Betty asked, "did you think about trying to barter a little longer with the supplier and perhaps pay less money for the food?"

"Yes, Betty, Case and I discussed it, and we were in agreement. If we find a supplier we trust, pay him a fair price and he can stay in business. He also knows if he serves us well, and at prices we will accept, we will continue buying from him. The best effort we can provide involves trusting the people we have faith in."

For Bill the process of setting up contracts was slow, but five weeks later, the Dykes family had signed agreements with wholesale food warehouses in fourteen large cities and seventeen smaller ones. As Bill drove away from Tallahassee, Florida, he said, "Children, tomorrow night we should be sleeping on our farm. After we spend a few days with the George Cline family and the children on the farm, God willing, we will proceed to our land beside the river and hopefully begin building our home."

It was past eleven Sunday morning when Bill parked the trailer beside the chapel. He said, "I believe everyone is inside, so let's enter quietly." The doors were open, so the family entered and took seats on the last pew. No one heard or saw them except the young man who was behind the podium, closing his sermon.

Bill's family recognized some of the people, but there were

several visitors they didn't know. After the young man closed his sermon, he said, "Praise God, this morning we have four new visitors. Welcome to the Lord's house."

When George's family and the children turned and recognized the Dykes family, they engulfed them with hugs, thanks, praise, and many salutations. George said, "For those of you who have not met the Dykes family, they are the ones who made it possible for us to have a home, food, and clothing. They're probably tired, but after they rest, they will answer our many questions and tell us about their travels. This is a cool morning, so our visiting neighbors are invited to sit with us and eat at the picnic tables outside."

While eating, members of the Dykes family asked the children questions about the farm and their daily lives. At the end of the meal, Bill said, "George, as soon as I get my binoculars let's walk around the farm so I can see the improvements that have been made."

While they walked, George said, "As you will see, everything we put in a letter for you has been completed. And, the hogs, tobacco, gum tar, and our boys who do contract labor are our money makers."

"George, how do you manage to sell so many hogs?"

George laughed and said, "Construction crews, grocery stores, schools, the WPA, and several other firms buy pork from us. And, at times we trade a few hogs for a piece of machinery or a beef cow. Bill, these children have had a rough start in life, but by working to survive, they learn quickly and do excellent work."

"What do you need hay for, George?"

"Bill, you can't see them from here, but we have ninety-four head of beef in a pasture and seven milk cows in a field next to the farmhouse. We feed them hay to supplement their grazing diet."

Later they stopped beside a pine thicket where several wooden drums had been filled with gum tar. "When will these be sold?" Bill asked.

"Those will be sold this week. We notify Hercules Powder Company when we have at least one hundred drums filled and their trucks and trailers will pick them up."

It was five o'clock before the men ended their tour. Bill said, "George, when we drove in here, and while we've been walking, I've noticed three farms on this side of the road and four across the highway for sale because of delinquent taxes. Next week I would like you to purchase all of them."

George was astounded and exclaimed, "Bill, did you find a gold mine while you've been away!"

Bill laughed, nodded, and said, "With the purchase of those seven farms, you will have almost three thousand more acres of cultivated land and another two thousand in timber. Since these young people are beginning to get married, we will need more farmhouses."

George nodded and Bill continued. "Tomorrow morning we will go to the general store, and I want you to tell Mr. Webster to order a large diesel tractor with the necessary farm implements, a pickup truck, and a two-ton stake body truck for the farm and a car for my family. I would like you to contact a doctor and ask him to come to the farm and give everyone a physical examination. Be sure to tell him to vaccinate anyone who needs the shot. Also have a dentist come to check everyone's teeth."

As George made notes in his pad they walked toward the farmhouse. He said, "It is almost time for our evening service, let's go into the chapel."

When everyone was seated in the sanctuary, Mark Wilson stepped behind the podium and prayed. After closing, he said, "This evening we will omit our weekly service. Instead, Mrs. Betty Dykes has consented to share with us the events in which her family has been involved since they have been away several years. Mrs. Dykes, the Lord and part of his worshipers await you."

Betty stepped to the podium and said, "Thank you. I will be brief because many of you already know most of our circumstances. After leaving here almost three years ago, we stopped in many towns, cities, hamlets, and roadside businesses where my husband looked for work. On different occasions he was fortunate, but a job lasted a few days, sometimes a few hours, and once or twice, a few weeks. But everywhere we went, transients were on the move, searching for food and jobs. Finally Bill went to work in an oil field outside Morgan City, Louisiana. However, he was let go a few weeks later when the oil well failed to produce oil or gas.

"But while Bill worked there, we became friends with Case and Myrna Mack, who were Christian people of good report. Case owned several thousand acres of property in the Rocky Mountains. He had tried to make a living searching for gold, but he was not successful because he didn't know how to use dynamite. Case learned that Bill was experienced at using explosives, so he offered my husband a share of anything they mined, providing he would move to the Rocky Mountains and work with him. I was reluctant about gold mining, or returning to the snow country, but after our family took a vote, we went to the mountains. Case, Clyde, Bill, and a fine old Indian, Chikata, went prospecting for gold. I truly believe the four of them were in the palm of our Lord's hand. Within a year they had found a fortune in gold, including what is called the mother lode."

The congregation sat in awe as Betty continued. She said, "However, possessing a fortune brings responsibilities of a tremendous nature. Their fortune was divided in thirds, but Case and Chikata gave over ninety-nine percent of their shares to Bill to be distributed among the poor people in this country. Since leaving the mountains, Bill has paid approximately forty-five wholesale food warehouses in different towns to deliver food to the kitchens for the needy each week for a year or less. Before the year is out, one of us will return to each city or contact them by telephone in order to pay for another year of supplies should it be necessary.

"I could tell you of the poverty, rejection, and sickness across this nation, but most of you have experienced it firsthand. I wish I could report that the economic conditions are improving, but that would be a falsehood. I will remind you of this, anyone living in this country that goes to bed at night with a full stomach and a roof over their head is very fortunate.

"My family returned here because we love and care for you, and we hope to expand and improve the living conditions here. We know that the Lord has entrusted a fortune to us; it is our responsibility to help his people," Betty continued. "One thing I have insisted on is the building of a small schoolhouse so each of you can get an education. Another piece of news is the size of this farm will triple in size next week, not only in acreage, but young farmers who need a place to live, worship, and grow will be settling here and they will need your help."

Betty paused, smiled, and looked intently at George and Sara before continuing. "We want to thank George and his wife, Sara, the couple who has worked hard for all of you by planning, teaching by example, implementing your good ideas, guiding, supporting, and loving everyone who has made this a successful farm. But remember, when new faces join you on this farm, please be as tolerant with them as George and Sara have been with you.

"Each of you will start receiving medical and dental treatment and a few material items you can use. You still have a job to perform, but better tools will soon be provided. When we leave, Bill plans to build us a house in Fernandina Beach beside a river. We will be located less than two hours from here by car so we will visit you often. And, God willing, all of you from time to time will come to our riverbank and visit us.

"While our house is being built, Bill plans to go south and north and establish food banks where they are needed," Betty continued. "Before the year is out, one of us will visit each charity we have helped and try to be of service in the coming year. In a nutshell, this is what has transpired since we left you. Does anyone have a question?"

A four-year-old girl said, "Mrs. Dykes, my name is Amy. What items will we receive?"

Betty smiled and answered, "Items such as new shoes and clothes, grooming supplies, a school with pencils, paper, books, and the luxury of having a new truck so all of you can go to the general store occasionally, a piano and hymn books for you to use in this chapel, a telephone in the main farmhouse, several board games, and assorted sports equipment. Please, never forget that this is your home, sanctioned by the Lord, and he wants you to be happy in his service.

"As we arrived here, my daughter read the sign posted beside the highway. 'Ring this bell if you need food.' Amy, our hearts went out to all of you for remembering to share your food. Thank you, and continue to walk a straight path."

Three days later, several vehicles arrived at the farm and Bill signed the necessary papers, paid the delivery team, and took possession of the new car. He handed George the keys to a pickup truck, a tractor, and a flatbed truck which had a trailer loaded with farm implements hooked to it. He said, "George, with these keys come responsibilities." He handed George an envelope filled with cash and continued. "Here is some money to pay for the supplies for a schoolhouse and the many items you will need for the children. Tomorrow we're leaving to build a house of our own and continue fulfilling our duty."

George looked inside the envelope before saying, "This is a lot of money, I'll do my best not to waste a penny."

The bell in front of the farmhouse rang and a small girl and three barefoot boys who were pulling a wagon containing their possessions waited beside the sign. George said, "Bill, if you would like to hear a pitiful conversation follow me."

The men walked slowly toward the highway as Mabel exited the farmhouse and passed them. The adults waited and Mabel said, "I'm Mabel Jones, one of the many workers on this farm and I assume you're hungry." The children nodded so Mabel turned toward the farmhouse and called out, "Christy, we will need four meals with milk. What are your names?"

The tallest boy pointed and said, "I'm Cyrus Johnston and these are my brothers, Hank, Joseph, and my sister Francis. We read the sign, and we're willing to work a full day for a meal."

"Cyrus, that won't be necessary," Mabel said. "Let's go to the porch and you can eat in the shade." George and Bill smoked their pipes as they waited.

When the children finished eating, the men approached them and George said, "I'm George Cline and this is Bill Dykes, the owner of this farm. My family and several young boys and girls work this farm. Their reward is love, food, clothes, shelter, and Christian training, but everyone is required to work on jobs he or she is capable of doing. Have you children been abandoned?"

Cyrus answered, "Yes, our parents stopped at a service station in Savannah, Georgia, and when we came from the restroom, they were gone. We stayed close to the station for two days, but they didn't return. We've been walking and living off of blackberries and rainwater for two weeks."

"I can offer you a Christian education, shelter, food, clothing, and a job, if you wish to stay here and work," George said.

"Thank you, sir," Cyrus said, "we accept your offer. We don't know anything about farming, but we'll work hard and behave ourselves."

"Mabel, take them to the storeroom and tell my wife to give them clothes and shoes," George said. "Then show them the shower stalls so they can bathe. Cyrus, all of you can rest for a couple of days and roam around the farm if you care to. Then we will find some work for you."

Betty cranked the new Ford and followed Bill to the highway. As they were driving away from the farm, an employee from the telephone company parked in front of the farmhouse.

Betty said, "Children, it looks as if they will soon have a phone and we will be able to stay in contact with our friends. Clyde, how long do you think it will take us to get our house built?"

"Mama, I don't know but it shouldn't take too long," Clyde said. "Anyone with money today can buy the best products and cheap labor. I know that you and Papa have already drawn a house plan to save time. When Papa goes north, he plans to hire Mr. Johannsen to look after the house while it is under construction."

Bill kept driving but Betty stopped each time she saw a

group of transients, so Mona and Clyde could hand them money.

Later Bill parked his truck a few feet from Winston's house and Betty stopped beside him. Winston, Gloria, Sam, and Cynthia were excited as they greeted them. Laughter and gaiety exemplified their conversation, and pure joy filled everyone as they went into the house. Betty picked up Christy and said, "Look how this beautiful girl has grown! And that reminds me. Clyde, go to the car and bring in the gifts for Christy and this family."

By sunset, Clyde and Mona were telling Sam and Cynthia about their life in the Rockies and their travels while Betty and Gloria conversed in the kitchen. Bill answered Winston's questions while they sat on the porch smoking.

When Bill finished, Winston asked, "Do you still plan to build a house and settle here?"

"Yes, I do. I would like to hire you to look after the house while it is under construction. I need to go to several states in the next several weeks and I can't be here. I also need your help on other projects in this area. I don't want you working with your hands, but you know the people in this area, and your knowledge of supervision and contracts is what I need."

Winston took a long pull on his pipe and said, "Of course, I'll help you. Sam and Luke have taken over our roadside business and they don't need me. When do we start?"

"Tomorrow morning we need to start hiring workers to construct the house, order building material, apply for a telephone to be run to our construction site, go to a bank, and take a look at my city lot. Where are the boxes I shipped here?" Bill asked.

Pointing, Winston said, "Those heavy boxes are buried on the high ground between those big oak trees. The last few boxes are still in the barn beneath the hay bales."

Before ten o'clock the following morning, Bill and Winston had accomplished everything that Bill had planned except for the last item. When they parked in front of the bank, Winston said, "I didn't know this bank was for sale."

After exchanging large bills for one-dollar bills, Bill and Winston met the president, Cecil Yarns, and the head accounting officer of the bank. With pencil and paper in hand, Bill said, "Mr. Yarns, I'm interested in buying this bank. What are the bank's assets? What are the bank's liabilities? What price is being asked for the bank? And, is all of the bank's stock for sale?"

As Mr. Yarns spoke, Bill recorded the figures he quoted answering his questions. Then he said, "Thanks, Mr. Yarns. After I do some checking, I or my representative will make you an offer for this property within a few days."

When they drove away, Winston said, "Bill, we need to visit Mort Yale. He's an attorney and holds a degree in accounting. Mort resigned from that bank a few years ago because of their president and their unscrupulous business practices. His office is in the next block."

"Winston, is Mort Yale an ethical lawyer?" Bill asked.

"Yes, sir, I've known Mort since his childhood. If anyone goes to him asking his help in breaking the law, he dismisses them."

Shortly Winston said, "Bill, this is Mr. Mort Yale, the attorney I spoke of. Mr. Yale, this is Bill Dykes."

After being seated in Mort's office, Bill told him about his meeting with Mr. Yarns and his intentions to buy the bank. Mort looked at the numbers Mr. Yarns had quoted and said, "Bill, I'll be blunt, if Yarns doesn't sell that bank within sixty days, he will lose it. These figures are astronomical. The amount of assets is probably accurate, but the property value and the stock amounts are inflated. Mr. Dykes, would you like me to negotiate this sale for you?"

"No, sir," Bill answered. "I would like to hire you to purchase the bank and operate it. I realize I'm asking a lot for your time and talents, but I'm willing to pay a fair price for them. If we can acquire the bank, will you take the job?"

"I'll be blunt again," Mort said. "The only business I've been paid for this past year is foreclosures. Do you have the assets to acquire the bank and pay me a salary of two hundred dollars per week if we close this deal?"

Winston took a deep breath, but Bill said, "That sounds fair to both of us. I know very little about the banking business, and I realize bank employees in today's economy have to say 'No' to most loans, but if we purchase this bank, I hope we can be negative in a nice way. As soon as you process the documents for my ownership, I will deposit a large amount of money in the bank."

"Being negative in an underhanded way was one of the reasons I quit that bank," Mort said. "Bill, if I accept this job, will I have a free hand with employees, loans, legal decisions, salaries, and working hours? And, to whom do I answer?"

"As I said in the beginning, Mort, you will be the manager and make the decisions operating the bank—hopefully you will make money. But every once in a while, I will look at the books and I want my wife, Betty Dykes, myself, Winston Johannsen, and my two children named as bank officers."

"Mr. Dykes, I accept the job. What is your address?" Mort asked.

"For the moment I don't have one, but my trailer is parked on Winston's property, so forward any correspondence to him."

Mort nodded.

"I will be here a few days before leaving town, and my next trip will last several weeks. The company is installing a telephone on my property so I will be in contact with you before I leave. Thank you for taking the job."

Mort looked at Bill intently, drew a circle around a front-page article in the newspaper, and handed it to him before saying, "You are the one."

Bill read aloud the headline in the paper. "Mystery man travels from state to state establishing food banks for the hungry." Bill shook his head and said, "Many people don't have food, shelter, or jobs. Mort, if you acquire the bank, we'll see you in a few days."

The following morning while Bill's family was establishing a homesite, Winston was supervising utility workers to install an electrical panel in order to have electricity at the job site for an eight-man construction crew. By the end of the day, concrete footings for the house and the brick storage shed were poured.

Bill said to his family, "Winston knows what he is doing, and with a telephone out there to order supplies, let's stay out of his way. At my request, the storage house with shelves will be finished first because that crew needs a dry place to store nails, hardware, and tools."

At the end of the working day, Bill's family was looking at the layout of the 3,800-square-foot house. He answered the phone, and Mort said, "Mr. Dykes, I've met with Mr. Yarns and made him an offer. He tried to negotiate the price, but I didn't bargain with him. If you can be at the bank at nine o'clock three days from now, your family will own a bank, and there are no other stockholders. The price will be five hundred sixty-four thousand dollars less than what Mr. Yarns quoted to you. Bill, if you buy this bank, I want to install new locks on every door, including the safes in offices and the vault."

"I will meet you at the appointed time and we should be in the banking business. Thanks again, Mort," Bill said.

"Betty, three days from now, we should own a bank and have a safe place to store the Lord's treasury. I will postpone my trip until we put our cash money and deposit the gold in a safe place."

Four days after Bill took possession of the bank, Mort had hired new employees and had replaced the bank's locks. At ten o'clock on Thursday, Mort was astonished when he watched Bill and his friends bring in boxes filled with one-hundred-dollar bills to be counted and placed on the bank shelves inside the vault. Next, the large crew broke open boxes, and the employees weighed sacks and rugged bars of gold before storing them in the vault. It was close to daybreak before the job was completed, the boxes hauled away, and the floors cleaned.

Bill signed a cashier's check and handed it to Mort. He said, "This is a twenty-million-dollar check so deposit it with the bank assets. I'll be leaving in the morning, but my wife will keep me posted, should you need anything."

Mort laughed and said, "Bill, when I report our assets to the banking authorities, the state bank examiners will be here within two weeks going through the books and trying to ascertain as to where the wealth came from. They will try to validate every transaction, to be certain it is legal. Have we broken any laws?"

"No, sir, I'm not a lawbreaker, so stop worrying, Mort. I'll see you in a few weeks."

"Just a moment, Bill," Mort said. "Within a week, I will have armored trucks from Tallahassee to begin picking up your raw gold in order to carry it to the smelter. After the gold has been melted, they will pour it into molds and return it here in a brick size. Of course, we will weigh each ounce before we load it onto the armored trucks and have the state workers sign for it. Bill, I wanted you to be aware of this job and have your approval before you left here."

"Thanks for reminding me, Mort," Bill said. "I forgot to mention a smelter when I was in your office. I will keep in contact with you while I'm away."

After bidding his family farewell the following morning, Bill approached Winston and handed him an envelope. He said, "This envelope contains money. You will need it for supplies, and continue taking fifty dollars per week for your services. Old man, that is some sturdy-looking framing for a house, you should be proud of yourself."

Winston laughed and said, "With the amount of screws, bolts, nuts, two-by-twelve floor joists, two-by-six studs, two-by-ten ceiling joists and rafters, you planned it to be strong. When will you return?"

"Winston, I plan to stop at the farm today and then try to

establish food banks on the east and west coast of Florida. I can't really answer your question, but you remain in that chair and continue supervising, not lifting or sweating."

As Bill drove away, he knew that stopping in less populated areas to help smaller groups of people would be time consuming, but Betty had said, "Now that we have the time and resources, let's try not to omit anyone who needs help to survive."

After spending the night with George, Sara, and the children, Bill left the farm early the following morning. Traffic was scarce and he remembered to keep his word to Betty—don't pass any children without helping them. And whether Bill encountered one person beside the road or a group, he stopped and prayed with them before he gave them money.

Essence of Love

For twenty-eight days, Bill stopped and asked different people in adjoining towns the same question, "Where can I find a large group of hungry people?" The people responded by pointing to a location or naming different churches, warehouses, auditoriums, and tent cities. Often a pedestrian rode with Bill in order to show him a group who had set up living quarters in a field or a patch of woods. On four different occasions, Bill persuaded homeless people to join others, making it easier for suppliers to feed them. At each place he secured a contract with nearby stores or warehouses to supply them food on a daily basis.

Several weeks later, Bill was returning home and stopped beside a man, woman, and eleven children within a few miles of his farm. They were the most pathetic-looking group he had seen since the depression began. All but three were shoeless, some wore rope belts, and six of the children were shirtless. Four of them each carried a small bundle in his hand. A small child was picking green blackberries, cramming them into her mouth, and all of them were covered with insect bites, sunburns, and skin rashes.

Bill stepped from the car and said to the man, "Sir, I'm Bill Dykes and it looks as if you could use some help."

"Yes, sir, I could, but I don't know where to turn. Mister, I'm Homer Wilson and this is my wife, Grace. Four of these children are mine and the other seven are transients who were abandoned, so they're traveling with us. I worked as a tenant farmer in South Carolina, but I lost my job. Sir, do you live in this area?"

"Sir, I own a farm just minutes from here. If your group will wait for me, I will send a truck back to pick you up and take you to my farm where you can get food."

The group took seats under the trees and Bill sped away,

thinking of the children's bulging eyes, skinny bodies, exposed ribs, and dirty faces that radiated disappointment and defeat.

Within the hour, George returned with the flatbed truck and took the transients to the farm where they ate, took a bath, put on clean clothes and shoes, and applied ointment to their skin rashes. Later George talked with the group and explained his farming operation and offered them a place to live, work, and worship. The entire group was thankful George let them join his family of farmers, allowing them to lead productive lives.

Bill spent the balance of the day walking around the farms, looking at a school building which was being built, and several pens and sheds for feed and livestock which were under construction at the new purchases.

Everywhere he went small groups of children were working on different construction projects or farming. He spent the night with George and Sara, and at supper he asked, "George, did the new transients decide to remain here?"

"Yes, all of them want to stay here. Seven of the boys are between twelve to fourteen years of age. Mr. Wilson is a farmer, but he's also a mechanic, which we will desperately need in the future," George said.

"George, while I was looking around today, I came to the conclusion that your hands-on working days are over," Bill said. "You have so many workers, crops, buildings, livestock, pieces of machinery, and different jobs to supervise, it's all one man can do to keep check on everything."

"Bill, so far, being a boss to these children has not been necessary, but usually some younger group needs advice. Has your recent trip been successful?" George asked.

"Yes, I like to think so because several thousand people will lie down tonight with food in their stomachs," Bill answered. "But I still have several thousand miles ahead of me, up north and west to complete our mission. When I get home, there should be a roof on our house so we can invite your family to visit and go fishing before too long. George, before I left home, we bought a bank, so I also have to check on that."

George shook his head, smiled, and said, "Bill, I've been reading a few newspapers lately about the many places a stranger establishes food centers to feed the hungry. When you left here a few years ago the Lord led you to become a rich man because he knew you would distribute his wealth and help his poor people."

The following morning Bill parked beside the trailer, and after embracing Betty, he asked, "Where are the children?"

"Clyde went to the creek with Sam and Luke to catch seafood. Mona is inside sketching on our house plan where she thinks we should put the furniture in the new house. How was your trip?" Betty asked.

Bill handed her a folder and answered, "I think it was productive, but when I traveled through the small hamlets and the back roads, it amazed me to find so many homeless people. Those documents are the locations and addresses of the different groups and the amount of money I paid to each food supplier. While I was on the road, I talked on the telephone with Mort Yale and he assured me that everything is running smoothly at the bank. Are there any problems with our construction crew?"

"Darling, when Winston hired construction workers, he hired a group of perfectionists. As you can see, the tin is on the roof and the brick masons are finished. The wiring is complete and today they will finish covering the walls and ceiling with tongue-and-grooved boards. The boards in each room are applied in different patterns. Tomorrow they will start nailing the oak flooring in place."

"Betty, I can see the stack from the fireplace, but is it finished?"

"Oh, yes, and the bricks have been cleaned with acid. The brick mason, Mr. Hammel, suggested we use bricks to seal the entire wall beside the fireplace. He also built bookshelves on each side of it. The workers poured concrete for a foundation and six days later, it was finished. Mr. Hicks, a former boat carpenter, built a gorgeous fireplace mantel and columns and installed them. Our fireplace has a five-foot opening and a damper with a brass knob just like the one in Case's log cabin."

"Who is that hammering in the storage shed?" Bill asked.

"Mr. Hicks is building cabinets and shelves for the bathrooms, kitchen, closets, and a gun and fishing rack for you. He's also going to build valance boards to go over the top of the windows. Bill, let's go through the house and see if it meets your approval."

After Bill and Betty inspected the house inside and out, he said, "This is a beautiful house, and anyone can see that perfection went into every piece of work. How did Winston find such perfect lumber for everything?"

Betty laughed and said, "I don't think you have ever seen the stern side of Winston. When he calls for a truckload of building material, the supplier knows he will be paid in cash. But if one piece of lumber is knotty or warped, the driver takes it back to the warehouse and returns with a good piece before he is paid. One thing about a great depression, it is a buyer's market. Darling, another thing about money Mort told me to tell you and I forgot to. After the Lord's gold was processed into brick form, the fortune is worth over thirty-two billion dollars. That is more than you estimated, and Mort said the price of gold has gone up."

Bill picked up a beige brick and said, "Betty, this brick is six by twelve by two and one-half inches high. Why did you decide on this size and color?"

"Because they are stronger than a smaller one, and I love this color!"

After supper, Bill, using lantern light, marked the routes on four different maps for his next trip to the northeast coast and then across the country as far west as Detroit, Michigan, where he would turn south and stop at different locations to supplement the needy. Betty worked at a table, recording names of towns, food suppliers, dates, phone numbers, and the amount of money Bill had paid for food on his recent trip.

Bill asked, "Betty, how often do you plan to contact the food centers we are supplying?"

"I will call them once a month, and I expect several of them to begin feeding a larger number of people in the months to come, which will not be a problem. And, some of them are already feeding more people since they started receiving help. Concerning some of the smaller groups on your last trip, you paid only thirty to forty thousand dollars to food suppliers because of the smaller numbers of homeless people. If our distribution of money continues to be processed properly, maybe you can cut down on some of the travel time by mailing a check to the food distributor instead of contacting them personally."

"I truly hope that will come to pass," Bill said, "but we won't know for some time. Betty, as soon as we finish setting up all of the food centers, we will know the total amount of money needed for payouts each year. Only then will we know how many years we can afford to support them. Tomorrow I'm going to check on our bank and discuss a savings plan with Mort. Our bank is the only possession we have that made a substantial amount of money the past few weeks."

It was past eleven the following morning when Bill, along with Mort, finished checking the bank's books. "Everything appears to be in order," Bill said. "The bank is making a profit, new depositors are opening accounts, and you are making worthwhile loans to a few sound businesses. When the bank auditors came a few weeks ago, did they find any discrepancies?"

"No, sir, and they checked on everything, even the currency and change in the vault. Three men came, and on different occasions, each of them asked me, 'Where did the owner of this bank get his money?' I told them I think you made your money out west, working at different jobs, but I could not swear to anything. Bill, I know you've been thinking about putting some money in a savings account. You know that many of the credit unions, banks, and every financial institution we can name with the exception of the United States Treasury have gone bankrupt. I firmly believe US Treasury bills are a sound investment. However, they're only yielding about 2 percent interest."

"Mort, what makes you think these T-bills are a safe place for a savings?"

"Bill, if the T-bills fail, our government will cease to exist as a business."

Silence permeated the room. Finally Bill said, "Mort, sell one hundred million dollars' worth of gold and purchase the T-bills in my family's names. Mort, how many out-of-town customers do we have?"

"Seventy-two, and each day new people come in and open an account. When your financial statement was posted on the bank window and reached the state capitol, the huge amount of money shown was exactly what people with money were looking for, a safe place to deposit it. And, the fact that you don't have one liability tends to make people think you are a genius."

Bill burst out with laughter before saying, "Mort, a genius would never sweat away years of his life working in a coal mine. Yes, I've been lucky; and I have been blessed by our Lord and many of the people I've met since the depression began. Mort, earlier I deposited a large sum of money to my checking account because I'm tired of taking the risk of carrying so much cash with me. When I take my next trip, I will write checks for food instead of paying with cash."

As they walked out to the sidewalk, Bill suddenly bent over in pain and then upchucked in the gutter. For several minutes his pain continued, and when he tried to stand straight, Mort had to grasp his shoulders to prevent him from falling. With a clerk's help, they put Bill in the car and rushed him to a medical clinic. A doctor immediately performed an appendectomy on him.

As a result of the ether, Bill felt sick and was vomiting after the operation. Three days later while Betty was driving him home, she said, "To my knowledge, this is the first time you've ever been sick. You will have to be careful not to lift anything or the doctor will be replacing those stitches. Darling, since you are in no condition to travel, in order to expedite feeding the hungry, I've been thinking about my making the trip northeast and to the west."

"No," Bill said. "Anyone with a few dollars in his pocket, visiting all those cities is taking a chance and it is far too dangerous for a woman. I'll be fit in a few days and be on my way. Betty, how many more days do you estimate it will be before our house will be finished?"

"The carpenters are installing the shoe mold and that will finish the construction job. Luke and our neighbors are going to help us clean the house tomorrow. The day after tomorrow, our furniture will arrive, and we can move in the next day. What are you going to do with the truck trailer?"

"Betty, the trailer is adequate for two people to live in comfortably. I think we should send it to George and let him decide if he can use it on the farm. In the future, some of his workers will be getting married and one day he won't have a farmhouse for the newlyweds. He can put the trailer on the ground and install flooring and the farmers will have another dwelling and a truck to use."

During the next week, Bill observed as his family occupied the house. His children had their own rooms, which was a first for them. His family and neighbors landscaped the yards and planted flowers, but he personally supervised Clyde, Sam, and Luke as they cleaned and arranged tools and other paraphernalia in the tool shed.

Bill's strength was returning and the second weekend after moving into their new home, Betty invited George, Sara, close friends, and several neighbors for dinner. After a short prayer, Betty and Gloria served fried chicken, fried shrimp, fish stew, and four vegetables with hot bread and iced tea.

While eating, Lace commented, "Bill, this is the largest dining table I have ever seen. Where did you buy it?"

Bill pointed to Betty and she answered, "Mr. Webster didn't have one large enough in his catalog, so we had a carpenter build it and the chairs. The painters applied three coats of black paint before putting black lacquer on everything for the final coat. As you can see, I ordered black hutches, sideboards, and chairs to match."

The meal was superb, with congenial small talk about what was right in the community, and no one mentioned the depression.

After the group ate dessert, Betty smiled and said, "You men probably want to smoke, so feel free to excuse yourselves whenever you like."

The men looked in all the rooms in the house and then went to the riverbank and packed their pipes. "Bill," Lace said, "Clyde told us that you are going on another trip tomorrow. Where are you going?"

"Lace, I plan to go up the east coast as far as Maine and then go west to Detroit. From there I'll turn south and stop at the larger cities and try to set up feeding centers for the needy. Before returning home, I plan to make a small detour and spend some time in the coal-mining area with some friends where I use to work."

"Heavens, Bill, there will be a lot of people happy to see you!" Lace stammered.

At breakfast the following morning, Betty said, "Darling, I need to go to the drugstore before you leave. I'll go with you to the bank and it will save me a trip later today."

Once inside the bank, Betty had a satchel full of one-dollar bills when she and Bill left the counter. Brian Harmon, an escape convict from a Georgia chain gang, brandished two revolvers and shouted, "Anyone who does not want to get killed, drop to the floor!" To Betty he shouted, "Woman, give me that satchel of money!"

Betty answered calmly, "The Lord does not want people to steal." Brian shot her through the lungs and grabbed the satchel. Betty fell toward the floor and Bill caught her, cradling her in his arms. As blood gushed from her, he stopped the flow by pressing his thumbs over the holes in her chest.

After forcing the bank clerks to fill sacks with money, the robber ran to a truck and sped away. Mort yelled, "Someone call the medical clinic and tell them we're on the way with a wounded lady. Then call the county and state police and report the robbery."

While Mort and the clerks put Betty on the rear seat of Bill's car, Bill kept his thumbs over the bullet wounds to control the bleeding. As Mort drove at record-breaking speeds, Betty opened her eyes and asked, "Bill, was anyone else hurt during the robbery?"

"No, no one, and we have a doctor and his staff waiting to take care of you. Please, breath deep and pray," Bill begged.

"Darling, this incident is horrible, but don't forget to pray for the young robber and his family," Betty mumbled. "They also need help. Bill, continue to be a splendid father and serve the Lord." She closed her eyes and was pronounced dead upon arrival at the clinic.

Bill had Betty's body moved to a funeral home for embalming before he obtained permission from Winston to bury her at his family plot. Then he went home to get burial clothes for her and to tell Clyde and Mona that their mother was dead. Before nightfall, Betty's body was placed in her home for viewing. Later a crowd of people arrived with covered dishes and offered their condolences to the family.

In earlier years, Bill and Betty had spoken reverently about what they would do should one of them be called unexpectedly to join the Lord. They both agreed that large or fancy funerals meant nothing, and they should be buried immediately without any pomp or large ceremonies. However, because of the humanitarian work of the Dykes family and news reporters communicating and writing stories about them, they had become household names, so many people, including writers, planned to attend Betty's funeral.

Privately, the crowd of mourners spoke about Brian Harmon being shot twenty-two times in a gun battle at Yulee, Florida, and the stolen money being recovered. The group's next subject was the number of kitchens in the different states for which the Dykes family was supplying food for the hungry. Finally the group got around to the huge fortune the family owned and many of them quoted different news reporters as to where they thought the money came from, but all of them were guessing.

In the living room at eleven o'clock the following morning, the Dykes family kissed and said their final farewell to Betty before Bill motioned for an attendant to close the coffin. Six pallbearers carried the casket to the cemetery plot with the family walking behind them. When the casket was resting across two sawhorses, Bill noticed hundreds of vehicles and throngs of people he had never seen. A few were standing on the hood of their cars to watch the proceedings.

The young preacher, Simon Coles, stepped upon the loose dirt beside the grave and said, "Let us pray. We are gathered here this morning to pay our final tribute to Betty Dykes, a chosen Christian who was exemplifying humanitarian work on the day her life was taken. Betty's compassion for her fellowman was unequaled as was demonstrated by her giving and loving. Yes, her earthly life is over, but her soul rests in the bosom of our Father. Amen."

After reading several verses from the Book of Psalms, the preacher said, "This morning, with the approval of Bill Dykes,

I've asked Winston Johannsen to speak. As we know, Winston is a man of wisdom, and he has had the privilege of becoming a close friend to Betty and her family. Winston, if you will step forward."

Winston stepped on the mound of dirt and said, "I have the honored privilege of speaking to all of you, not only about Betty's life but also about her being a wife, a mother, and a great humanitarian. I will give you an insight to her life as she constantly helped others. If Betty were standing here this morning, she would say, 'Please, this is a time for rejoicing, because another soul is in heaven. Remove those morbid looks from your face, wipe away those tears, put away those handkerchiefs, and rejoice.'

"Betty Dykes possessed great attributes that she put into action, not only with words and the giving of herself, but the compassion and guidance she had for everyone. Above all, her finest quality was the unlimited love she bestowed upon everyone she encountered. A love with action spread across half of this country, which came through her from our Lord, and she passed it on with her last dying breath.

"By now most of us have read or heard the stories about Betty and her family leaving the coal mine after it shut down, looking for work. The news stories detail the Dykes family stopping sometimes for hours, a few days, and several times working a few weeks until a job played out, and the family moving on to another state. The first time I saw Betty and her family, they parked here to help my pregnant daughter, Gloria, out of their trailer. Mistakenly, I was moping around in a foggy gloom feeling sorry for myself and blaming my troubles on the depression.

"However, the Dykes family not only suggested to me a profitable business venture, they worked and helped me implement it. A few months later, Bill Dykes delivered my granddaughter, Christy. And Betty had taken charge of the chores in our household during the latter part of my daughter's pregnancy. When Bill Dykes was laid off from the fertilizer plant, he saw to it that every needed repair on my farm was fixed before they drove away.

"It was several months before we heard from Betty because her family was constantly moving, looking for work. While Betty was out west, we learned that immediately after leaving here, they purchased a farm for a family of four and sixteen abandoned children in order to provide food and shelter for them. Betty persuaded her husband to help the transients beside the highway although they were not a rich family at that time.

"When Betty and her family became rich and started their

return trip to this riverbank, one of their first stops was Boys Town, Nebraska, where they gave monetary help. The rest of the Dykes story you know, the Dykes family has donated money to feed the poor in large cities, small towns, and hamlets in almost a hundred different locations. What you don't know is the morning Betty's life was taken, she had just withdrawn one hundred thousand dollars in one-dollar bills for her husband to give to abandoned children along the highway on his trip to the northeast and midwest.

"There is no point in our trying to outguess Betty because she said, 'Many people need help and we need to act.' When I think of all the people I've known in my lifetime, if all their attributes were confined into one person, it would not produce a lady like Betty. The only thing she hated was sin and any form of injustice. She truly gave of herself for the good of others.

"Once in a private conversation with Betty, I was complaining and she said, 'Mr. Johannsen, I must remind you that you have access to Jesus Christ, a Holy Bible, and the Constitution of the United States. These three are the greatest treasures that you will ever possess. Pray, read, and study the three.'

"Not once did I ever hear Betty say anything that caused me to be ashamed of her. If Betty were here this morning, I think she would say, 'Get on with your lives, continue to love and care for your families, but don't neglect the needy, because God wants their souls to join his heavenly family. I will be waiting for all of you. My prayers and love to all of you.'"

Simon Coles said a prayer, and Betty was lowered into the earth, covered with dirt, and a cross mounted at her head. Very slowly the congregation dispersed into small groups and talked before driving away.

Bill led Mona and Clyde to the edge of the creek, and they took seats on a log. He said, "Your mother's, and my wife's, earthly life has come to an abrupt close. I will hire two people to handle the cooking and other chores for us. Winston will help us secure workers who are capable of doing this, especially while I'm away. I want you to continue to live your life as if your mother was always beside you. And never forget to always make her proud of anything you do."

Bill desperately needed a housekeeper, a bookkeeper, and someone to maintain his twelve acres of land and to perform repair jobs at the bank and his other buildings. The following week he hired a married couple, Mack and Grace Sorrow, who would work under Winston when Bill was away. Grace, a former bookkeeper, had the responsibility of maintaining the records for the charity institutions, cooking, and taking care of the house as well as the children. Mack, an out-of-work carpenter, maintained the grounds, ran errands, and worked with the construction crew next door to where Bill was having a house built where the Sorrows would live.

The following Monday, Bill drove away, finally heading northeast, in order to establish food banks for the hungry. He glanced at the satchel on the floor which contained one-dollar bills and remembered Betty saying, “Don’t forget to stop and give the abandoned children money. And above all, pray for them.”

About the Author

Jack E. Cauley was born during the Great Depression on September 19, 1931, in Brunswick, Georgia, at a cost of five dollars. Jack's father was a heavy equipment operator who also held a liscence to pilot ships, so the family was constantly on the move, going from one job to another. As a small boy, Jack lived on Sapelo Island, Georgia, for almost two years alongside eight white families and four hundred African American whose forefathers had moved to the Island for one reason, freedom.

On Sapelo Jack heard many stories from the black race which was handed down from their forefathers and grandfathers about slavery and the despicable U.S. government. At the age of eight, Jack moved from Brunswick, Georgia, to Plattsmouth, Nebraska, where his father helped build a military air field in Omaha. Just over a year later, Jack was living in Colorado Springs, Colorado, where his father was helping to construct another air field for the U.S. government. While living in Colorado Springs, the Japanese Empire had Pearl Harbor and several other areas in the far east bombed, drawing the United States into a world war.

This traitorous act by the Japanese enhanced Jack's curiosity about peace, politicians, history, war, men with delusions of grandeur, and survival. Jack became an avid student of history, especially fishing, war, dictators, and ranching. After the air field was finished in Colorado, Jack returned to Brunswick, Georgia, where his father worked at a shipyard as a gantry crane operator until the end of World War II. When Jack graduated from high school, he joined his father working on a shrimp boat off the cost of Mexico for almost two years.

Jack worked as a deck hand and the fishing trips lasted between thirty to forty days and nights. What time Jack had onshore, he constantly visited stockyards and ranches, because he was fascinated with bullfighting. Jack had a birthday on a Sunday and received a draft notice on a Monday, notifying him that he had a two week's notice before he was compelled to report to an induction center in Jacksonville, Florida. Jack joined the U.S. Army and became a paratrooper, simply because it paid more money. While in the paratroopers, a Mexican gunboat committed piracy and seized his father's vessel and six others that were anchored in international waters exactly twenty-three miles offshore of Tampico, Mexico.

At the time Jack wrote to a Texas Senator on behalf of his father and the other seamen trying to have their case heard in an international court of law, however he received no answer. President Truman ordered the Mexicans to release the fisherman and their boats but they refused and kept the seamen in a dungeon. This was Jack's first hard lesson about politicians, journalism, and U.S. law. After fourteen days of brutal treatment the seamen were fined and released, but their boats had been stripped of their seafood, radios, depth recorders, nets, hardware, tools, anchors, spare parts, and ninety percent of their fuel had been pumped from their tanks.

After being discharged from the U.S. Army, Jack returned to fishing for another year. During that year he survived one violent hurricane at sea, and watched a seismograph boat being blown our of the ocean. However, Jack's most humiliating experience was a Mexican gunboat boarding his vessel and at gunpoint stealing his seafood. Two weeks later, Jack watched the Mexicans sell his product to a seafood house on the U.S. Mexican border at Port Isabel, Texas. The U.S. government began importing shrimp from foreign countries causing the price to drastically drop so Jack quit fishing.

Disgusted with government, Jack returned to Brunswick,

Georgia, and joined Hercules Incorporated for thirty-seven years and worked at analyzing, producing, and then supervising the production of terpene and synthetic products for the world market. Jack's education consist of high school, courses in law, bookkeeping, management, and chemicals.

In 2017 the author self published a biography, "The Call of the Sea," and a novel, "Olga." The author now tries to avoid liberals and politicians.

Other Books by Ozark Mountain Publishing, Inc.

Dolores Cannon
A Soul Remembers Hiroshima
Between Death and Life
Conversations with Nostradamus, Volume I, II, III
The Convoluted Universe -Book One, Two, Three, Four, Five
The Custodians
Five Lives Remembered
Jesus and the Essenes
Keepers of the Garden
Legacy from the Stars
The Legend of Starcrash
The Search for Hidden Sacred Knowledge
They Walked with Jesus
The Three Waves of Volunteers and the New Earth
Aron Abrahamsen
Holiday in Heaven
Out of the Archives – Earth Changes
James Ream Adams
Little Steps
Justine Alessi & M. E. McMillan
Rebirth of the Oracle
Kathryn/Patrick Andries
Naked in Public
Kathryn Andries
The Big Desire
Dream Doctor
Soul Choices: Six Paths to Find Your Life Purpose
Soul Choices: Six Paths to Fulfilling Relationships
Patrick Andries
Owners Manual for the Mind
Cat Baldwin
Divine Gifts of Healing
The Forgiveness Workshop
Penny Barron
The Oracle of UR
Dan Bird
Finding Your Way in the Spiritual Age
Waking Up in the Spiritual Age
Julia Cannon
Soul Speak – The Language of Your Body
Ronald Chapman
Seeing True
Albert Cheung
The Emperor's Stargate
Jack Churchward
Lifting the Veil on the Lost Continent of Mu
The Stone Tablets of Mu
Sherri Cortland
Guide Group Fridays
Raising Our Vibrations for the New Age
Spiritual Tool Box
Windows of Opportunity
Patrick De Haan
The Alien Handbook
Paulinne Delcour-Min
Spiritual Gold
Holly Ice
Divine Fire
Joanne DiMaggio
Edgar Cayce and the Unfulfilled Destiny of Thomas Jefferson Reborn
Anthony DeNino
The Power of Giving and Gratitude
Michael Dennis
God's Many Mansions
Carolyn Greer Daly
Opening to Fullness of Spirit
Anita Holmes
Twidders
Aaron Hoopes
Reconnecting to the Earth
Victoria Hunt
Kiss the Wind
Patricia Irvine
In Light and In Shade
Kevin Killen
Ghosts and Me
Diane Lewis
From Psychic to Soul
Donna Lynn
From Fear to Love
Maureen McGill
Baby It's You
Maureen McGill & Nola Davis
Live from the Other Side
Curt Melliger
Heaven Here on Earth
Where the Weeds Grow
Henry Michaelson
And Jesus Said – A Conversation
Dennis Milner
Kosmos
Andy Myers
Not Your Average Angel Book
Guy Needler
Avoiding Karma
Beyond the Source – Book 1, Book 2
The History of God

For more information about any of the above titles, soon to be released titles, or other items in our catalog, write, phone or visit our website:
PO Box 754, Huntsville, AR 72740|479-738-2348/800-935-0045|www.ozarkmt.com

Other Books by Ozark Mountain Publishing, Inc.

The Origin Speaks
The Anne Dialogues
The Curators
Psycho Spiritual Healing
James Nussbaumer
And Then I Knew My Abundance
The Master of Everything
Mastering Your Own Spiritual Freedom
Living Your Dram, Not Someone Else's
Sherry O'Brian
Peaks and Valleys
Riet Okken
The Liberating Power of Emotions
Gabrielle Orr
Akashic Records: One True Love
Let Miracles Happen
Victor Parachin
Sit a Bit
Nikki Pattillo
A Spiritual Evolution
Children of the Stars
Rev. Grant H. Pealer
A Funny Thing Happened on the Way to Heaven
Worlds Beyond Death
Victoria Pendragon
Born Healers
Feng Shui from the Inside, Out
Sleep Magic
The Sleeping Phoenix
Being In A Body
Michael Perlin
Fantastic Adventures in Metaphysics
Walter Pullen
Evolution of the Spirit
Debra Rayburn
Let's Get Natural with Herbs
Charmian Redwood
A New Earth Rising
Coming Home to Lemuria
David Rivinus
Always Dreaming
Richard Rowe
Imagining the Unimaginable
Exploring the Divine Library
M. Don Schorn
Elder Gods of Antiquity
Legacy of the Elder Gods
Gardens of the Elder Gods
Garnet Schulhauser
Dancing on a Stamp
Dancing Forever with Spirit
Dance of Heavenly Bliss
Dance of Eternal Rapture
Dancing with Angels in Heaven
Manuella Stoerzer
Headless Chicken
Annie Stillwater Gray
Education of a Guardian Angel
The Dawn Book
Work of a Guardian Angel
Joys of a Guardian Angel
Blair Styra
Don't Change the Channel
Who Catharted
Natalie Sudman
Application of Impossible Things
L.R. Sumpter
Judy's Story
The Old is New
We Are the Creators
Artur Tradevosyan
Croton
Jim Thomas
Tales from the Trance
Jolene and Jason Tierney
A Quest of Transcendence
Paul Travers
Dancing with the Mountains
Nicholas Vesey
Living the Life-Force
Janie Wells
Embracing the Human Journey
Payment for Passage
Dennis Wheatley/ Maria Wheatley
The Essential Dowsing Guide
Maria Wheatley
Druidic Soul Star Astrology
Jacquelyn Wiersma
The Zodiac Recipe
Sherry Wilde
The Forgotten Promise
Lyn Willmott
A Small Book of Comfort
Beyond all Boundaries Book 1
Stuart Wilson & Joanna Prentis
Atlantis and the New Consciousness
Beyond Limitations
The Essenes -Children of the Light
The Magdalene Version
Power of the Magdalene
Robert Winterhalter
The Healing Christ

For more information about any of the above titles, soon to be released titles, or other items in our catalog, write, phone or visit our website:
PO Box 754, Huntsville, AR 72740|479-738-2348/800-935-0045|www.ozarkmt.com